RIDING
HIGH IN
APRIL

A NOVEL

RIDING HIGH IN APRIL

JACKIE TOWNSEND

SPARKPRESS

Published by SparkPress, a BookSparks imprint,
A division of SparkPoint Studio, LLC
Phoenix, Arizona, USA, 85007
www.gosparkpress.com

Published 2021
Printed in the United States of America
Print ISBN: 978-1-68463-095-0
E-ISBN: 978-1-68463-096-7

Library of Congress Control Number: 2021908292

Interior design by Tabitha Lahr

For Sean

PROLOGUE
JUNE 2010

A BLACK, CHAUFFEURED EQUUS was parked in front of the nameless, back-alley establishment when Stuart and Niraj arrived at the private club to which they'd been invited. A woman with porcelain skin and long silky black hair showed them to a nondescript room with a low wood table surrounded by leather couches. In one of them sat JS, dressed in an elegant suit, trim, impeccably groomed. A bottle and three glasses sat prominently on the table. JS poured, and they began the evening by each downing three shots of Ballantine's seventeen-year-old whiskey, because that was how things worked in South Korea. Everyone had to be at the same level of inebriation so that no one was above embarrassing himself.

Stuart had already called Marie in San Francisco and told her that they shouldn't bother speaking to each other before bed, as was their custom. "Be careful," she had said. "You're not twenty-five anymore, Stuart."

Why did she always need to remind him of that?

Things got loose right away—why waste time?—and Stuart relaxed and reminded himself that he liked JS. JS was engaging and intelligent and, most important, down to earth—you would never know his family were practically South Korean royalty. JS and Niraj had been cohorts at the Stanford Graduate School of Business more than a decade earlier. JS had gone on to work at Cisco in San Jose for some years, before returning to Seoul to reengage in activities more appropriate for his status and rank. He knew networking and infrastructure, owned a variety of South Korean enterprises operating in the sector, and coveted Stuart's technology acumen (if Niraj was Jobs, Stuart was Wozniak).

More shots went around. Plates of fresh fruit and dried squid arrived. They talked about the evolving state of technology, car clouds, open-source software; the death of Cisco, HP, and IBM; how cloud computing was changing the world and how Stuart and Niraj could be drivers of that change, and the great heights to which they could take their as-yet-undefined endeavor—if they played their cards right. JS had some serious ideas about the markets they should go after, the connections spanning far beyond South Korea he had to offer them, and the people he could introduce them to. At one point, and maybe it was the Macallan 18-point, Stuart got the sense that JS wanted a bigger stake in what he and Niraj were doing, one that went beyond introductions and connections, though this was not the place for such a discussion, just as it was not the place to discuss the crisis that had erupted that day at Korea Telecom, Stuart and Niraj's first and only client, thanks to JS. The delicate matter of a rogue resource was what had brought them together tonight. But why taint the mood? No, no—all that could be solved tomorrow. For now, let the pretty Korean women arrive, which they soon did, pairing up with each of the men—for window-dressing purposes only—and the discussion about how they were going to change the world ended.

CHAPTER 1
JUNE 2010

THE DREAM TEAM, AS STUART had begun calling his three-string band of network engineers, had been working on the proof of concept (POC) for three months now, and the demo was almost ready, when suddenly Dr. Kwak, their client sponsor, called Stuart and Niraj into his office, all gaga about this cloud phenom he'd just heard about. This guy's company had just secured $20 million in funding—did Stuart and Niraj know him? His secure cloud-to-cloud VPN? Could they get him over to Seoul for a meeting? Stuart cleared his throat, and Niraj listed to one side. Hadn't they come to Asia to get away from all that Silicon Valley bullshit? Niraj, very carefully and before Stuart could open his mouth and unleash something foul, counseled Dr. Kwak that while, as independent consultants, they were obligated to remain unbiased and open to all vendor options, they were intimate with the Phenom's platform and felt it had yet to be fully proven. Dr. Kwak nodded, as he always did, and then flew the Phenom over anyway.

What could Stuart and Niraj say? They weren't even a company, let alone funded. They couldn't say that the Phenom's platform was a piece of shit—something Stuart knew because he'd worked on that piece-of-shit network component for the Phenom at one point in his illustrious—he used that word facetiously—career. Stuart never practiced in discrediting peers. He was a collaborator, and anyway, you never knew—perhaps the Phenom had fixed the issues by now. He wasn't stupid, just an ass.

Fast forward two weeks. Stuart was kicking himself. Had he forgotten? Did he really believe that the Phenom would show up in Seoul with a filter? That he wouldn't be the exact bombastic, fat-fuck Silicon Valley CEO that he was? One of the first spewers of cloud, a member of the clouderati, as they'd come to be called, a badge less of honor than of derision. Most of those spewers, full of shit to begin with, were just using the cloud as a means of self-promotion. And apparently, Stuart *had* forgotten. Not only did the Phenom show up at Korea Telecom (KT) knowing nothing about Korean culture and having made exactly zero attempt to garner any, but he proceeded to insult KT's data management team directly to their faces in their first meeting with the CTO—a big no-no in a country that was all about saving face.

And then it got worse. KT had strict standards about how to enter the data center—the first of which was to take off your shoes—but the Phenom went in there with his cowboy boots on. The CTO was so pissed, he threatened to shut down the Dream Team's POC and look at other vendor options. (Thanks a lot, Kwak.) Other options? There were none. Network vendors knew shit about cloud infrastructure, and cloud infrastructure vendors (of which the Phenom's company was one) knew shit about networks. That was Stuart's niche, what he and the Dream Team brought to the table that no other vendor could: they crossed borders between the two. It was one thing to build a distributed cloud, but to make network access to it secure and redundant was something else, not to mention at the scale and scope that a large enterprise like KT required. Even the Phenom couldn't purport to offer that, though, thankfully, he got no chance to purport to offer anything—Niraj sent him and his cowboy boots packing back to Silicon Valley the next day.

Nevertheless, the Phenom had tainted the well, and for the next two weeks, Stuart and Niraj spent much of their precious POC time saving face with the Koreans—a lot of face. This meant many soju-sodden dinners with Dr. Kwak and his team and one ridiculously long karaoke fest. Relationships—deep and meaningful, soul-searching relationships—were how business was done in Asia. You should see these guys belt out their songs. It was both exhausting and exhilarating, especially a few mornings later, when Dr. Kwak, bleary-eyed and hungover, pulled Niraj and Stuart aside before their POC presentation and told them that the CTO had made a verbal commitment to Phase II. The Dream Team hadn't even presented their findings yet or showed Dr. Kwak's business managers their demo, and Stuart hadn't given them his software-defined-everything spiel, but apparently it didn't matter. What mattered was that the managers liked the Dream Team. They trusted them.

Be careful what you wish for, Stuart and Niraj chided each other on the way back to their corporate apartment in a cramped, kimchi-and-garlic-smelling cab. Six months, five engineers, $1.8 million. Now they had two proposals to get out this weekend, SingTel being the other one. The largest telecom in Singapore, government funded—and not just any government, but one that doled out ridiculous incentives for startups to come to its country and utilize its workforce and facilities and programs. Once they landed SingTel, this would all become real. Whatever "this" was, beyond the nebulousness of Stuart and Niraj's passionate discourses about the future of "software defined everything" and the anti–Silicon Valley tenets with which they would rule this world, had yet to be defined. A startup? Fine, call it that if you must, even though Stuart despised the word. Javelina—their endeavor's code name—was no startup. He'd been working on it for five thousand years. It was an old beast, as ancient as he was.

"We're going to need a bigger boat," Stuart said.

"Let's not load up the boat before the boat can hold the load," Niraj responded. Meaning, "Let's not go on a hiring spree when neither deal has been signed yet." While Silicon Valley believed in evangelicals (like the Phenom), Stuart and Niraj believed in customers, making sure they were solving their problems, adding value, delivering on what they'd promised, and generating a steady stream of revenue—yes, people, *revenue*—while doing it. Right now, that meant getting these two proposals out the door.

Back at the corporate apartment, Niraj went right to work on the SingTel numbers while Stuart began sketching out a proposed KT network topology architecture for the Phase II proposal. The rest of the Dream Team had already dispersed to their respective territories in the three-bedroom condo: Liam in his room, scouring security résumés; Franco in the living room, in front of the TV, configuring the demo server for scale; and Arman? Who knew what Arman was doing? Probably downstairs, smoking a cigarette. An Aussie, an Argentinian, and a Persian—Javelina project members 3, 5, and 27, respectively—had been toiling away in various corners of the world before Stuart, using their GitHub addresses, hunted them down.

The television was on, mostly to drown out the din of everyone's idiosyncratic personal noises—a stomach groan, for instance, or the flushing of a toilet, a stifled belch, and other disturbances. It wasn't until the clock struck 7:45 p.m. that Stuart and Niraj looked up from what they were doing and realized they'd not even had a drink. Hadn't even thought about having a drink, one of those fuck-all, Friday-night-in-Gangnam kind of drinks, until this moment, when they threw on their shoes, left the kids to fend for themselves, and headed up the elevator three floors to the lounge on 29 because drinks were half off for only fifteen more minutes. They were on a budget, after all.

Dim, smoky, tall windows looking out onto a hazy city skyline, bottomless bowls of wasabi peas and boiled peanuts, the din of drunken Korean businessmen—this was where Stuart and Niraj came each night to debrief and decompress after another challenging, if not slightly bizarre, day at the KT's offices in Seoul.

Two doubles were before them, just under the wire.

Niraj handed Stuart his phone. "Did you see this?"

Liam had posted the latest Gartner industry report on their "morons" Slack channel, and Stuart smirked. "Gartner—what a bunch of jokers." He refrained from a verbal tirade and began typing it into his phone instead. He was in no mood for an idiot's guide to the top ten strategic tech trends for 2010. Not after the past two weeks, not after the Cowboy, as the Phenom would now forever be called, had almost derailed them with those stupid boots. Stuart shot off a response, then flipped open his laptop and checked the Javelina GitHub project for any new code releases.

"Brilliant," Niraj said, having just read Stuart's Slack response, which essentially eviscerated those top ten trends. "Come on—fabric-based infrastructure? Virtualization for availability?"

"I've been writing about 'hybrid fucking IT' for more than two years, and no one's been listening. Now Gartner gives it a name, and off we go."

"The name means nothing until someone gets it, and no one's getting it."

"Least of all KT. These telecoms are sinking ships. We need gamers, data streamers, or traders, companies running multiple software-as-a-service platforms in the public cloud and in data centers, with offices all over the world. These are the guys who are going to see Javelina for what it can one day be: a way to optimize and manage distributed cloud infrastructure with redundant, secure connections."

"Speaking of which, I've started the process of patenting our IP."

Intellectual property, theirs consisted of code that the Dream Team was presently creating outside the Javelina project, code that would become part of a proprietary platform they would rebrand as COMPASS. Niraj already had fifteen patent applications open for it and counting, even though they were still three months from a beta version. Why wait? Stuart released a latent smirk. His partner did not mess around.

"By the way," Niraj added, swallowing his drink, "JS wants us to use his guy on KT Phase II."

"What guy?"

"A McKinsey guy."

"What did I say about McKinsey?"

"McKinsey Korea. There's a difference."

"Not a good one."

"Look, he's a local—insurance that we don't fuck up on the cultural front again. Blood is thicker than water, especially in Asia. He can help us maneuver through the maze."

Stuart was just about to reassert his no-stuffed-shirt McKinsey policy, when his cell phone rang. He stared at the name, then at his watch: four in the morning in San Francisco. He stood up and told Niraj to order him another double, then paced off to the far window and picked up the call. "Go back to sleep, Marie."

"I can't."

He pictured her naked warmth all tangled up in the sheets, hair everywhere, and his heart swelled, just like that. Ache and burden.

"How did it go?" she asked.

"They want a proposal for Phase II."

"That was easy."

"What can I say? They like me."

A whooshing sound on her end. Movement, street sounds. "Where are you?"

"Here," she said.

"What do you mean, 'here'?"

"What I said. Here."

He felt himself stepping backward from the window, the knowledge gripping him, consuming his eyes. God, he was tired. A different kind of tired than the Silicon Valley bullshit kind, but tired nonetheless. "Where. Exactly. Are. You?"

"I'm on the airport bus. In a minute, I'll be walking into the InterContinental."

A moment of white space before his brain took the signal. She would do this. "Stay there. I'll come to you."

He told Niraj, in a combination of nonchalance, panic, and uncertainty, that Marie had just shown up in Seoul and said he'd be back. Still not fully processing what was happening, he walked at a fervent pace three blocks through the sprawling maze of the underground COEX, an extravaganza of glossy stalls and shops and restaurants and delicacies and any other Korean kind of craziness you could imagine, to the InterContinental hotel, where he'd told her to wait until he came to get her because he was certain she'd get lost trying to make her way back to him through that COEX, where he and his team were staying at the much more economical but not entirely unglamorous Oakwood Apartments.

Was he ready for this? Where would she stay? With the five of them, jammed into their three-bedroom condo?

"YOU'RE PALE," SHE SAID when he walked up. She was
seated on a purple velvet sofa that sat starkly singular in the
center of the cavernous, retro-decked lobby. Like a scene out
of *The Great Gatsby*. A massive, ticking clock. Her heart
pounding in her ears. She'd been so certain thirty-six hours
earlier. "Bad idea?"

She stood up, and he pulled her into his arms. "You're here.
I can't believe you're here."

Now, she was anything but certain. June, ninety-five
degrees with the humidity outside, and yet Stuart felt cold,
clammy. She fell further into his embrace, feeding him her
warmth, though it soon became clear that Stuart was the one
holding her up. He brushed his finger across her cheek, wet,
and pulled back to get a look at her. "You're crying."

"I'm not crying."

"What happened? Did something happen?"

It took her some more swallows before she could form
words: "Nothing happened. I simply reached the conclusion
last night that I had two choices: I could be home in San
Francisco, alone, or I could be here, with you."

He pulled a clean tissue from the back pocket of his
jeans, the ones he kept on hand as a result of perpetual sinus
issues, and handed it to her.

"I chose the latter, and yes, I'd had some wine."

He held her again, until her breath steadied and her trembling subsided.

There was less of him, literally—his waist felt thinner.
And he smelled of sweat and cigarettes and, now, tears. She
looked up at him. "You don't look well, Stuart."

"It's been a long couple weeks," he said in a tone that
meant he had made the understatement of the century.

And now he has me to deal with. This is idiotic. Marie blew
her nose with the tissue. "I can stay here, Stuart." She nodded
over at the hotel's gleaming white reception area, imagining, after

twelve hours of middle-seat coach travel, a gleaming white bed to go with it. Though she knew she shouldn't. They shouldn't. She needed to be frugal. There'd been times with Stuart when she'd not had to, but this was not one of those times.

"Come on," he said, grabbing her suitcase.

The reality struck her—she was such a private person. "They won't care, will they?"

"They don't give a shit."

"I'll do my own thing," she said, and then, "I don't want to be apart anymore."

He squeezed her hand in the whole of his until it hurt.

CHAPTER 2

TWO YEARS EARLIER, STUART had started the Javelina project as a ruse. A fuck-all Silicon Valley manifesto of sorts—if the VCs wouldn't fund his Javelina platform, then fine, he'd give it away for free. He opened a project on GitHub, an online community where programmers freely contributed and shared code as they deemed fit for whatever their purposes were. In Stuart's case, the code he threw out to the community represented three years' worth of his mission to design a secure and reliable way for enterprises to connect their systems to distributed cloud infrastructure, a connection that went far beyond the flimsy public internet connections that had so far been the norm. His Javelina project garnered little interest at first—in 2008, enterprises could barely say the phrase "cloud infrastructure," let alone see the need for a safe connection to one. Only a few techie rebels had glommed on and become avid contributors (Liam, Franco, and Arman, aka the Dream Team), plus some hackers, curiosity seekers, intellectuals, philosophers, haters. Open-source software projects had been around for decades by the time Javelina was born, but it was still anathema in Silicon Valley. You were not to give away software for free. Microsoft called open software projects cancer, if not outright communism. Stuart was no communist. He wanted to make a million just as much as anybody, *had* made a million, even two—and then there'd been that ten (on paper)—before he'd lost, not to mention spent, all of it in various ways, shapes, and forms, but that was another story.

Suffice it to say that for more than eighteen years, open software had been Stuart's rebel cult. It was also how he'd met Niraj. In 1990, fresh out of Berkeley with an engineering degree, the first thing Stuart did was purchase a very old x86 machine and download a copy of BSD on it—which was not technically free at the time, but as a Berkeley grad, he had connections. BSD stood for Berkeley Software Distribution, an operating system based on Unix and developed by professors at Berkeley. It was the precursor to OSF/1, the first open-source platform to enable true portability and vendor neutrality, and on which a mentor of Stuart's, Jack, had worked after graduating from MIT. Stuart had met Jack through online chat channels and made a cross-country bus pilgrimage to Cambridge the summer before his senior year at Berkeley just to meet him. He'd ended up bunking on Jack's floor for three weeks, during which time they'd spent many evenings at the newly opened Cambridge Brewing Company in Kendall Square, discussing the virtues of open-source, how stupid AT&T and SUN were for not joining the foundation, and so on. (Jack had gone on to spend so much time at the brewery that his name was now engraved on one of the barstools.) Stuart stayed in touch with Jack through his senior year, charting the progress of OSF/1, which was released in December 1990, helping Jack with some of his implementation needs, specifically with the networking stack, which came from BSD, which Stuart was intimately familiar with, since he worked with it at Berkeley. That relationship was what solidified Stuart's belief that open-source was the future of computing.

The problem was, he didn't have the cash to upgrade the hardware on his x86 machine as his programs got more demanding on the system, so he went straight to the only person he knew who might own a more powerful x86 machine: a classmate from India he'd butted heads with a few times in one of his many failed attempts as a recreational cricket player. Wealthy, arrogant, stubborn, with a mountainous nose, Niraj had just graduated from the business school. Stuart showed up at Niraj's dorm room to find him packing up his things and getting ready to spend his summer at home in Delhi, before returning to San Francisco to work as a management consultant for Price Waterhouse. It didn't take much persuading to get Niraj to let Stuart load BSD onto his computer and begin playing around with the source code. It didn't take long for Stuart to blow up the computer, either. Not literally, meaning, it didn't ignite into a ball of flames, but for many days, Stuart could not get the machine to boot up again. Niraj left the machine with Stuart and said he would retrieve it, ideally fully intact, upon his return. And that was how Stuart, and Niraj by default, discovered the best thing about open-source software (which it technically wasn't called at the time): the online community of rebels that came with it. Over the course of the next few weeks, with the help of people from all over the world accessed via Usenet, Stuart put that machine back together. From then on, especially after the advent of Linux a few years later, Stuart would never pay for a piece of software again.

Fast-forward eighteen years, and the Javelina GitHub project, after its slow start, grew to more than one hundred contributors and more than two thousand commits. Networks were exploding, and hacking had grown rampant, thanks to more complex and distributed clouds. There was no going back from Javelina, but Stuart was running out of money—and, by the way, he was not twenty-five and running out of money; he was forty and running out of money—and something snapped, Marie, for one, who'd been hinting about his getting a "real" job, and Stuart, for another, who, for the first time in his life, began looking for a "real" job. And then, just when he was about to land said "real" job at Chase Bank, he did what he always did in times of transition or uncertainty or, in this case, outright panic: he went to Niraj.

"You'll last a month in the IT department at Chase," was Niraj's dead-eyed response.

To this day, Stuart wasn't sure he even liked Niraj. He wouldn't call them friends. Niraj was simply the guy Stuart had always gone to for straight answers. But on this day in 2009, Niraj had been in a particularly wound-up state. Burned out from what was now the behemoth PricewaterhouseCoopers and, as always, under pressure from his family to return home to Delhi, he very articulately and succinctly laid out for Stuart how he could package Javelina, rebrand it as COMPASS, and sell it to large enterprises—all those things he'd learned in business school that Stuart had no patience for. Amazon Web Services may have invented the cloud, but it had its heads up its ass when it came to delivering cloud to the enterprise. Cloud was complex, and companies needed help, which meant services, consulting, *people*. And what did Silicon Valley VCs hate more than people? Well, nothing. VCs didn't want people; they wanted iPhone apps and energy drinks and CEOs under the age of twenty-five. Fuck the VCs, Niraj, who rarely cussed, had barked back at Stuart. *He*, Niraj, knew consulting; *he* knew how to build a services arm around COMPASS. They'd start with telecoms, because those companies were the first to look seriously at adopting cloud and knew absolutely nothing about how to deliver them. Telecoms in Asia were even better, since Niraj, through JS, had serious contacts there.

Six weeks, Stuart had told Marie. They'd been sitting side by side on their bed, staring into their hands, his suitcase by the door of their twentieth-floor SOMA tower apartment with the sweeping bay views that they'd long stopped being able to afford. Spending weeks apart was not new to them, so they'd been assuring each other on and off for the past few days. This was who they were. Own beings. Battling the pursuit. Fifteen years of it. Unmarried, childless, secure about their relationship as it existed, separate and apart from the world. They were to think of this as a repose, a way for Stuart to make some gig money and recover some of their losses.

"It'll be over before you know it," Stuart said, and stood up at last.

She noticed his golf clubs by the door. "You're taking your clubs?"

He stared at the clubs. Then at her. A lump in his throat. He'd never felt so alone.

Six weeks turned into three months.

"Is everything okay?" Niraj lit a cigarette and examined Stuart through the smoke.

Unsure how to respond, Stuart fell into the lounge chair that still held his imprint and downed what remained of his scotch, before starting on the second one Niraj had ordered. It was the first time either of them, going back eighteen years, had made a direct inquiry about the other's personal life.

"Everything's fine," Stuart quipped.

Niraj grinned, a grin that said, "We've no time for baggage now."

If only the sobbing hadn't unnerved him. Not to mention the fact that Marie had been in Seoul only one hour and he'd already abandoned her. He needed Niraj to know straight off that with her here, nothing changed, including these nightly status-scotch sessions. Nor would it change the fact that their weekend was basically shot, what with the two proposals due on Monday. Liam had just emailed Stuart some cloud network résumés; one guy from Juniper looked great, and he suggested they not wait, because this guy was hot and soon he'd be gone. Stuart and Niraj talked about it and other hiring options, but Stuart couldn't focus.

He shot Marie a text: "Where are you?"

She'd wanted to shower and was then going to join them, but he knew her better than that. When he'd asked her if anyone knew she was here, her response had been "Who would I tell?" Marie, the loner. Had she always been this way?

"Someone told me drinks were half off here."

Niraj startled. Even Stuart was a little surprised.

It hadn't been easy, but she'd gotten her ass out of bed and gone to the bar. She'd have to be different. Better. Make an effort. Do as she was told. All those things. "Don't mind me." She plopped down into the oversize leather chair next to Stuart and facing Niraj, as if there were no need for introductions, even though she'd never met Niraj before. "I'm just here for the scotch."

Stuart motioned to their server.

This was, after all, a work session. Stuart had warned Marie of that. And, true to form, Niraj continued their IP discussion as if she weren't there.

HE HAD DARK EYES and lashes and thick, bushy eyebrows. A blazer and slacks, no tie, he appeared relaxed, if slightly weathered, like Stuart, from some recent storm. He wore an easy, entirely unreadable smile, and could barely look at Marie as he spoke. Part of her wondered if she'd flown across the world just for this, to meet the man she liked to call Stuart's guru, the man Stuart refused to call his friend, even though they spent more time together than a married couple, especially these past three months at KT: sixteen-hour jaunts on planes together, business dinners, business drinks—lots of drinks—lunches, laundry. Still, Stuart claimed to know little about Niraj's inner workings: where, for instance, he spent his evenings after they parted ways every night. Not to bed was Stuart's guess—this was Gangnam, after all. "What happens in Gangnam?" Marie had inquired once, to which Stuart feigned innocence and asked how would he know?

She swallowed her drink and interjected, "What's IoT?" if only for effect, if only to see Niraj glance at Stuart the way he just had. She knew what IoT was, the definition, anyway: internet of things, which meant things connected to the internet, like her thermostat, so that she could control it from anywhere. How could she not know this after living with Stuart for fifteen years, not to mention that she was, or had been, in her day, someone who knew her way around a technical document? Anyway, she just wanted to hear how Niraj might explain it to her, and he did, sans patronizing, with eloquence, clarity, and, above all, the kind of patience for her deep-dive inquiries that Stuart often lacked—"It's not true just because you said it," she would often have to remind him. Anyway, the guru had passed. After all, hers had been a test.

"Okay, I'm starving." Stuart said finally, already craving her naked warmth beside him in bed that night. He stood up. "Let's go eat."

Marie stood, but Niraj stayed seated, staring critically at his phone.

Marie nudged Stuart, who nudged her back. She nudged him again, and he cleared his throat and said to Niraj, "We're going to get some dinner. Join us?"

"Nah."

"Okay."

"See you."

"Yep." He did not look up.

THAT NIGHT, AFTER DEVOURING the Korean pancake, the pork dumplings, and the noodles made by the fat and sweaty Korean lady in her shop above the 7-Eleven that overlooked the Bongeunsa Temple's Godzilla-size Buddha statue, after their long discourse on whether it was the Chinese or the Italians who had invented pasta, Stuart and Marie lay stretched out on their sides on the bed, facing each other.

"It's going to be different this time," he said.

She could smell the scallion on his breath and the pork on his flesh. She didn't ask him what was going to be different. She'd already taken him down that road, and it had brought them to the bottom.

She closed her eyes.

Stuart rubbed her head until she fell asleep, her dreams erratic.

CHAPTER 3
JULY 2010

WHEN THEY LANDED SINGTEL as a client, Stuart flew Marie to Jeju Island for the weekend. Ninety percent rock and home to a dormant volcano, an hour by plane off the southern coast of the Korean peninsula, it was where the exiled had been sent in times past to live among the fishermen. They checked into a nondescript hotel and spent hours walking along the craggy, windswept shores.

When they spotted what they thought were seals floating in the jagged pools along the shore's edges, Marie climbed far out onto one of the jettisoning rocks to see, Stuart following from a distance—he was not a strong swimmer. The waters were rough, and when he called to Marie to come back, she only scrambled out farther.

"They're divers," she said, returning at last.

He wiped the mist off her face and took her hand, wet, in his. They continued down the shore, until they came upon a bronzed statue of a woman wearing the same kind of body-suit and *Twenty Thousand Leagues Under the Sea* breathing apparatus as those they had just seen below the surface. Sea women, they were called, according to the plaque. Once the island's main breadwinners, these women were legends now, though a dying breed, what with the resorts having taken over, the women's offspring having fled to the mainland for work.

They walked over to a tarp-covered outpost, where the few remaining sodden and ancient sea women sat crouched before buckets, cleaning their catches. Stuart went up to one of them and knelt beside her. Since he'd begun working in Korea, he'd become fascinated with the language—his love for decoding all-consuming and pervasive and beyond ones and zeros—and the fact that Korea's founding fathers purposely made the alphabet easy and accessible to all their people. Stuart had found mastering basic proficiency easy and as such was able to exchange some words with the sea woman. Soon enough, he was walking away with a round, spiny creature in his palms, its bristles writhing, its body breathing, even after she'd slit it open. Marie's face screwed up in both horror and delight when he came at her with it. He'd taught her to love raw fish in all its forms, but not like this. She put a hand over her mouth. "Now's not the time to be squeamish, Marie."

She removed her hand. "Are you sure?"

He dug his finger into the wet, tonguelike flesh and fed her.

The next morning, Marie woke at dawn to go back to the shore to watch the sea women. There were only a handful of them; she watched them squiggle and contort around the mossy rocks along the water's surface, disappearing and reappearing with the crashing swells. Hunters and gatherers. One more succulent mollusk. Searchers of the purest form.

Marie. Her name echoed in a crashing wave. She turned. It was Stuart calling her to come back. Come back.

When he'd come to find her—he knew where to look— she was farther out on the rocks this time, staring out as if at any moment she might dive in, or as if she were waiting for a wave to pull her in. But then he'd called out and she'd turned, beaming and full of life as he'd not seen her in some time, her hair whipping in the wind, streaked amber in the morning light. She stumbled her way back, falling and catching herself and laughing.

"I thought you were going to jump in," he said, smiling quickly, as if he might be joking.

"Oh, Stuart," she said, their eyes holding. "It doesn't matter, don't you see? I'm done with all that."

He didn't see. Didn't always want to.

She grabbed his hands. "I'll go back to work."

A wave sighed in the distant depths. He looked past her, toward the pale horizon. She'd been saying that since her mother had died. The two had grown unbearably close in the end, as Marie had let her career fall away, though she claimed that by then her career had long stopped being one. She pimped herself out on high-priced consulting gigs for an eccentric ex-boss who had a penchant for deals that never came to fruition. That was the "career" she'd left. She hadn't worked in years, and, as enticing as her noninconsequential income might have been to them both, she didn't want to go back to the fight, and he wasn't going to make her. He loved her. He had vowed to take care of her. "But don't you see? You don't have to go back to work. Not if we live here."

"In Seoul?"

"Singapore. I'll take you, Marie. You'll see. You can decide for yourself."

He told her about their plans for COMPASS while the sea raged on, the great body of tumultuous gray, the clear white light of everything.

She *had* thrived. That was the thing. Part of her really did want to go back to work. The challenge and the pace. "You go show them, dear . . ." had been some of her mother's last words. But the other part of Marie, no. No, no, no, no. The part she had kept from her mother, who came from a different era, where working was a privilege and there were no excuses; her mother, who never once did not work a day of her working-age life. Literally, she was seventy-two years old and headed to a board meeting when she pulled over onto the shoulder of the 101 freeway and rested her head back. She was done.

"I'll go anywhere, Stuart. Just tell me where. Singapore? Fine. Singapore it is."

"But you haven't even seen it."

"I don't need to."

She held his eyes, imploring him, with all her being, to read what she was trying to tell him, which was that there was no longer anything of her that wasn't his. Children. That's what she had meant by "I'm done with all that."

He followed her eyes as they turned toward the sea. He did not want her to change for him. He loved her exactly as she was . . . and yet this thing about children. The fact was, he'd never wanted kids, though he'd assumed that would change with maturity, with age, as it had for his friends. And he had tried, for a while. He'd participated in her quest, which had turned into an obsession as she recovered from the loss of her mother, then desperation as the years stretched on and no child materialized. She had fallen into a black hole, one deeper, darker, and more distant than the others, and, honestly, he might have taken the project in Korea to be free of her. To get some space.

"I want to show you something," she said.

He grabbed her arm to steady her as she led him along the shore, pointing out little rock pyramids here and there. Man-made, all shapes and sizes.

"What do you think they're for?" she asked, and he said that perhaps they were prayers, offerings, of some sort.

She knelt, picked up a stray rock, and placed it on a patch of hardened ash from which weed and bramble sprouted. He did the same, and they kept on like that, thoughtfully placing one atop or aside the other, until the formation felt as solid as it did not. Complete. And ready to tumble over. Ready to be swept out to sea in the next storm.

CHAPTER 4
JULY 2010

WHEN STUART AND MARIE returned from Jeju, Niraj was waiting for them with a check from his father for $150,000, carrying certain unwritten terms with which Niraj told Stuart he need not concern himself. Stuart knew that Niraj came from serious money; that his father had founded one of the largest low-tech, cash-cow, steel-manufacturing-parts businesses in India; that Niraj, like Stuart, was forty, and, also like Stuart, should probably give up on frivolous passions, and, unlike Stuart, should return home to take the reins of the family business and settle into an arranged marriage. For years now, Stuart had heard rumblings about a fiancée back in India. Perhaps Niraj had made some sort of arrangement with his father and now his clock was ticking. Whatever the reason for the money, Stuart didn't care. The point was that neither of them had more time to waste; what with Niraj's receding hairline and the strand of gray Marie had discerned on Stuart's pillow that morning, the window for making their mark was closing.

Stuart, wanting an equal amount of shares in the majority, cleaned out his savings to match Niraj's father's $150K. They hired two Singaporean network architects, plus a cloud engineer Stuart had worked with in the States, and opened up shop in a two-room space in a row of repurposed, single-story teahouses and mah-jongg parlors in Singapore's old Chinatown, because the rent was dirt cheap and the country was English speaking and centrally located to their Asian markets. It took them a month to apply and receive the government's matched funding, at which point they doled out options to the Dream Team, bought a few folding desks and chairs—comfortable, but no Aeron, mind you; no bean bags; no Ping-Pong tables or Hacky Sack balls, no balls of any kind—and began building a business around the second coming of Javelina: Vita, Latin for "life."

Stuart, as CTO, took charge of building the COMPASS platform, while Niraj, as CEO, built the services arm, which included managing the ongoing projects at KT and SingTel and now, possibly, cross their fingers, Toyota. JS had arranged the introduction to the Toyota Cloud VP through a Japanese conglomerate with which JS often transacted in business and the exchange of favors. Stuart did as JS instructed and sent Stuart to Tokyo on a Saturday with his golf clubs. "Go easy" were his last words to Stuart—meaning, "Let them win." Stuart, who was pathetic at all other sports beside this one, thanks to his father, was a two handicap. Or used to be, anyway—he'd not had time to play in a while and was rusty. And slightly nervous, standing outside his hotel near Tokyo Station in the dark at six in the morning as a black Toyota Highlander, fresh off the manufacturing floor, slid up alongside the curb. A round of golf in Asia, Stuart would soon learn, was not a casual Sunday affair. In the backseat were Fumitaka-san, VP of Cloud at the Japanese conglomerate; Hideo-san, Toyota's VP of Cloud; and Koichiro-san, the CEO of Dashi Corp Asia, a large data service provider JS had thought it in Vita's best interest to befriend. All were dressed in blazers over polo shirts, pressed slacks, and fine leather shoes and matching belts that blended with the Toyota's interior.

The SUV made no sound as the driver pulled away and headed for the exclusive course at which Fumitaka-san and Hideo-san were members. The Highlander was part of the new "connected" series, the first Toyota vehicles able to send data back to the company's central databases, as well as share it with other cars. The issue was what to do with the data once you had it, hence the quotes Stuart always put around the word "connected," for being "connected" was one thing, and converting mountains of data into intelligence that powered in-car services entirely another. For that, you needed the right cloud infrastructure, not to mention secure connectivity, and after some preliminary discussions with JS and Fumitaka-san, Stuart was certain Toyota didn't have either. Meanwhile, Hideo-san was proudly pointing out the new cloud features that had been incorporated into the car's GPS and voice recognition system, such as automatic crash notification and roadside assistance, all of which made Stuart feel less safe. Bells and whistles, he thought, wondering how long it would take him to hack in and change the radio station from that grating disco music. Yet he nodded all the while, with great intrigue.

An hour later, they were cruising into a serene suburban enclave of delicately undulating hills full of trees bursting with autumn. They pulled up to a *ryokan*-styled clubhouse, which stood elegant and unassuming before a vista of wide, perfectly manicured fairways. Lakes were positioned treacherously here and there, with floating geese and mist still lurking along the surface as dawn broke open the sky. They checked into the locker room, stored their blazers and bags and changed their leather shoes, and met in the dining room for a breakfast of steaming hot bowls of rice porridge flecked with bonito and whitefish. They went to the range for a half hour to warm up. It was nine o'clock when they teed off; the fog had lifted, the grass smelled pungent, and it was peaceful and quiet. Stuart felt so far away as to feel brought close again to his father and Fremont, the crappy public course they'd no money to play on, the one sodden most of the time because of poor irrigation. Carts were pointless. As they were here, apparently, but for other reasons. The four of them strolled along the fairways with caddies following, carrying their clubs. Noises of great admiration were made each time Stuart teed off. There were few other golfers out, so they moved along at a languid pace. It took two hours to play the front nine—every putt lined up and taken seriously on account of the betting—at which point they paused for a leisurely lunch back at the club restaurant and each drank a generous amount of Japanese beer.

Stuart didn't play so well on the back nine, as had been his intention and for which the beer had been strategic. When they were finished with the round, they returned to the locker rooms to scour themselves clean in baths alternating between scalding, icy, and lukewarm. Back in blazers and fine leather, they met in the lounge to analyze each other's swings, tally each other's scores, and, of course, drink more beer. Stuart handed over 2,000 yen to Fumitaka-san, of whom he'd grown quite fond as they'd made their way around the course. Fumitaka-san was compact, fit, and a gentleman of the highest order. He took great care to point out to Stuart the areas of the fairway he should avoid, and which ways the putts tended to roll. His face was flushed from the beer now; it had been a nice day, and they were all having a good time. The beer began talking, and soon Fumitaka-san was telling Stuart, privately, about his boss's request that he relocate to the States to run their Asian operations there. He admitted that he was somewhat daunted by the idea, as he was fifty-five, after all—news that shocked Stuart, who had guessed midforties—and admittedly had not the energy and ambition of his youth and would have liked to have taken it easier at this age. After some silence, Stuart asked what he planned to do, and Fumitaka-san said that there was nothing *to* do; when your boss asked you to do something, you did it.

Stuart nodded.

They were all slightly buzzed on the drive home. Kichiro-san and Hideo-san were dropped off first. Next up was

Fumitaka-san, red-faced from the beer and resting his head back on the seat. At one point, he roused himself to ask Stuart how he had become such a good golfer. Stuart told him that as a fireman, his father had received free tokens for the range down at the Fremont public course. He and Stuart had gone every weekend his father was not on duty. Stuart couldn't help laughing as he described to Fumitaka-san how he used to drive his dad nuts. "Just relax and hit the ball, son," his father would say. "You're thinking too much." Stuart, being Stuart, had applied an engineer's mind to the whole endeavor. He ran the calculations of flight trajectory, speed, and club arc, and by the time he was thirteen, he'd made his own seven-iron, the only club he'd played with until he was in his twenties and working and could afford a set of his own. By that point, he told Fumitaka-san, his dad had had to retire from the fire department because of a knee injury and couldn't hit balls anymore. Well, actually, he *could* hit balls, Stuart said—he just didn't want to. He was unhappy about a lot of things by then.

The car hit a bump, and Stuart felt something move in his intestines. When the waiter had come to take their lunch orders, Stuart, going first, had ordered the bento box. Everyone else had gotten the burger with fries, and Stuart felt immediately idiotic, wondering if they had done so for his sake. When his box came, it consisted of rice, seaweed, pickled vegetables, and fried chicken, none of which surprised him and all of which he devoured, to the surprise of those around him. As it turned out, though, they'd ordered the burgers not for his sake but for their own. Since the war, the Japanese had become big beef eaters; in fact, the number-one destination for a meal in Tokyo was now McDonald's. Stuart learned this as Fumitaka-san now, and in what Stuart presumed was a rare foray into personal detail, began to talk about his grandfather. Struggling to survive after the war, Fumitaka-san's grandfather, living in a small village on the island of Hokkaido, got involved in helping to facilitate the Americans' importation of beef into Japan as a push to rebuild. Through his scrappy hard work and cunning, his grandfather dug himself out of poverty, moved to Tokyo, and raised a family. Thanks in part to him, Japanese teens were now on average two inches taller than they were half a century ago.

The driver pulled up in front of Fumitaka-san's house. By now, the fried chicken and the beer were raising alarm bells in Stuart's bowels. He knew that it was far from appropriate, possibly even deal-breaking—even Niraj had never been invited into JS's home; *gaijin* (foreigners), friends or not, were kept apart and separate—but the drive to Stuart's hotel was still thirty minutes away, and there was just nothing else he could do. "Fumitaka-san, I must ask you this great favor. Please forgive me, but may I use your bathroom?"

He must have seen the desperation on Stuart's face. "But of course," he said. "Please, let us not wait here any longer."

Fumitaka-san led Stuart up to the door and into the foyer, where they were greeted by his wife, who bowed and stepped back. Stuart slipped off his shoes, and she showed him to the bathroom, where he proceeded to evacuate his entire bowels in a not-so-gentle manner. If only there had been a candle to light, something, anything, but, alas, after washing his hands, he shut the door behind him and, after some swift goodbyes and nods and bows, skulked guiltily out the front door, mortified. It was almost nine o'clock, and he spent the ride to the hotel slouched far down in the backseat, so as not to be spotted by anyone, least of all himself, chewing his finger intermittently and thinking that he wouldn't be surprised if they never heard from Fumitaka-san again.

The next morning, Niraj called Stuart to tell him that the Toyota car cloud team had agreed to take a meeting.

CHAPTER 5

THEY TOOK A NINETY-MINUTE Shinkansen bullet train out to the middle of nowhere—Nagoya—where Toyota's sprawling IT facilities were located. Unlike in Korea, Stuart and Niraj didn't have to pass through ten levels of security and release their cell phones and other electronics before being granted access to the conference room; rather, visitor conference rooms were located directly in the building lobby, just past next year's Lexus and Avalon releases. When they entered their prescribed room, they were confronted by ten unsmiling Japanese men and one translator. The senior Toyota cloud team member gave them a cursory overview of the company's car cloud strategy, clicking through slides that were almost childlike and that reminded Stuart of the Japanese variety show he'd stared at the previous night on TV. When Stuart and Niraj spoke, the men remained standoffish and asked few questions. They shared no details about the constraints or difficulties they were experiencing and might have needed help on. Everything was going according to plan, and it soon became apparent that the team had taken the meeting only because it had been dictated from above.

Disillusioned and frustrated, Niraj and Stuart went to the United lounge at Narita and, while waiting for their return flight, brainstormed ways they might win over the Japanese. Stuart at one point flippantly suggested that they rent the exact same car and let Liam—who'd made a career of hacking into enterprise systems from his village in the outback before meeting a Singaporean tourist on the beach in Melbourne and following her home—loose to hack into the car's system and show these guys firsthand why their car cloud was neither safe nor secure. Ha!

Stuart swallowed his drink while Niraj went silent. Very silent. So silent that the Japanese announcer calling for flights over the loudspeaker grew jarringly loud. Niraj waited for her to finish. "We'd have to do it in such a way that the Japanese wouldn't lose face."

"I was joking, Niraj."

"Why? It makes perfect sense."

"Is it even legal?"

Niraj got out his phone and called JS, who then called Fumitaka-san, and after some back-and-forth it was decided that Fumitaka-san would call Hideo-san and offer the idea in a way that would make Hideo-san look like a hero. While his team wouldn't know about the fake hack, Hideo-san would, and thus all faces would be saved.

Three days later, they had the go-ahead. Stuart was still wary about it and part of him wished he'd never said anything to Niraj. Liam was little help—all doom and gloom about it (he and his wife were in the middle of trying to adopt newborn Korean twins, and they didn't need anything tripping that up). "Oh, cheer up, Liam," Niraj chided. "Try to have a little fun."

Stuart had met Liam under the alias Charlie Brown back when Liam had joined the Javelina project, and his character wasn't far from the cartoon version. Dry-humored, glass half empty, exacting when it came to networks—there would be no breaches on his watch—and so not the best with clients because clients needed options. For Liam, there was only ever one option: the right one. His wife, the Singaporean beauty he'd met that day on the beach and soon thereafter married, rented them the Toyota hybrid car, and Stuart,

Niraj, and Liam drove it far out of the city to a vacant empty lot. Niraj had the brilliant idea to videotape Liam hacking to show the Japanese exactly what steps they had taken and prove it had really happened and that they were the ones to do it. After an hour of pounding on his laptop, Liam had the doors unlocked and the trunk popped and had taken full control of the dashboard. Two hours later, he'd managed to intercept data from another Toyota nearby, and, most impactful of all, upload to the car software that gave him access to the Toyota network, if he so chose to do so.

Afterward, they drove back to Chinatown, returned the car, and went to their favorite pepper-crab restaurant, where they proceeded to sketch out Toyota's network vulnerabilities on chili pepper–stained napkins. Stuart then returned to the bodega and spent the night working on diagrams and documenting the process they had gone through and the risks Toyota had unknowingly opened itself up to. How, for instance, once a hacker took control of the car, there was no reason why they couldn't then upload a virus from that car to Toyota's core network and bring it to a screeching halt. Liam had proven just that.

No, those unsmiling men would not like to hear that. Stuart wondered how Hideo-san might punish his team once he found out and couldn't help envisioning what might be the only option: an honorable seppuku ending. Stuart couldn't understand the Toyota team's staunch resistance to COMPASS in the first place, why they had refused to listen to the theories Stuart had put forth, preferring instead to focus on the minutiae, like the literal translation of every last word in the presentation. Not to mention the questions, those bordering on the medieval: How can a network function without brand-name components like Cisco or Juniper or Brocade? How do we know your solution is secure if it doesn't use Check Point firewalls? How can we conceive of sharing a platform with your other clients, potentially competitors? They needed their walled gardens. The problem was, there were *no more physical assets*, but no matter how Stuart put it to them, they couldn't conceptualize it in any other way but that they were losing control. Change was glacial in Asian markets—and Stuart had thought the VCs were bad. Everyone, for that matter, remained unable to comprehend COMPASS. Was Stuart not articulating it properly? *What* was he not articulating? He chewed on his cuticle for a moment, staring at his screen but not seeing anything, because it always came back to the same thing. Networks as they existed needed to be blown up and re-created with an entirely new sound—a new way for people to hear.

"What is a car cloud, anyway? A car that floats on clouds?"

Stuart looked up, startled to see Marie standing there in the moonlight, in her robe, her hair matted from sleep. "Don't try to be funny, Marie."

"I thought you said that if you're pulling all-nighters, you're doing something fundamentally wrong."

He sat back and huffed. "Come look at this."

"You sent everyone home so you could do all the work? It's three in the morning."

"This isn't work."

She sighed and came over.

He moved to the side to let her in. "It's just an outline. It needs a lot of work."

Her eyes were having a hard time adjusting to the screen. "Outline for what?"

"Just read it."

It took her a few paragraphs to understand what it was: his book, the one he'd been threatening to write for years.

"People aren't getting it, Marie. All night I've been thinking about the best way for them to get it, and I think this is it."

"As if you don't have enough to do."

"That's where you come in."

"What does that mean?"

"I thought you could help me write it."

Her response was to respond in no way whatsoever.

"You said you wanted to go back to work."

"What do I know about virtual networks?"

"Don't pretend you're dumber than you are."

"I'm not sure that's a compliment."

"I'm organizing all my notes and posts in a Dropbox folder for you."

"How romantic."

There was a pause.

"Really, Stuart, I've been out of the telecom world for so long, I can barely update the software on my cell phone without your help."

He whirled out a few commands on his keyboard and then fell back. "I just sent you the Dropbox invite. It won't be complicated. Just some basics, because people *aren't getting it* and *we want them to get it*."

"You already said that."

"Well, I'm saying it again."

"Will anyone even buy it?"

"We're going to give it away."

"Sounds like a solid business model."

"If you don't want to help, just say so."

"I want to help."

He shut his laptop and, before she could change her mind, turned her in the direction of bed. Sleep would be the best course of action at this point, even if it was only a few hours. Perhaps some scotch to dull the adrenaline surge. He poured a glass along the way, and they moved through the dividing wall of slatted wood doors to the bedroom. The bodega they were renting in Singapore—a tenth of what they'd been paying in SOMA—was tucked on a quiet side street off the glossy shopping thoroughfare of Orchard Road and had been designed to stay cool at all hours of the day, shaded by the eaves and windows positioned for the cross-breeze. Marie's robe fluttered to the floor as she stood at the window, taking it in, stripped bare in the moonlight. He could see all the nicks and marks peppering her flesh, the scars, the spot on her inner thigh where the tattoo had been lasered off. Broad shouldered, long, the skeletal remains of a swimmer's body. God, she was beautiful.

"Stuart?"

Sultry, almost. The slow whirl of the ceiling fan.

She was looking at him strangely. "Do you want me to turn on the AC?"

"Do you like it here?" he asked.

"What do you mean?"

He went over to her and got on his knees and pulled her in to him. "I want you to like it here."

CHAPTER 6
AUGUST 2010

THE NEXT MORNING, AFTER Stuart left for the office. Marie went to the kitchen, poured herself an espresso, and took it with her to the table. She opened her laptop and stared out the window at the Japanese garden. There was a thick layer of dew over everything and water dripping from gigantic leaves, even though there had been no rain. She took a deep breath of moist air and opened the Dropbox folder Stuart had shared with her, planning to call his bluff—she knew he knew she didn't want to go back to work, even when she might insist that she did, and he knew she knew that when he told her she didn't have to go back to work, he secretly wished she would. Was writing this book a test of their respective wills?

Back in San Francisco, as Stuart's six-week stint in Seoul had turned into three months, it had struck Marie that Stuart might never be back, not in the way he was before, anyway. *They* were before, not that that would be a bad thing—they'd grown out of sync, to say the least. He had Javelina, and she had . . . what, exactly? No career, no mother, no child, what? So, as she sometimes did after a couple glasses of wine failed to dull the self-loathing, she drafted an email to Jim, one of her first bosses and the only one who kept managing to track her down for the occasional high-priced gig. Jim would hook her up in an instant. This was what Stuart wanted for her and what she needed for herself. But then, as she always did after drafting an email to Jim, she deleted it—this time, slamming her laptop shut for emphasis. Then she got up and went to the window to check the seams for cracks or fissures, because up here in the SOMA tower there was only ever one temperature—bitter cold. Famous bridges shrouded in fog. Wind howling through the skyscrapers clustered so closely to hers that she could almost reach out and touch them. No fissures, just shitty insulation and poor heating. She could never get warm, not even in the warmest months. She poured more wine. From the more modest abodes of their late twenties and thirties, they could hear the foghorn, the ring of a distant cable car, even the howls of a sea lion, on occasion, but up here in this tower, there was only the whistle and whirl, the rattling panes.

She took her wine back to the couch and, calmer now, reopened her laptop. Maybe she was doing this all wrong. Jim was the queasy, dreaded, easy out. What she needed to do was start over, rebuild herself from the beginning. You know, do things the hard way. Start as an analyst, a minion, and work her way up through the ranks again, with no one she knew expecting her to be something she was not. Yes, that was what she'd do. Fueled with this new plan, she hunted down an old résumé from years back, tucked in a forgotten folder, and read through it. Would people notice seven years—poof—gone? How much longer could she pretend? She spent the next two hours massaging her work experiences as best she could—always the question of whether to omit the blow-up firm or not, as it did have some cachet. She ripped off a cover letter and sent it, along with her résumé, to the HR department of the last firm she had worked for, the one that had since been acquired, merged, and then been sold again. She had no idea if any of the partners she'd worked with would still be there. She'd not kept in touch—had had zero desire to.

Submission received!

In the days that followed, she wandered up and down the hills of her birth city—Nob, Russian, Telegraph, Rincon—past all those old abodes, bracing against the wind off the bay and waiting for a response from the firm. Back in the tower, she'd often find herself frozen in some banal activity, like examining her face in the mirror or repositioning the space heaters or gazing into the rooms of the Four Seasons, looking for couples arguing in their underwear; caught up in the image of herself rushing through an airport, or staring into a closet full of dark, ominous clothing, or addressing a conference table filled with stone-cold executives, trying to convince them of something she was not so convinced of herself. It had been seven years since she'd tried to convince anyone of anything. This idea of persuasion, of getting people to see things the way she saw them, or her team saw them, what their research pointed to, the moment the telecom industry crashed and she'd been escorted out the door—that instinct had gone dead. Even in her subsequent gig work for Jim, something was missing, hollowed out. It had become her belief that people knew everything they needed and wanted to know already, and so, at last, after having made some money with Jim, she'd stopped returning his calls and emails. She'd gone quiet, devoid of voice or opinion—a break from the world that had turned into a way of life.

A week later, the firm responded, short and sweet: Marie was not what they were looking for. She was, to say the least, stunned. It had never occurred to her that she would be rejected, which was probably why she'd failed to mention to Stuart that she'd sent her résumé in at all, not wanting him to get his hopes up if, in the end, she decided to turn down the offer. How utterly mortifying.

She released her eyes from what had been their clenched-shut position—back to the present—and clicked open the

Dropbox folder Stuart had sent her. She began reviewing his manuscript outline. She read over his blog posts, some articles, lectures, and random notes and texts. It was slow going at first. She knew the intricacies about networks from her days working in telecom and from her interactions with the network engineers and network system administrators at her enterprise clients. Routers, switches, and hardware were how systems communicated with each other back then— not so different from how post offices got letters to where they needed to go. Back then, infrastructure was what it was, infrastructure, as opposed to today, when infrastructure was code, software, "virtualization." She'd missed that wave. Cloud computing, they now called it. Instead of flipping a switch or reconnecting a wire, a network engineer created a machine, aka a server, by writing a piece of code. The problem was that today's network engineers *did not know how to code*. Nor did they want to learn how to, and so the telecoms that employed them, the main users of those physical routers and switches—and the companies that made them, Cisco, Juniper, who cared?—were going extinct, this time really extinct, versus the market crash of 2002, when telecoms lost $2 trillion in value and half a million people lost their jobs, including Marie. This time, we were talking wiped-off-the-face-of-the-earth extinct.

Marie looked up suddenly. Was she just like them, all those soon-to-be-extinct network engineers? Had she, too, become obsolete? She looked down and started typing, just like that, cutting through seven years of fog, connecting and interpreting and massaging the information. What was the story? There always was one, a story for investors, clients, customers—game-changing words and catchphrases. Her job was to find it, to create something out of nothing. Smoke and mirrors. It was what she excelled at, though she'd never written a book, per se, just garden-variety, overhyped product reports that led analysts to overhyped valuations. By noon, after drafting a new outline and a three-page thesis statement, she hated herself again. All of them. For being liars. Fakes.

Stuart said it was going to be different this time, but she wondered.

She shut her laptop. She knew what he was doing. He was trying to get her to engage again, to put her back together the way she had been because he would never believe the truth of what had really happened; that she had closed her eyes—to a lot of things. She was as much to blame as everyone else.

She went for a walk, not knowing where she was going, gazing absently into the high-end shop windows of Orchard Road until she reached the end and found herself wandering through jade meadows and moss-filled lakes, down tangled, wooded paths, and deep into a forest. The distant sounds of city life were suppressed by a lushness so profound, it became a sound of its own. She crossed over a series of walking bridges, through a maze of vertical gardens. She came upon a villa tucked discreetly inside the foliage, Mediterranean-style, sleek with wealth and status. Then another. And another. Farther on, carved out of the jungle, was a marble-inlaid lap pool—elegant, tasteful, pristine, secluded from view. Two teak lounges and a low table sat askew. Without thought, she stripped down to her bra and underwear and dove in, swimming along the bottom to the other end and back, before surfacing through a cluster of lilies, gasping, smoothing her hair back from her face. Birds were singing. A rustle came through the leaves. She dove under again. Lap after lap, she didn't stop, until perhaps an hour had passed and she was spent and exhilarated. She slid her clothes back on and made her way out via the same path from which she'd come, only to find herself not back at the botanical gardens but in the Shangri-La Resort, with all its colonialism and wicker and sour-smelling guests. She walked out the pillared front entrance, her clothes sticking to her, past the line of Rolls-Royces and Mercedes, no one paying her any notice.

Later that evening, at the bustling, cavernous Suntec City food hall, Marie and Stuart sat at a communal wood table among a sea of other communal wood tables, slurping up the soupy noodles they had just watched the old and gentle-mannered Singaporean hawker make with his bare hands. It was a mesmerizing process that started with a ball of dough that he folded over and over and over again—never, not once, did he cut the dough. He simply kept folding it, a hundred times, it felt like, until the noodles had reached the perfect width and length and were ready to drop into the hot soup. It was like a magic show.

Singapore organized its street vendors, those offering any and all kinds of food—Indonesian, Thai, Singaporean, Malaysian—by rounding them up in halls like this one to control the health, hygiene, and quality of food. The hall at Suntec was located at the base of four office towers, in the center of which stood the infamous, space saucer–shaped Fountain of Wealth. It was here, in between slurps and over the sounds of raging water, that Marie told Stuart about the pool she'd discovered earlier.

He promptly dropped his chopsticks. "Marie, this is Singapore. They throw you in jail for chewing gum; how do you think they're going to feel about trespassing? Don't you remember the sign I pointed out to you at the airport?"

Death for Drug Traffickers Under Singapore Law. Yes, she remembered.

"You've got to be more careful." His face felt hot and clammy, though that could have been from the steam.

"Calm down. I couldn't find it again if I tried."

"Liam's wife belongs to the Cricket Club, if you want to swim. There's also the American Club."

"You know I'm not a club person."

His look to her: "I know." Then he picked up his chopsticks. "Did you look at my outline?"

This surprised her. She'd thought he might have forgotten his request by now. And anyway, wasn't it her job to reject such notions dreamed up in the wee hours, usually under the influence, in this case, of sleep deprivation?

"I thought it was good," she said finally.

The noodle slipped from Stuart's chopsticks and fell back into the bowl, almost scorching his face. "Good?"

She looked around for a napkin, always mysteriously absent in these places—not a small problem, especially when you were eating spicy food.

"It's missing the real story, though," she added. "The fact that you *are* Javelina. Why don't you talk about Javelina in the book? Why you started it as an open-source project. Everything you went through to get it up and running, and how it took off like it did."

"Niraj wants to distance us from Javelina. I've burned enough bridges in Silicon Valley already."

"Well, maybe this is your bridge back."

He swallowed his beer. "Javelina is an open-source project, Marie, and there's still a lot of resistance."

"I thought you said that cloud has exploded the demand for open-source projects. That this utilitarian way of creating and building technology would become the norm. That there was no going back from open-source."

"Well, I was wrong. You can tout the advantages of egalitarian software development as much as you want, a free and open exchange of ideas and code in a safe, nonthreatening environment, but the reality is, it's bullshit." He looked purposefully at her. "Big cloud. You know who they are, Marie." He paused to get a cue from her that she did and then continued, "Facebook, Amazon, Netflix, Google—FANG—have skewed all the wealth in their favor because of open-source software more than anyone could ever have imagined. They take the free software, throw their money on top of it, push out the little guys who invented the software in the first place, then exploit the shit out of that software for the benefit of their customers, who pay a nice fee for it, directly or indirectly."

"But—"

"The only money being exchanged in the open movement is between big cloud and their customers, and the rest of us can go fuck ourselves. How do you think Google's grown so huge? Free, *open* software, that's how. They don't have to reinvent the wheel; they don't have to train their programmers. They already know what's going on out there because it's all out there. They're probably trying right now to figure out a way to make a nice chunk of change off Javelina, if only their high-priced engineers could understand it."

Her mouth had clamped shut. Now was not the time to interrupt him.

"I've been working with open-source projects for two decades now, Marie, and the reality is that most tech startups that use an open-source project at the core of their product usually fail. So why fund them?"

"You are not making me feel all warm and fuzzy about our future."

He shrugged a shoulder. "Have I ever?"

She had to smile at that. Then, "Seriously, Stuart, how do you plan on surviving?"

"We've got a jump start here while everyone, including big cloud, still has their head up their ass when it comes to COMPASS networks—a year, maybe two, before Amazon Web Services catches on. So why not go for it? What, are we all supposed to roll over and die because of companies like Facebook?"

She didn't answer. She watched him bring the bowl to his lips and slurp, wondering, as she had been more and more since they had moved to Asia, if he'd been switched at birth. "Do you really want to write this book, Stuart?"

He set down the bowl, gasped, and studied her. "Yes."

"You asked my opinion, and if you really want it, it's this: Tell the truth—the complete and absolute truth."

"Ones and zeros don't lie. Technology is the essence of truth."

"I'm not going to make shit up anymore."

"I didn't ask you to. Where is this coming from?"

She sighed. She didn't know. "I'll need to talk to your guys."

"And one gal."

She gave him a second glance. "It's about time. In fact, where *are* the women?" she wanted to know. "Shouldn't they be flocking to open-source projects in droves? Isn't this the perfect environment for them to excel in because of the collaboration it needs? Women are good at collaboration, communication, all that stuff you espoused in that blog post you wrote about not coding in a vacuum. You say you want to write the truth? Well, the truth is that the lack of women in tech—not to mention African Americans and every other nonwhite, male group known to humankind—is creating a technology bias. And, by the way, I don't understand how you can't find women engineers. I think that's a cop-out."

He stared at her, stone-faced, for a few moments. Then, loudly, viscerally, and for all the Singaporeans to hear, Stuart told her, "Don't lecture me about women, Marie. Make no mistake: Some of my best bosses have been women. If you were to ask me, I'd say women should be running all the companies. It's the misogynistic, myopic, asinine males in the boardroom who are destroying our world."

The Fountain of Wealth abruptly stopped gushing, as it did intermittently throughout the day so that people could walk around its smaller, inner fountain three times, for good luck. Marie had an instinct to head over, but then Stuart pounded on the table. "Vita wants women, Marie. Just tell me where to find them, and I'll get them."

Without the sound of rushing water to drown out Stuart's increasingly vehement discourse, people around them turned and stared.

Stuart sat back and caught his breath for some moments, before coming at her more calmly. "Why don't you meet Laurie at the Tokyo conference next month? Meet everyone, for that matter. Talk to them. Get their opinions for yourself. It's the first time everyone from our little virtual startup will all be physically together."

He'd never asked her to meet any of his colleagues before. He preferred to keep her locked in a closet, where she preferred to stay, but she'd done it now. She blew air out through her lips, which were burning. She was going to regret this.

CHAPTER 7
SEPTEMBER 2010

OPEN-SOURCE. OPEN WORLD. One minuscule piece of code evolving and becoming part of a greater code, every singular piece of code now part of every other piece of code, joined together, no more silos. Everything connected. The circle of life. Who needed children? This was Stuart's legacy. His way of continually filling the gap. After five hours combing through Javelina chat forums and a few books Stuart had recommended, this was what Marie had come up with. You had to go deep inside the code and then even deeper, into the coder. These were the people running the world. She looked up from her laptop. This was her problem: she read too much into these things.

It was one o'clock. She threw on her swimsuit and a sundress and set out in the swelter for the botanical gardens, in hopes of retracing her steps to that pool. She started with the wooded paths and walking bridges, the lily ponds and meadows, but this time she was confronted with a locked gate that hadn't been there before, or one she didn't remember, anyway. It was draped in bougainvillea and had a tiny sign that said PRIVATE VILLAS; NO TRESPASSING. Perhaps last time it had been left open and she'd not noticed. She could climb over it, she thought, though her skin might get ripped to shreds. And then she remembered Stuart's caution: *Death for drug traffickers.* She was about to turn around and go back, when the lock clicked open. A woman behind her, wearing Jackie O. sunglasses, a three-string choker of pearls, and the largest hat Marie had ever seen, slipped her card key back into her purse, waited for Marie to pass through, and then followed, the gate closing shut behind her.

"I forgot my key," Marie said.

"Are you new here?"

Marie nodded, because it was partly true.

"I'm new here myself. Should we be friends?"

Marie smiled in a way that could have meant anything.

They walked single-file along a windy, narrow path, Marie following the woman, whose foreign-sounding voice fluttered up through the trees. "Fresh off the boat from London. I had this vision of succulent blue skies. I'm a person who needs light, lots and lots of it; otherwise, I'll get depressed. It's my Danish blood. London almost killed me. I was so glad to leave." The woman stopped and turned back, and Marie almost ran into her. "Should we exchange numbers?" the woman asked. Then she kept walking before they did so. Before long, surprisingly, pleasingly, they came upon the peaceful little pool Marie had hoped to find again. "We live over there," the woman said, pointing high up into the thick, verdant leaves, though Marie could see no structure. "And you?"

Marie twirled her finger toward some other direction.

"I must confess, I was watching you swim yesterday. That was you, wasn't it?"

Marie blushed. The woman's eyes had a mischievous look.

"You swim with such purpose. I was watching you from my balcony."

Marie glanced up and around in search of a balcony.

"I drank my afternoon mocha, took a shower, fixed the kids a snack, and watched a TV show with them, and when I returned to the balcony, there you still were, swimming laps. Lap after lap after lap. Not a soul in the world but you."

Marie was silent.

"I'm a swimmer myself. Or used to be. I haven't gotten in the pool in ages, but I must say, you've inspired me. Are you going to swim now? If you need a suit, you can borrow one of mine. Though you might be swimming in that, too!" She let out a cackle that could have split open the sky. She was a big woman, bones, laugh, and all. "Hell, maybe I'll join you."

"I wore my suit," was all Marie could manage to say.

"I'll go check on the kids. You won't leave until I get back, will you?"

Marie shook her head, and the woman sauntered off. She'd not even told Marie her name.

Her instinct was to flee, but Marie could not resist. She stripped down, dove in, and swam along the bottom in search of that unending silence. Then, lap after lap after lap, oblivion. At some point, she felt vibrations of a body sliding into the water, displacement, hard and heavy thrashing beside her, and Marie surfaced. The Dane had a strong stroke but little form, and she tired easily. After only four or five legs, she stood, looked around, and asked, "Is this the off-season?"

"I believe September is the high season."

"It feels so empty."

"Vast. Infinite. Everything. And nothing. What emptiness feels like."

The Dane narrowed her eyes.

There were cookies on one of the lounges. A bottle of wine.

The Dane got out and dried off and poured them each a glass. When she reached for a cookie, her fingers were trembling. "I don't know what I thought moving here—that it would be sunnier?"

"There's some light over there." Marie pointed across the pool at a sun ray streaming through the bougainvillea.

"I feel like someone needs to cut a hole in the sky."

"It is rather thick, yes," Marie agreed.

"But it's good for the skin, I hear. The moisture. I mean, look at you. Your skin is practically glowing." It didn't seem to occur to the Dane to eat the cookie. "You see, it's important that we be happy here. Settled. He promised that we would be settled here. Though he promised that about London, too." She looked at Marie. "Do you have kids?"

Marie shook her head, and the Dane nodded, as if that were the answer she'd expected. "I just need to know that we won't pick up and move right away."

"What does your husband do?"

"He's starting a hedge fund. Though why he's brought us here to start it, when he could just as well have started it anywhere, I couldn't say. To tell you the truth, he's always moved from big bank to big bank, but this last move, I don't think it went well. He didn't part on good terms with the company, and I'm concerned that he's deposited us all here as a facade. Something about taxes."

"I see."

"I told him we could give up some things, that he didn't need to work. I told him this, but he didn't agree."

"You should join the Cricket Club," Marie offered, wanting to change topics. "I've been told it's quite nice. Lots of people and gatherings and events and things."

"Are you going to join?"

Marie shook her head.

"Then why would I?"

Some moments passed.

"I guess I should be going," Marie said.

"It's only two o'clock."

"I have some work to do."

"Tomorrow, same time?"

Marie opened her mouth to speak, but nothing came out. When she finally got up to go, the Dane asked, "What work do you do?"

Marie paused. It was a question she'd avoided like the plague for seven years. What would it be like to become a completely different person? "I'm a writer," she said.

CHAPTER 8
OCTOBER 2010

"YOU SHOULD GO," MARIE SAID.

Stuart's eyes rested on hers. "I've got a few more minutes."

They were seated outside a sake bar on child-size chairs, holding tiny wooden cups.

Sometimes this was all it took, a few moments like this to refuel and reset and remember why he was here, doing any of this. It had been a long week—a good week, but a long week. He and the team had spent it back at Toyota's IT facilities, under the microscope, the Japanese scrutinizing the résumés Stuart had brought them and continually demanding a detailed list of the exact problems COMPASS was going to solve. Wasn't that the point of the scoping project itself? To figure that out? Granted, defacing the Toyota network engineers in front of Hideo-san might not have been the way to form relationships with Toyota's cloud team, as Stuart had intuited, and the daggers shooting out of their eyes made the meetings more grueling and longer than they already were.

He'd done a lot of prep work to keep the strategy simple and inclusive. 1) Franco would send his network topology program to crawl through Toyota's car cloud to get the lay of the land. Then 2) they would go about deconstructing the IT silos to automate the provisioning of the "infrastructure as code," which would effectively change everyone's job as they knew it. Not. One. Smile. Thank God they'd decided not to show the videotape. Nevertheless, by the end of the meetings on Friday, Vita had a six-week, $250K Toyota COMPASS POC in hand, mostly because Hideo-san, and before him Fumitaka-san, and before either of them JS, Stuart was pretty sure, had said it to be so.

Stuart was practically giddy with relief to be free of the project, for a while, at least. He and the team had joined up with the other Vita employees for the Software Defined Network global conference in Shinagawa, where Marie had met him. It was her first trip to Tokyo, though Shinagawa was not Tokyo. It was more like the fringes thereof, its biggest draw being its massive conference center. Tall, uninspiring hotels sprawled five blocks down the side of a hill with chain restaurants catering to foreigners at every turn, McDonald's and Denny's being representatives from Stuart's country. At the bottom, everything and everyone funneled into a supersize train station that served as a transit hub for commuters headed to and from the Tokyo city center and beyond.

Their hotel was the least swanky of the five, more like a crappy old Hilton whose lobby was cavernous, and it was packed because it was where all the events took place. Ten thousand conference attendees from all over the world, milling around while parades of uniformed Japanese flag–waving conference minions marched in packs to some unknown destination. After dropping Marie's luggage with a quick "Sorry about the room," Stuart led her back down the elevator, out a side door, and down the massive hill, but in the direction opposite where the hordes were headed, into a tangle of alleys someone had told him about, where all the locals went for ramen and sake fests, so they could have a few moments alone before he had to set off for a work dinner.

"It's nice to be back in civilization," Stuart said, some-what facetiously, as two suit-wearing Japanese men spilled singing-drunk down some nearby stairs.

"Is that supposed to be the Eiffel Tower?" Marie nodded at the gaudy neon replica in the near distance.

Stuart glanced at his watch.

"Really, Stuart. You should go."

"I've got some time."

He was meeting Fumitaka-san and Yahoo! Japan in thirty minutes, but Stuart had no desire to go. Not just yet. Marie had only just arrived, and tomorrow the conference would begin and he would be flat-out. This was to be Vita's official coming-out, a way to announce itself and COMPASS to the world, in whatever meager, organic, self-funded way it could. Signing Toyota for the POC had upped the company's game; even if it was for only $250K, no one needed to know that. What they needed to know was that Vita was strategizing a car cloud for one of the biggest carmakers in the world. And after the boost in revenues from KT Phase II, Niraj had opened his purse strings to fly everyone, including their three new hires in India, out to Tokyo. One of those new Indian hires was Niraj's cousin Arman, whom they called Smally because they already had an Arman whom they now called Biggy. Smally might have been small, but he was tenacious, if not high-strung. A jack-of-all-trades, he worked out of his parents' home in Delhi while he and Niraj searched for office space clandestinely, the full scope of their India strategy highly sensitive and still on the down-low. Anyway, Smally was the kind of guy who would do anything for you, and that meant *anything*. It was Smally who had managed to finagle a discount on an exhibit booth for the conference, had banners designed on the cheap, same with the brochures and swag, while everyone worked their ass off to get up a website that wasn't laden with bugs and spelling errors, thanks to Liam, who was presently up in his hotel room, frantically inputting the fixes.

"I'll have Smally scrounge you up a pass so you can walk the exhibit floor tomorrow." Stuart poured Marie more sake, holding the bottle with two hands per custom, as opposed to Korea, where you held the wrist of the hand pouring the bottle. In either case, you never poured for yourself. "It will be just like old times." She dulled her eyes and returned the favor, pouring him more sake—no wrist, two hands. He swallowed it in one gulp. "Maybe this time you won't be so standoffish."

"I wasn't standoffish."

Yes, she was. "You were cold as a stone."

"I'd been in telecom for a whopping three weeks. I was petrified you'd see right through me."

"And I did."

She smiled tightly, thinking of herself back then. "When's your keynote?"

"Day after tomorrow."

"Are you nervous?"

"If you know what you're talking about, there's nothing to be nervous about."

"I used to think that, too. Do you want to practice it on me?"

Now he looked nervous. She could be quite critical in her day. "I'm going to come," she said, and, before he could say anything, "I'll wear a hat and sunglasses."

"Okay, but no heckling." He nodded down the alley. "There's Laurie." She was headed into what looked like a coffee shop across from them, but who knew what any of these places really was until you entered? It could also be a massage parlor or a kiddie-porn theater. "You remember Larry?"

Marie's face said no.

"Plum-wine Larry?"

"Oh, him. Of course. That stuff was gasoline, but he was nice. For once, one of your network guys actually looked me in the eyes when he spoke. He'd just had his second kid, I remember. His wife was Croatian, and they were considering moving back to Dubrovnik to be near her family."

"When we started Vita, Larry was the first guy I thought of. He's one of the sharpest network architects I've ever worked with. I shot him an email. I was surprised to find him available. He responded right away: 'Count me in. Send me wherever. Laurie.' I had to blink at the name a few times before it registered." He paused so that it could register with Marie now.

"So, this is how it's done?" she asked.

"Apparently. Anyway, whatever—'he' or 'she' or 'they,' I don't care, so long as the quality's the same. Plus, we could use another woman at the company, given what happened with Jasmine, the Singaporean coder Liam hired. Turns out she can't code."

"How is that possible?"

"Good question, one Liam and I had a heated debate about. How was it that we, coders, could possibly have hired someone for our product team who couldn't code? Apparently, so Liam deduced after some sleuthing, it was Jasmine's husband who had taken the coding test Liam had sent out, not Jasmine. She'd been using her husband to get by like that for the entire month she'd been with us, before Liam caught on."

Marie's look was beyond incredulous.

"We replaced her, and the ordeal is behind us, but not really, because she was a woman, one bad seed who, unfortunately, reminded me of all the women coders or engineers I have worked with in my lifetime who ended up leaving within the first three months—and these were honest women; creative, intelligent, and idiosyncratic women, but for the fact that they simply couldn't deal."

"What, do you guys smell or something?"

"You're funny," he said, studying her. He brushed her cheek with his hand. For a moment she thought he was going to kiss her. But then, no, he wouldn't; even though this bar was obscure and it had grown dark out, they were still in public. He swallowed his sake and extracted himself from the kiddie chair. Marie watched him go, and it was as if all the sake patrons had gone with him, though maybe it had only ever been them there—she wasn't sure.

She stared across the alley, thinking, now was as good a time as any. She crossed over and entered where Laurie had entered. Laurie was in a booth in a far corner, hunched over her laptop. After a moment of standing there, thinking about what to say, Marie went over. Laurie, in flip-flops and jeans and a tight-fitting COMPASS T-shirt, must have been twenty-eight or so now, Marie thought. Her long brown hair snaked down over tiny breasts that hadn't been there before. Her mouth was parted, her face illuminated angelically by her screen. "DevOps." Marie read the word aloud from the header on Laurie's PowerPoint slide.

Laurie looked up with bleary eyes and blinked at Marie with some distant recognition.

"It's Marie," she said. "Stuart's Marie."

"He didn't tell us you were here."

"No. He wouldn't have."

Then, after some moments, Laurie smiled, as if relieved to see a friendly face.

"No parties tonight?" Marie asked, sitting down.

"I'm speaking on a panel tomorrow. Stuart asked me to do it, but I told him I'm not good at panels."

"He wouldn't ask you to do it if he didn't think you could do it."

Laurie turned her laptop toward Marie. "Does this sound logical?"

Studying the slide, Marie said, "Looks spot-on to me."

"Really?"

"No, but only because I know nothing about DevOps."

"Right."

"But if you explain it to me, I can help you put it in layman's terms. Hold on a second."

Marie went off and returned with two beers and slid into the seat across from Laurie, who took a sip of the beer Marie had set down before her. It seemed to revive her.

"It's just like it sounds—'development' and 'operations' as one word, 'DevOps.' You see, today, and going back to the beginning of time, *development* teams coded applications and *operations* teams kept them up and running on physical servers, and there was never any reason for the two groups to meet. Until now. Now, with everything moving to the cloud, there are no more boundaries between development and operations, or between any other IT departments, for that matter. All the walls of IT are coming down, and jobs are merging. A network engineer can't just be a network engineer anymore. Now he's got to be an operator, a coder; plus, he needs to understand the purpose of the application. He's got to *care*. It's like training a man to become a woman, and vice versa."

Marie looked at her. "A new sex entirely."

"Yes, basically, and people are going to get pissed and scream and cry. But it's going to happen. Someday, anyway. Before I came here to Tokyo, I spent some time with Biggy at Korea Telecom, where we were attempting to implement the DevOps workload of COMPASS that incorporates networking, but it turned out to be a ridiculous endeavor, given how entrenched Koreans were inside what already was. Their idea of solving a problem was to throw more bodies at it." She typed in some changes she'd just thought of. "I like that thing you said about a new sex. Should I use that in my presentation?"

"I'd keep sex out of it."

Laurie nodded.

Marie said, "So what you're saying is that the people are the problem."

"The code works, the infrastructure's there, and so, yes, that's what I'm saying—it's the people driving technology, contrary to popular opinion, not the other way around. And they're not driving very well."

"But that will change soon, once technology figures it out and gets rid of the people, no? Once it destroys what's in the way? Isn't that technology's end goal, putting the people out to pasture?"

A moment passed while Laurie looked at Marie and seemed to think about it.

"Do you think it will?"

"Nah," she said finally. "This stuff is too hard. Intricate. Nuanced. They're going to need us plebes forever."

Marie swallowed some beer. "Do you like what you're doing?"

Laurie sat back and let out a groan, as if it hurt. "I love it."

Marie helped her with a few slide headers and some formatting, then went back to her room and started on a chapter of the book with the working title "And Then There Were None."

When Stuart returned from his ten-course kaiseki dinner, awash in a waft of intoxicating scents, Marie was seated at the walled window, staring out at the jewel-speckled skyline, dark shadows of the river snaking below, a vast garden built by some shogun or samurai, eating rice triangles and drinking from a bottle of convenience-store sake. He came and stood before her.

"What?" she said.

He looked like he'd seen a ghost.

"What is it?"

"They want to invest."

"Who wants to invest?"

"Fumitaka-san and Yahoo! Japan."

She stayed still, steadying visions of dollar signs that had only ever brought trouble. "I thought you weren't going out

for a round yet." She paused, but not for long. "And all that pontificating about growing organically? About using the revenues from consulting to fund COMPASS so you wouldn't have to compromise on your vision by bringing outside investors onto your board? What happened to all that?"

"If someone offers me money, Marie, I'm not going to turn them down."

She stared at him, then handed him the bottle.

"Look, Marie, there's something I've not told you, because at the time this all started it was just talk, but now it's becoming real."

Here we go, she thought, then said, "I'm on the edge of my seat."

"Our plan has changed—that is, the endgame." He cleared his throat. "You see, it's a plan that goes beyond COMPASS as a platform to COMPASS as a service. Today's network engineers are never going to get COMPASS. They can read all the books they want, but they won't change. They are hardwired for hardware, and COMPASS is software. We've seen it at KT and SingTel, and now at Toyota. The hardest part of this whole cloud-computing equation is the network, because of the lack of skills and the engineers' unwillingness to embrace software. That, combined with the sensitivity of the network, which is the gateway to the crown jewels . . . If it's compromised, then . . . well, good luck. The *only* way this is going to work is if we take an enterprise's network and manage it ourselves on COMPASS. And the only way we can do this efficiently and cost-effectively is out of India. MNS, Marie, will enable recurring revenues."

"Why does everything have to be an acronym?"

"Managed network services"—he enunciated it very slowly—"is Vita's master plan. It's where the real money is and the only way we can be sustainable as a company. But it must be in India, where the labor economics work and the talent is smart and hardworking. Niraj has already flown over and begun scouting out office space. We're no longer just feeling things out, Marie, and the point is that if we're going to do this, we need money. Lots of money."

"And you didn't tell me this before because . . ." She paused so that he could interject, but then continued before he had a chance to. "Because you don't think I'll get it? Because you don't remember that I've been down this exact road? Re-engineering people out of their jobs? Is this what you'll be talking about in your keynote speech tomorrow?"

"Jesus, Marie, why are you attacking me?"

She stepped back at the sound of her own foul tone. "I . . . I don't know." She felt her eyes widen with shame, innocence. She really didn't know. "I'm sorry. I don't know where that came from." She paced to the other end of the room and pushed at her temples. "Probably because I'm writing this book, *your* book, and I'm trying to create a story, and this seems like a dramatic moment in the story, one that will improve the arc of the book—you know, really get readers engaged—and yet you don't want to talk about it."

"Leave MNS out of the book, Marie."

"Right, of course. Don't listen to me." And then she thought, *Why did I just say that?* Why were those so often the first words out of her mouth?

CHAPTER 9
OCTOBER 2010

STUART SET THE ALARM for five. Marie was up at four thirty, waiting for his eyes to pop open. They dressed in the dark and then found their way to the Tsukiji fish market, a maze of alleyways cluttered with hawker stands selling just-off-the-boat delicacies, counter-only sushi restaurants with queues already three hours long. They watched a fisherman slice apart an eight-foot tuna with what looked like a samurai sword, the fish's severed head displayed proudly on the table. Stuart fed Marie chunks of the just-cut meat with a toothpick from a wobbly paper plate as the moon grew into the faintest memory.

They had vague plans to meet up with the team, but they were hard to find, having already scattered about in search of the freshest catch. Many had found it easier to stay up all night than to set their alarms. Stuart and Marie finally ran into Smally, Niraj, and the Singaporeans—hungover, punchy, delirious—waiting in line for still-moving eel. The three new hires from India were nowhere to be seen, but they found Franco holding hands with a pretty, dark haired woman half his height. He was trying to be courageous, if only his face hadn't gone as gray as the oyster on his plate. Franco was an enigma—Stuart's description. Little was known about him, other than that he lived with his cat and was a reader of literary fiction who in his spare time liked to go hot-air-ballooning. Argentinian with a Thai influence, sort of androgynous, he rarely spoke about his personal life (but then who of them did?), so when he introduced the tiny woman he was holding hands with as his girlfriend, that he'd flown her over from Korea to be with him, everyone pretended not to be shocked that he would have let his worlds collide like this, that he would have revealed this secret part of himself.

Marie and Stuart left the others waiting in line and went off in search of the purveyor of that oyster, so big they had to share it, Stuart sucking down one half, Marie the other. Moving on, they came upon a not-so-small Japanese man torching a clam the size of his big, meaty palm on a tiny makeshift grill. He sliced it into four pieces, poured vinegar and spices on top, put the shell on a plate, and handed it to them. Stuart put the shell to his mouth and slurped. Then Marie did the same. All around them, vendors called out in a language they didn't understand.

At eight o'clock, they stumbled back to their hotel room and fell face first onto the bed, where Marie dreamed of the erotic flavors of her beginnings. It was nine thirty when she woke again. Stuart, already dressed in jeans and a blazer, dropped a floor pass onto her pillow. Marie let out a groan, turned over, and fell back to sleep.

The maids kicked her out at eleven after giving her a few minutes to throw on clothes and brush her teeth. She headed down to the exhibit floor. It was chaotic and jarring and blasting with air-conditioning and whatever else they were shooting into the space, and the bad coffee had not done its job. Big, flashy booths for Docker, Google, VMware, Red Hat, GitHub, Netflix, and Amazon Web Services confronted her at every turn, as if to say: "And what have you done lately?" She listened to a guy from Google AI speak to a group of two hundred wide-eyed twenty- and thirtysome-things, mostly men. Someone from the Linux Foundation spoke to a lesser, more professorial crowd of thinkers and philosophers. She saw a few women wandering around. Marie always liked to take a count. Ten on her watch. Fifteen. She saw a flyer posted for a women in tech cocktail event that night. She told herself she would go, knowing she wouldn't. She didn't recall wearing jeans to these events in her day. This was how old she was.

It took her a while to find the Vita booth, tucked in a corner off the beaten path, by the bathrooms. Biggy—she presumed—and one of the Indians were in the middle of demoing the network monitoring module to a small group of people. She came up and listened. Another Indian guy—Smally, she presumed—wearing a suit that looked sewn by the deft hands of a loved one, came up to her and handed her his business card. She introduced herself as a trade writer doing a piece on how "software defines everything." A month earlier, she had known zilch, but she was armed with knowledge now. She asked a few probing questions as Biggy gave the demo and a few of the onlookers turned and scrutinized her, as women tend to do of other women, which was when Marie realized that this group surrounding Biggy was mostly female. She turned and took a closer look at Biggy, quickly understanding. Tall, striking features; thick, wavy hair; black eyes with long lashes; and, most important of all, an affable, self-deprecating demeanor. No question was too silly or dumb for Biggy, those he answered in a deep Middle Eastern accent. He did not look like a coder. Smally, standing right next to Biggy, had to ask Marie a couple of times if he could get her anything, before she heard him. "What I'd really love is a Starbucks," she responded finally. "But don't tell anyone that."

A few of the women groaned in agreement before moving on to the booths with the big, flashy logos. The others left, too. Then Smally disappeared, and for a while it was just Marie and Biggy and the Indian named Raj, who was on the floor untangling a mess of cables. She was not one for charades, so she admitted to Biggy that she was here with Stuart. "Ah, Marie!" He gave her a bear hug, for which she was wholly unprepared. "He didn't tell us you were here."

"No, he wouldn't have."

"I've heard so much about you."

She pulled away from him, skeptical. Then she positioned herself so there was some space between them.

"I remember when he first met you. He went dark on the chat channels for three days straight, which he'd never done before. We'd been working on a piece of code for the Linux guys, and I finally wrote, 'This better be because of a woman,' and it was."

Marie, blushing, said, "All roads lead back to Linux."

He laughed, a big, hearty laugh. "Linux is how Stuart and I met, twenty years ago. I was still living in Iran and was experimenting with Linux, and we ran into each other on the chat channel. I knew Stuart as Javelina back then, that piglike, hoofed beast he used to use as his picture. He was trying to break apart a piece of the operating system, and I helped him. We developed our own encrypted language, in which I communicated to him my plans to escape Iran. I'm part of Baha'i, a small religious sect persecuted by radical Muslims in my country. Stuart hooked me up with a roommate of his from Pakistan, the route I took on my footed flight. From Pakistan, I went to London and then to the States, where I received asylum and then was granted a scholarship to MIT. After I graduated, I sold out for the big money—as Stuart likes to remind me—and went into mortgage swaps. Stuart and I stayed in contact. I've been following his career for years and was one of the first contributors to Javelina. When he asked me to come to Asia, I, sick of finance, hopped on the next plane. It was the first time we had ever met in person. I didn't even know what he looked like."

Stuart had said that Biggy was a talker, but that was a lot to unpack. "Ugly little beasts, aren't they?" she said, referring to the javelinas.

He did not disagree.

Some people came up and wanted a demo. Marie said that she'd better let him get back to work, and then suddenly there was Smally again, sweaty and out of breath and handing her a steaming-hot Starbucks from a carrier holding four Venti cups. Smally was looking around for the other women. Marie stared at the cup. The nearest Starbucks was a ten-minute sprint down the hill to the train station. She'd not meant for him to *actually* go there. "I don't know what to say." The crooked smile he returned was almost majestic. Marie reintroduced herself as being "here with Stuart," and he nodded as if he already knew that and went and got her a compass. They were giving them out as swag.

"We will see you in India soon," he said, shaking his head no, which meant yes, and Marie found herself nodding along with him, as if it were a foregone conclusion. India. Of course. Absolutely. Then she got hold of herself, and using the compass he had given her, she found her way off the floor before she nodded herself onto a rocket ship bound for the moon.

She burst through the hotel doors into an anticlimactic swath of gray. Her nose was frozen, and she couldn't feel her feet. She was dying for a beam of sunlight, but polluted air would have to do. October. Cool, breezeless, and gray. That never-ending gray. Like her mood now; for some reason she couldn't pinpoint, she was feeling obscure, like all those network engineers wandering around on that floor, looking lost and bothered.

Soon, she was at the bottom of the hill and then on a train headed to the Yanaka district, thanks to her phone's GPS. She looked for a bathhouse turned artist studio she'd read about, but she couldn't find it after detraining and wandering around for an hour through perfectly quiet, narrow streets lined with cubed homes with slatted front doors that brought to mind all those Japanese movies Stuart had made her watch: *Yojimbo, Rojimbo, Akimbo*—she could never remember their exact names. Was there ever a moment without him in it?

At some point, she discovered herself lost deep inside the bowels of a cemetery, where dilapidated tombs loomed large and insignificant and engraved wooden slats signifying swords were stacked everywhere. She kept looking behind her, thinking someone was there, but it was just those swords, slapping against each other in the wind.

STUART HAD SET A DATE with Marie for sushi that night, but at six he texted her to say that he and Niraj needed to go to dinner with a potential client.

Stuart: "Sorry."
Marie: "No worries."

She grabbed a rice triangle and a bottle of sake from her stash in the mini-fridge and fell asleep at eight o'clock. She woke again at nine, then ten. At some point, Stuart was leaning over her, as if in a dream. She asked if he'd been smoking. He stood up and stripped off his jacket. "It was a Japanese yakitori place," he said.

Marie said nothing. She watched him change into boxers and crawl into bed and enfold her with his laptop, wanting to watch an episode of *Mad Men* so that he could decompress, but she could barely keep her eyes open. "Are you sleeping?" He kept looking at her and asking. In the morning, she would not remember what happened on *Mad Men*, just the sound of his voice. "*Are you sleeping? Are you sleeping? Are you asleep?*"

AROUND ONE O'CLOCK THE next the day, returning from a sightseeing excursion, Marie was making her way to the hotel elevators, head down so she wouldn't run into anyone because all she wanted was to soak in a bath and lie horizontal for an hour before Stuart's speech, but then she spotted Laurie seated among the myriad oversize leather lounge chairs that looked tossed about, as if after a storm. Tomorrow was the last day of the conference, though it seemed already to be on its last legs. As was Marie.

Franco was beside Laurie, their heads bent over one of their laptop screens. Marie went over and fell into the couch opposite them. "Have you guys been to the Imperial Palace?"

They both looked up at her, then at each other.

"No, I suppose you wouldn't have had time for that."

"Was it fabulous?" Laurie wanted to know.

"Funnily enough, I can't say. You see, I set out to see it this morning when I left the hotel, but I couldn't find it. I know that sounds weird—it's the Imperial Palace, after all. It must span three miles of city blocks. I walked all the way to what I thought was the entrance, only to find out that it was on the completely opposite side. So I walked what must have been another two miles in that direction, where, high in the distance, I could see a stream of people flowing over an ornate wooden walking bridge into what I presumed was the entrance to the grand structure, but once I got there, there was no entrance at all, as if Pied Piper had already shut the forest doors. Where I found myself, finally, was in the much more subdued and anticlimactic Imperial Gardens, where I fell facedown on the manicured grass, spent and exhausted from three hours of searching."

"They say that's the whole point," Franco said.

"I did feel rather as if I'd accomplished something."

Franco smiled and went back to what he was doing.

Marie asked Laurie how her panel had gone.

"It went well," she said. "I kept getting distracted by the translator waving her arms around right next to me. And then there was this little Japanese guy in the front who filmed me the whole time on his iPhone. He came up afterward and gave me his card and said, in very broken English, that he wanted to publish my speech on his podcast tonight, at a party that he invited me to." She looked at the card. "It's in Akihabara."

"Oh no," Franco said.

"What's Akihabara?" Marie asked.

"It's hard to explain," Franco said.

"Try," Laurie said.

"It's a mix of electronics, gaming, and schoolgirls who are really women dressed as schoolgirls."

Laurie ripped up the card.

Marie said, "Do you think these conferences serve a purpose other than the partying? Do you guys learn anything here?"

Franco shrugged, as if he had no idea. Laurie said that the OpenStack panel had been worth going to. Franco asked Marie if she'd gone to Shibuya Crossing yet and said he thought the whole trip to Tokyo might have been worth it just for that.

"What's Shibuya Crossing?" Laurie asked.

"It's in Hachiko Square," Marie explained to Laurie. "Where a dozen or so metropolis streets intersect, hub and spoke–style. When the lights turn green, traffic halts from all the spokes at once and the pedestrians charge forward in one massive, chaotic crisscrossing. Though, strangely enough, when I crossed, it didn't feel chaotic. More like transcendent, monumental, as if, during the time it took me to get to the other side, the sky opened up and down rained this great white light. *His* light. We, the show, et cetera, strutting and fretting . . ."

Laurie stared at Marie and said, "*Her* light." Then she got busy again on her laptop, promising to send Marie a secure link to Vita's proprietary DevOps documentation.

Marie went back to her room and, while drinking a syrupy Coke and still loopy from her excursion that morning, laid out the next chapter, only to have an idea that had nothing to do with DevOps or network monitoring, which fueled another idea, and the writing wouldn't stop. When she looked up from her screen, she had an hour until Stuart's speech and decided to go on a clandestine excursion for that infamous American coffee Smally had collected for her the other day.

She left the hotel and walked at a brisk pace down the hill, pausing at a light that she might not normally have stopped at—Japan tolerated no errant street crossings. A swarm of bodies poured in around her—dark suits, hair, shoes, cases, more and more of them, a building mass—and when the light switched to green, they crossed in one big swarm, headed to the escalator that transported people up great heights to the train station entrance. Bottlenecked at the bottom, Marie ran up the adjacent stairs and remerged with the bodies moving down the main station hall, cavernous, domed, a football field in size, shoulder to shoulder—the suits, the hair, the shoes, the cases. The station clock said five o'clock. Rush hour. Big mistake, at which she'd have laughed if it had been funny. She looked around for a way out of the rush, but there wasn't one. Good, industrious people, people just like Stuart and everyone she knew who journeyed home every evening via public transit from a long, hard day at work, but there just happened to be a *billion* of them. *Breathe*, she reminded herself.

It helped. It wasn't long before she began to feel cocooned, protected inside all these purposefully plodding commuters. No rushing, no shoving, everyone scoured and neatly dressed. She jumped up to see where all this was going, at which point she saw the sign on her left. *Now or never*, she thought. She bolted left and made a series of staccato steps to reach a narrow gap where the stairs to the Starbucks were, crawled past more bodies up the steps, waited in a long line to buy her coffee, then sat with it at the balcony railing, from which she had a full view of the streaming masses below. They kept coming. And coming. No breaks, gaps, or lulls. One constant stream, until they disappeared around that bend and off the side of a cliff.

When she at last made it back to the conference center, Stuart's speech was over. She went back to her hotel room and watched the YouTube video of it that Liam had posted on Vita's website, immediately discerning all the things he could have said differently. When it was just the two of them, facing each other across the table, he spoke so passionately, succinctly, his eyes boring into hers, holding her rapt. Why couldn't he speak to his audience like that? Why this filter? Why sugar-coat the reality of what was going to happen to many of these individuals? But then she reminded herself that at least he had the courage to get up there at all. At least he was still trying.

At six, she went back down to the exhibit floor, looking for people, but all the booths were in a state of abandonment and disarray, the tables overturned, crumbled conference badges and deflated balloons littering the purple-and-gray carpet. By seven, the lobby was a ghost town. Only a few post-conference stragglers remained, sleep-deprived twentysomethings wandering around in four-day-old company T-shirts.

The high-end hotel next door had a swanky bar, and Marie went there because that was where everyone usually found themselves every night at around this hour, but the place was empty. The bartender shrugged at her. "Closing-night parties."

Of course, she thought—everyone was with their team right now, Stuart included. She ordered a martini and sat on a stool, nursing it while the bartender pretended to be busy at the other end of the bar. He seemed embarrassed for her, too.

She got out her phone and watched the recording of Stuart's speech again on Vita's Twitter feed, 521 views and counting.

She read late into the night—no word from Stuart—a book she'd picked up at the airport, about a marriage told from his-and-hers viewpoints. It was heartbreaking, gorgeously written, though the characters felt unreal, strange, obsessive. The female protagonist left Marie disconcerted—all that she had kept from her husband, all her manipulation and cunning and devotion, her admiration and self-loathing and disdain, her sexual appetite. Her husband's sexual appetite, his devotion, his rage. A profundity between them that Marie couldn't place but that kept her from putting the book down. Did the wife really love her husband or not? Was that even the point?

Have we put a label on something that can't be labeled?

Stuart stumbled in at two. She pretended to be asleep.

At seven the next morning, Stuart's phone alarm blared and he flailed around wildly, as if fending off some imaginary beast. She took his phone and threw it across the room.

A moment of white space followed, in which her head pounded from last night's vodka. Her breath was rancid, her hair all over the place. *"Why do you destroy things?"* she could hear him say, even though he'd stomped wordlessly to the bathroom. *Do I destroy things?* She'd busted her laptop once back when she'd worked as an analyst, pulling an all-nighter, stressed and panicked because her model wasn't generating the numbers she wanted. Without warning, she'd banged her fists on the keyboard long enough to destroy the machine and all the work she had done.

CHAPTER 10

DECEMBER 2010

TWO MONTHS HAD PASSED since the Japanese conglomerate, aka Fumitaka-san, hosted that exclusive conference closing-night party in Vita's honor, atop a downtown Tokyo skyscraper with 360-degree views, an ocean of the finest sushi, and barrels of the oldest sake, on which everyone had gotten wasted (and Stuart had forgotten to text Marie, which had been a mistake, particularly for his iPhone, the one she'd thrown across the room). It was after that party that Fumitaka-san and Yahoo! Japan had each verbally committed to investing $3 million in Vita. Their actions had prompted JS to subsequently commit his own $3 million, though all of them later clarified that they would put in their money only after someone else did. Theirs was a circular problem, and Stuart and Niraj found themselves back at square one, hunting for that first $3 million so that they could close their series A round at a post-money valuation of $30 million.

"It can't hurt to hear what the VCs have to say," Niraj suggested, "if only to practice our pitch and gain market perspective."

Stuart's speech at the Tokyo conference had gone viral, according to Liam, who kept posting Stuart's YouTube hits on Slack. Suddenly, Niraj and Stuart were getting blind calls from VCs, tech presses, and other news outlets, not to mention prospective clients, and they had no bandwidth to support the influx. While Toyota was giving them great visibility, it meant straddling three countries, which was spreading their resources thin. They needed to hire, but hiring was a vicious cycle. Once they hired people, they would need to have a pipeline of work to keep those people billable, and neither Niraj nor Stuart had had enough time to dedicate to that objective. They needed a sales team for that. A COO, CFO, CMO, and a variety of other acronyms—not to mention a product manager and two more engineers in India.

"What perspective have the VCs ever had to offer about open software?" Stuart asked.

Niraj gritted his teeth and reminded Stuart to keep his enemies close, and when Stuart still balked, Niraj pulled out his business card, something he liked to do in situations like these, and pointed to the letters below his name: CEO. Then he let out what had grown, along with his stress, into a half-pack-a-day laugh, and Stuart sucked on his cheeks. He couldn't give a shit about being CEO, except for times like this. He swallowed his drink and called over their waitress to refresh the wasabi bowl. They were back in Gangnam, dealing with a scope-creep problem at Korea Telecom that had taken a stranger-than-fiction turn.

Stuart and Niraj had both flown to Seoul the previous night, having received a call from Dr. Kwak about an impromptu meeting the CIO had called to discuss changes in the Phase II milestones. That morning in the KT offices, present in the conference room had been the following: from Vita, there were Stuart, Niraj, Liam, Hung Su Kim (JS's ex-McKinsey guy), and their translator, Jae Yung (JD) Suh; from KT, there were the business units spearheading the platform buildout with their leader, Dr. Kwak, plus KT's internal IT group, including the CIO, not to be confused with the CTO, with whom they'd already been working. The CIO was bringing with her an ax to grind because to date the business units had kept her out of the loop on what was to be a critical, strategic direction for the company.

Hung Su Kim seemed like a sharp guy and a good addition to the Vita team in the few weeks they'd already spent working with him. He understood strategy and the importance of corporate buy-in, and he, Niraj, and Stuart were all on the same page about what they wanted the CIO—Karen was the English name she used—to take away from the meeting, which was that her demands were far beyond what they had signed up for in their statement of work.

It was a contentious meeting, and for the most part Hung Su Kim did the interceding so that the message could be delivered in Karen's own language, even though Karen made it seem as if she understood English very well. Stuart's role was to remain quiet unless a deep-dive technology question arose. A few did, and when he answered them, Karen nodded, even though Stuart was sure she knew little about what he was saying. When Niraj spoke, Hung Su Kim spoke over him, and Karen nodded at that, too. It was hard to tell what was really going on, though they appeared to be making progress. At the end of the meeting, Karen seemed placated; Hung Su Kim gave Stuart and Niraj a nod, as if all were under control, and then followed Karen out of the room.

Stuart was heading off to work on his three-page to-do list, somewhat relieved—there had been only $1.8 million in revenue at stake—when the translator cornered him. JD, just out of law school, had always been very solicitous of Stuart and his team—she translated all their deliverables into Korean, and vice versa. She was always quiet and rarely spoke if not spoken to. "Stuart," she said, head bowed.

"Yes, JD?"

"There is something I think you should know."

"Speak freely with me, as always."

"It is not my place to interfere."

"Please, interfere away."

"It's Hung Su Kim."

"What about Hung Su Kim?"

She still wouldn't look up. "He spoke to Ms. Karen, not in your favor."

After a pause, he asked, "What do you mean?"

"In the meeting just now, right in front of you, Hung Su Kim told Ms. Karen that neither you nor your team knows what you are doing."

There was a moment of white space; then Stuart screamed, "What!"

The walls might have reverberated. Niraj, amid a sidebar with Liam across the room, looked over.

"Hung Su Kim told Ms. Karen that the assumptions you are operating under regarding the technical architecture are flawed, and so is the technical architecture."

Blood pulsed up through Stuart's neck. That was why all the business unit managers had looked at him so strangely. He couldn't speak, for fear of what he might say. "Thanks for telling me, JD."

"Sorry," she said in Korean. She seemed embarrassed, though for Stuart or for her countrymen, it was hard to tell.

"What is it?" Niraj came over and asked.

"I need a cigarette," Stuart said.

They went outside. Standing in a doorway, their collars up to block the cold wind, Stuart told Niraj what JD had told him.

A good minute passed before the reality of what this meant caught up with Stuart's partner: they were looking at losing Phase II and 50 percent of next year's target revenues. "But why would he so overtly try to sabotage us? What could he possibly get out of it?" Niraj asked eventually.

"Phase II," Stuart said. "He wants it for himself."

"But that makes no sense. He can't do Phase II. He's got exactly zero technology depth."

Stuart shrugged. Nothing came as a shock to him anymore. "I want him out of here."

"You know we can't do that."

"Then call your buddy JS and have him do it."

Niraj ditched his cigarette. "Let's go talk to Hung Su Kim. Maybe we're misinterpreting."

"Fine, but—"

"I'll do the talking."

They went back inside and hunted down Hung Su Kim in his private office, nearby where the Dream Team worked out of a small, windowless conference room.

"They're rethinking Phase II," Hung Su Kim said right off, standing up from his chair and backing up against the window.

"I thought you said things were under control," Niraj said calmly.

"They're not buying into the technical architecture. They want to move in another direction."

"And what direction would that be?"

"I can't say right now."

"We didn't hire you to talk to them about the technology." Stuart couldn't keep his mouth shut. "You have no basis to talk about cloud or networks. No basis at all."

"You're idiots!" Hung Su Kim screamed. "You understand nothing about KT, Korea, or the industry. KT's never going to replace its network engineers with ones in India."

He went on waving and yelling and spitting and frothing. Stuart didn't know what the hell was going on—they'd yet to mention MNS India to KT, as they knew they weren't ready to do so. Who had said anything about India?

Niraj pulled Stuart from the room and told him there was no point, but Stuart couldn't forget the look on Hung Su Kim's face, the rant that came out of nowhere and exposed the deep-seated loathing he'd had all along for the Americans, and Indians too, apparently. It was an eerie reminder that in some ways Asia was no different than anywhere else when it came to stomping on someone else's turf.

Now they were in a bind because they'd have to take the Hung Su Kim issue to JS, who had recommended Hung Su Kim to them. And now was not a good time to deface JS, what with his $3 million on the table. They decided that Niraj would meet JS for drinks alone, because it was a very delicate matter about which Stuart couldn't be assured to contain his composure.

It worked. The next morning, bleary-eyed and green in the face, Niraj confirmed that JS would be "taking care" of Hung Su Kim. Stuart was about to ask what that meant but then decided he didn't want to know. He told Niraj that the only thing he cared about was never setting eyes on Hung Su Kim again. As for JS's $3 million? According to Niraj, JS was still in, but they needed that other $3 million first.

"I've got someone I can call," Stuart said.

"Well, you better get on it," Niraj responded. "I've committed to JS that we'll close the round by the end of the month. After that, he turns into a pumpkin. They all do."

CHAPTER 11

"ABSOLUTELY NOT. I'LL NEVER hear the end of it."

"He's a fund manager. He understands the risks."

"I'll sell my jewelry. My body, if I have to—"

"Oh, stop it, Marie. This isn't funny."

"I'm not being funny. I barely talk to my sister as it is." They'd gotten Larry, Marie's brother-in-law, in on some friends-and-family options many years earlier, for one of Stuart's ventures—options worth zero after the company went bankrupt. Though it was only a drop in the bucket of Larry's net worth, the loss remained there, like a wedge.

"I thought you said you already had the funding committed."

"They won't commit until someone else writes a check first."

"That's ridiculous."

"No one's saying it's not."

"We're at the beginning again."

"Sort of."

"Take my money if you need it."

"I'm not going to take your money, Marie. Besides, it wouldn't make a dent."

One hundred eighty thousand dollars was the sum total of Marie's personal assets remaining from her career days. Her mother had worked hard but had spent hard, too. Mostly with charities. The equity in her house barely covered her debt. "In fact, that reminds me," Marie said. "Ben called. I have a note coming due."

Ben was their investment advisor, an old friend of a friend who had coveted her and Stuart's business at one point but now seemed bothered only by the fact that their dwindling assets weren't making him any money. This was the third time he'd called about that note coming due in Marie's IRA, and she was loath to talk to him. Who cared anymore? This was how far she was from the days when she had checked the quotes every few hours to see if an option of Stuart's had quadrupled in value. They were as informed as two individual investors could purportedly be, and still she and Stuart had gotten it all wrong. When to buy and when to sell—who the hell knew? She'd finally just given up. "What should I tell him?"

"Bonds, Marie—just tell him to put it into bonds."

Stuart got another call. He looked at the number but didn't recognize it. It had come through on the company line, their version of a receptionist, calls routed to whoever was available, and guess what—it was his turn. He told Marie he'd call her back.

"STUART?"

"This is he."

"It's Jim."

It took Stuart a minute to process. Such a common name, yet he knew no other Jim. Jim, Marie's old boss, whom neither Marie nor Stuart had seen or heard from in years, not since Stuart had accompanied Marie on a visit to Jim at his chalet in Austria and he'd almost killed them all by speeding up a mountainside in his ATV.

"I saw your Tokyo speech in one of the chat rooms, and I have to say, I was floored." Jim's tone was animated, distinctively nasal, and as dialed in as ever.

Stuart didn't know how to respond. Jim was never floored. "Well, I actually thought—"

Jim stopped Stuart right there. "Let me tell you what *I* thought." He proceeded to deep-dive into his own meditation on hybrid IT and software-defined networking and what he knew to be the defining answer to it all. Jim had never been anything but 1,000 percent sure of himself, though not in a cocky way—in a way that made people listen.

And Stuart was listening, or at least trying to. Thirty minutes into Jim's esoteric dissertation, Stuart had processed only 10 percent of what Jim had said. Marie was the only one who could ever understand him.

"How is Marie, by the way?"

"She's great."

"Is she working on anything?"

Stuart stiffened. What would Marie want him to say? It was critical that he get it right. "She's writing a book."

After a pause: "I'm intrigued. Tell her I said hello and to call me when she's available. I might have something for her."

"Sure. Okay."

"But anyway, that's not why I'm calling you, Stuart."

Jim had made his mark by developing one of the first pieces of arbitrage trading software designed specifically for the telecom industry and had eventually sold it for a lot of money. He'd not needed to work since, but he was the kind of guy who couldn't survive without a game-changing intellectual problem to solve. He dabbled in a variety of startups, sat on advisory boards, and was a personal friend of Larry Page. Jim's brain worked in complex and mysterious ways, and while everyone clamored for his brilliance, they mostly didn't know what to do with it.

"Look. I sit on the advisory board of the Exchange, and I'm calling you because we've got a problem and I think you guys are the only ones who can solve it. I can't tell you any more about it until you get out here. How quickly can you get your team to London?"

Stuart got the feeling it wasn't a question.

CHAPTER 12
JANUARY 2011

SHE'D BEEN YOUNG. She'd had no idea. They'd been working closely together on a deal, she a new analyst, Jim some sort of savant, a hotshot trading specialist—he hadn't had a title, nor had he wanted one. A basement office—this was early in his career, long before he'd made himself. Marie had been running all these numbers for him, and she supposed he'd not before seen the possibilities as she had laid them out for him. She'd surprised him.

Side by side, they worked analyzing the deal's alternatives. He'd scribble a scenario on the wall-size whiteboard in his office. She'd then decode it because Jim was an enigma and everyone else was a human. There was a balance. She could ask only so many questions, which didn't much matter anyway because he'd already designed the solution in his head. The next day, she'd have those designs turned into spreadsheets and graphs. He made no note or acknowledgment of the all-nighter it must have taken her to provide those materials—the thought would never occur to him. He would glance at the files, expecting them to be insufficient. It was fun to watch his eyes connect with something he'd see there, the story that it told, a twist in the plot. She wondered if he'd ever worked with a woman before—or someone thoughtful, with all the patience in the world, and who did not give up. She could sense him wanting to give up, at times, but she would not let him. Her analyst peers shied away from Jim, but Marie wasn't afraid.

Jim rarely ate, and so neither did she. When they did eat, he'd order in, and always from the same two restaurants, one seafood, the other Japanese. He always did the ordering. She'd tell him what she wanted, and he'd order the same thing. Steamed sole with broccoli, hold the butter, no fries. Sashimi, never sushi. They also shared a penchant for scalding coffee and often ran into each other reheating their mugs at the office microwave, where Jim would continue his arbitrage discourse as if she'd never left his office. One time, when she ran into him standing before the gleaming silver box, upon sight of her, he smiled—something he rarely did—and then removed his coffee and replaced it with hers. While he waited for it to heat, he assured her not to worry— he'd already done some research and neither of them was going to die of radiation poisoning. She told him that was good news. It was the first time he'd said anything non-work-related to her.

She supposed she knew what was happening. He was growing a crush on her. Maybe, barely, she would assure herself. It was innocent. He was a family man, had a wife and a newborn and a clean life. He went to church. He'd never come to happy hour with the team before, and then one night there he was, drinking a beer with her and the others, his face already pink, as if that beer were his first ever. She snuck out early from the bar, as she always did, to meet Stuart. Her coworkers thought her elusive; they had no idea of the capacity with which she could love. Except Jim. Stuart had jolted Marie to life, and it was as if Jim got shocked by the undercurrent, discovered an emotion in himself he'd never known he had. He began questioning himself. His life. His marriage. He and his wife argued, and he began confiding in Marie, who tried to deflect all personal discussion—her modus operandi, and why she'd never mentioned Stuart. Something she regretted in hindsight. But if you were a woman and had a life outside work, you weren't taken seriously, and she wanted to be taken seriously, keep things focused on the job, on getting the deal, after which Jim was promoted and came to her and said that he was terribly unhappy. He was thinking of leaving his wife and baby, and did she understand what he was saying?

She looked at him in horror. No. No. She did not—could not—think of him in that way. He went into marriage counseling, and two years later left the firm just before the industry collapsed. He'd tried to warn Marie what was to come, but by then she was doing everything she could to avoid him. So, while Marie went down with everyone else, Jim moved to London and made himself hundreds of millions. He remarried. Had more children. They kept in touch because one never knew when one might need someone again. After the crash, another firm wanted her, thanks to Jim. And when that was over, she did a project for him every so often, the work lucrative enough to make her forget that it had ever happened, Jim's abandoning his first wife and newborn because of something she had or had not done. She could never get that innocent little baby out of her head.

Then there'd been that thing with the ATV. Once he'd discovered there to be a Stuart, he had extended many invitations to Marie and Stuart to visit his chalet in Austria, for which she'd always come up with an excuse. She'd finally run out; plus, Stuart wanted to go. He was curious. Marie had the feeling Jim wanted to confirm Stuart's existence, and he did. By almost killing him.

When Stuart told Marie that Jim had called out of the blue after all these years, she couldn't shake the slightly unhinged feeling that in fact it wasn't out of the blue but that he'd heard her argument with Stuart about funding, her call of distress, and had come to find her. It all felt very fated and doomed, this little favor Jim was doing for Stuart—introducing him to the Exchange—and she couldn't help believing it was really meant for her.

LIAM WAS THE ONLY one in the Chinatown office, and with his headphones on, he barely noticed Marie enter. She knew well not to disturb a coder in the middle of his work, so she pretended to be busy looking for something on Stuart's desk, until at one point Liam stretched back, cracked his knuckles, and released a long groan or sigh—it was hard to tell.

"It seems as if you guys need more comfortable chairs," she said.

He looked at the chair, as if he'd forgotten it was there.

"Maybe a print or two on the wall."

"You don't like the javelina?" he said.

She gave it a glance. "I have nightmares about that thing."

Some moments passed.

"Do you miss Melbourne?" she asked.

He gave it some thought, but not much. "I grew up in the outback with five brothers and two rooms. I don't miss that."

"Not much Wi-Fi in the outback, I take it."

"I just got my mom to use an iPhone, but she's got to drive into town to get any service."

"How did you become a programmer?"

"I was fourteen when my older brothers got their hands on a clunker PC." He used finger quotes for "hands on." "We took it apart, and then they got bored and smashed it to pieces with a baseball bat. They moved on to stealing radios and hotwiring cars, but I was never the same—I needed to figure out how that machine worked. So I rode a bus to Melbourne and went to the library at the community college, where they had some PCs in a back room that nobody knew how to use. Soon I was helping run them, and in exchange they let me take programming classes at the college for free.

A year of that, and I was at university, getting a degree in CS, the first one in my family to finish high school, let alone go to college."

"Do you miss them?"

"PCs?"

"Your brothers."

"The ones who aren't dead or in jail, sure, I miss them."

He had a twinkle in his eye, and Marie couldn't tell if he was serious. "I guess it's a stupid question to ask if you like what you do," she said.

"I get paid to solve puzzles all day; it could be a worse job."

She went over some of the edits she'd made on Liam's chapter about network security. Well, basically she'd rewritten the whole thing, using his concepts, and assured him not to take it personally. He smiled and said that he never understood how people wrote books. "It's not unlike programming," she said. "Solving a puzzle, as you described it. Figuring things out. Tumbling in darkness. Free-falling in the great abyss. And for what? A happy ending? There is no happy ending with technology, is there?"

Liam didn't answer.

"We all should have become doctors," Marie said.

Liam said, "I was once hired to do a network security review of a small medical-device company. It was run by a bunch of doctors. They all thought they were God. One of them used the pacemaker he'd designed himself and was bombastically proud of. I hacked into the simulated version of it and changed the settings to prove a point. Nobody is God."

Marie bit her lip to keep from smiling. "I'm going to date myself here," she said, "but I remember how euphoric it all was, the dawn of the internet, the obliteration of the middleman. I could buy my own stocks and make my own travel reservations. Any information I ever needed was right at my fingertips. My job as an analyst involved talking to people—industry experts, CIOs, CTOs, and CFOs—to predict trends, hurdles, critical success factors. But with the internet, I often had more information than those people could give me; I had to decipher what was good information versus bad. Talking to them face-to-face became more of a courtesy. Now, I was the one in control, and no longer would I have to endure their patronizing, why-is-this-woman-wasting-my-time silences. It all made me realize, over time, how much I disliked talking to people in the first place. What I didn't realize was that *I* was also a middleman. The further I clicked through on that road to oblivion, the closer I got to disappearing. I was disintermediating myself."

Liam was leaning so far back in his chair she thought he might fall over. Marie went and grabbed two beers from the mini-fridge.

"Is it true," she asked, "that when you write a piece of code, you leave something behind, either for someone else to find or as a means for you to find your way back?"

He swigged from his beer.

"Or is that only a myth? Am I just being naive to think you might want to communicate with someone out there in cyberspace, leave something funny or clever for them to remember you by? It must get lonely working in a silo of your own mind. So you write yourself into the code; you leave this little piece of yourself: 'I am here, people.' You can tell me if I'm being absurd."

"It's called an Easter egg," he said. "And we do it all the time, though it's illegal and we could get fired. There was a notorious one in the first 1983 Macintosh operating system. If a certain combination of keys was typed, pictures of the team who built the OS popped up. No one could find the egg or figure out how to take it down."

Marie left him alone to his program. She had no idea where her question had come from. She'd never asked Stuart that, in all these years—what it was that he left behind in all those lines of code he wrote, two decades' worth, a little egg floating out there in the world with his sperm in it.

CHAPTER 13

THAT NIGHT, MARIE WAS about to open a bottle of wine, when her phone rang. It was the Dane.

"I thought you might be lonely. Should I come over?"

Marie knew that it was the Dane who felt lonely—her husband was out of town again, and she often put forth the frustrating assumption that she and Marie were in this thing together. Hell, maybe they were. "Sure," Marie said, "if you want—"

Ten minutes later, she was at Marie's door, dressed in a chic beige pantsuit that looked like it needed a trip to the dry cleaner. Her long, dirty-blond hair was flipped over to one side, and she was holding a box of chocolate chip cookies and a bottle of wine, even though she didn't particularly like wine, she confessed to Marie now. In fact, what she preferred were those vodka drinks with the lemon syrup. The ones that had sugar on the rim and tasted like candy. She handed Marie the bottle. "Do you think Stuart's going through some kind of midlife crisis?"

"If only network software were that glamorous."

"I'm only asking because I'm pretty sure Giorgio is going through just that."

"Someone once told me that marriage is an illness."

The Dane thought about that for a moment. "Giorgio watches porn on his computer, instead of coming to bed."

"Like I said."

"He wants me to watch it with him, and I do, but I'm not into porn." A pause. "Are you into porn?"

"Not into porn."

"Are we prudes?"

"Porn is for people who wear pajamas to bed. Do you even know how the internet promulgated?"

"No. I don't."

"It promulgated because of porn."

"That's a lot of pajamas."

"It is."

"What does Stuart do in secret?"

Marie wondered if the Dane expected her to actually answer.

Yes, she did.

"When Stuart's depressed, he reads Hemingway's stories about the bullfighters. 'The poor beasts,' he'll look over and howl at me, as if it were all my fault. 'It's barbaric, Marie! Did you know that they torture the bull to the point where he's almost dead before the great matador even steps into the ring?' I'm pretty sure he identifies with those bulls in some primordial way."

The Dane carried the bottle and the cookies with her as she wandered around, taking in her surroundings, which didn't last long. She seemed both enamored and flummoxed by the bedroom with the silk-screened peacock doors that Marie and Stuart left open so the bodega basically turned into one open space.

"No guest room?"

"We never thought we'd have guests."

The Dane examined Marie while Marie examined the Dane's five-carat diamond wedding ring.

"There's this thing about working for a startup," Marie said. "It's called a startup salary." She bit the inside of her cheek until it bled.

The Dane plopped down on the small green love seat. "I keep telling Giorgio that that villa he's got us in is far too big and gaudy, that less is so much more—and I don't mean 'less' as in *less*. This place is so cozy, Marie. It speaks so much of the two of you."

Cozy? Marie thought back to their SOMA loft, dinners at Bix, drinks at the Four Seasons, Prada labels in her closet, tickets to Warriors games, golf at the Olympic Club, a facade Marie was embarrassed to admit she'd kept up long after it had come down. Things hadn't always been this cozy. She left and returned with a wine opener.

The Dane was waving at her face, which had grown moist and sweaty. "Is the air-conditioning broken?"

"We keep the windows open instead." Marie went over and shut them, then turned on the AC window unit, which rattled. The Dane wasn't satisfied until the room was frigid. Marie had to put on a sweater.

The Dane wanted ice with her wine. Marie went and got it.

"When I told Giorgio about Stuart, he googled him right away. What's this thing about a pig?"

"Javelina. It's not a pig. It's a . . . well, I'm not sure. An ugly, blind beast that tried to kill me once."

"Seriously?"

"We were in Tucson, golfing, of all things. As you know by now, I'm not a land-sport person. Anyway, we were on the fairway at seventeen; it was dusk, not a soul around, a dizzyingly vast sky. I was just about to hit my next worm burner, when a family of javelinas came trotting across the grass—Dad, Mom, and all the little kids. I'd never seen a javelina before, but Stuart grabbed my arm and warned me to stay still. The ugliest creatures in the world, by the way—a cross between a boar and a pig, dirty black and hairy, and on top of that, they're blind. They move around using their scent, and if they smell or sense you, especially with their babies around, they'll come after you. And one did. The mother, surely. She came trotting right at me, as if she could smell the rot in my womb, and Stuart grabbed his seven iron and we hopped into the golf cart and tore off. It chased us for a bit and then stopped. I was laughing and crying all at once. It was the most ridiculous, humiliating thing."

"Giorgio said Javelina was some kind of technology."

"Oh, yes, that, too."

Some moments passed.

"You know, Giorgio's starting this new hedge fund. That's where he is right now. In Frankfurt, raising money. Surely you and Stuart should invest."

Marie made no expression whatsoever.

"Trust me. He's good at this. He usually makes people tons of money."

Marie was suddenly reminded of all the films she'd seen before that began with this premise.

The Dane, who had eaten three cookies, said, "Wouldn't it be cozier if we curled up on the bed under a blanket and watched television?"

Marie poured more wine, and they moved to the bedroom. The Dane slipped off her sandals and crawled into bed while Marie set the wine and what was left of the cookies on the side table. "See, isn't this cozy?" The Dane selected another a cookie. "This is what you needed, Marie. A little girl time. Don't you feel better?"

Marie, who hadn't been feeling poorly until a few minutes ago, sat on the edge of the bed and began flipping through channels until she found *Baywatch*, her guilty pleasure. It was always on, Pamela Anderson and David Hasselhoff speaking in dubbed Malaysian with Korean subtitles.

And maybe it was all the mixed signals flying back and forth between tongues and nationalities, but out of the blue the Dane said, "I'm not Danish; I'm Bosnian."

Marie didn't say anything. She wasn't sure she'd heard right.

"I escaped Bosnia when I was eighteen and emigrated to Denmark, where I worked as a nanny for some years, until

I met Giorgio on a dating website. The kids are his from a first marriage."

Marie turned and looked at the Dane, who spoke to the TV.

"More and more, I wonder if Giorgio married me because he needed a nanny for his kids." The Dane grabbed another cookie. "I was in love with him once. And I had this ridiculously naive notion that one day he would love me, too."

Marie turned back toward the screen, and they continued staring at it for another minute. Then Marie muted the sound. "It was our last day in Tokyo," she said, "at the conference I told you about, and everyone was getting ready to depart on evening flights back to their respective tech hubs in the world. But before they all left, we met up to say goodbye at a converted train station in the Ebisu district. It was a cavernous tunnel lined with artisanal shops and hipster eateries along a quiet canal—something straight out of San Francisco, but for the fact that across the highway was a cluster of tall buildings slathered with flashy, alluring ads that preyed upon sorry men with a penchant for violence and kiddie porn—or at least that was my interpretation.

"Spread around on tiny, mismatched furniture, we were all sipping our amber beers, munching on exotic panini, and trading crazy conference stories. Stuart was telling us about the closing-night party he and Niraj had gone to the previous evening, hosted by a Japanese conglomerate that Stuart had managed to charm. A stage had been set up to conduct a demonstration of the virtual reality technology in which their fund had just taken a large investment stake. The board members were all seated on the stage with headsets on, on some virtual roller coaster trip to the moon or something, and one of them—not just anyone, but the CEO of the conglomerate—got so disoriented that he fell backward off the stage. And I'm not talking just any fall, according to Stuart. I'm talking about a backflip somersault." Marie rolled her eyes at the Dane. *Dorks.* "The team was falling over laughing at this point in Stuart's story, but it was Niraj whom I couldn't take my eyes off, the way he was hanging on Stuart's every word, his eyes alight in his partner's golden reflection."

Marie stood and went to the window. "It hit me in that moment." She turned back to the Dane. "You see, Niraj has always been shy around me, going back to the day I first met him in Gangnam. He never looks at me when he speaks, for instance. I'll see him for drinks with the team occasionally, but he won't ever come here to the bodega, even though we've invited him many times. I chalked it up to his feeling like a third wheel, which was ridiculous. *I was the third wheel.* He was afraid of women, was my next rationale—I'd never seen him with one. He's got a fiancée back in India, apparently. An arranged marriage. At one point I even thought he might have a little crush on me. He pretended to be unaffected by me, but I could tell back in Gangnam, after a few scotches and dry exchanges, that something about me had gotten under his skin. All of this was no big deal, mind you, just something I harbored in the back of my mind, until Tokyo. Across from those disturbing buildings, when I saw that look in his eyes as he gazed at Stuart, it struck me all at once—it wasn't I who'd gotten under his skin at all."

A moment passed.

"Do you think Stuart knows?"

"I brought it up with him once, lightheartedly. 'I think Niraj is in love with you,' I said."

"What did he say?"

"He asked me, evenly and sternly, never to say that again."

They watched the rest of the show. When it was over, Marie told the Dane that she'd be interested to hear more about Giorgio's hedge fund. That she had a note coming due on a bond and might need to get back in the game.

CHAPTER 14
FEBRUARY 2011

"THE FEAR'S ALL BULLSHIT," Stuart said, clanking his cup down on the saucer that the tailor had brought him. The tea had scorched his lips. "Remember Y2K? Everyone thought the world was going to end." He huffed. "Engineers aren't stupid. The world didn't end because we figured the shit out, we ignored the hyperbole and worked methodically to slog through layer upon layer of legacy software, and guess what? We got there. The banking system didn't crumble. No one lost their life savings. This too will be done."

The tailor stepped back.

Niraj said, "That jacket fits you nicely."

Stuart examined himself in the mirror. "The shirt's a little snug."

"The kids are all about slim fit these days."

Stuart put a hand on his belly and pushed.

They were in a men's clothing store in the basement of the five-star Shard Hotel, a blade of glass that stabbed through the clouds and overlooked the London Bridge. The Exchange had spared no cost—$100,000, plus unlimited expenses—for Stuart's team to spend two weeks performing an under-the-radar diagnostic of its networks after having experienced, two weeks earlier, an unexpected outage that halted trading for an entire day, the longest outage in the Exchange's history.

Those two weeks were over, and Stuart and Niraj were about to present their findings to the interim CEO—the residing CEO had been fired for the breach because someone had to be—and his senior management team, in the CEO's executive offices, no less. Niraj was insisting that Stuart step up his fashion game. If Niraj was the face of the company, Stuart was its metronome. It was part of his job to play the geek—if he walked in to see a prospective client and was wearing anything but jeans, sneakers, and a hoodie, they wouldn't take him seriously, which was why he wore dress shirts and leather shoes. He would play no part, until this moment, apparently.

"How about these loafers?" Niraj asked, holding them up.

"I liked the other shoes better," Stuart said.

"Do you think they have any idea?" Niraj asked, setting down the shoes and passing Stuart a belt.

"If they don't, they're idiots." Stuart tried on the belt. "My guess is they have no idea."

The tailor slipped the jacket off Stuart.

"Every CTO in the finance industry knows there's only one right move here: blowing up the football stadium–size data centers and distributing the data and code onto servers in the cloud. They just can't admit it, for fear of losing their big, hairy-ass bonuses when it comes time to put their money where their mouth is and things don't go as planned, which they inevitably won't because that's how progressive change happens—disruptively."

Stuart exited the store in a dark suit, white dress shirt, and bold tie, plus some Italian shoes and a belt to match, none of which he felt exactly comfortable in or could afford, but Niraj had been insistent and infectious as he picked out things for himself too during this enjoyable little repose from the normal course of their relations. It almost felt as if they'd been clothes shopping together all their lives.

As for Marie, Niraj insisted Stuart get her something, too, as they walked by a Montblanc store. They went inside, and Stuart bought her a black lacquered pen with gold trim and a nice, heavy weight to it. For the writer, he would tell her. Oh, how she would hate him for saying that. He smiled just thinking about it.

They had time to kill before their meeting, theoretically. (Technically, they had no time to kill for this or anything.) Niraj suggested they hit the Borough Market for some of that famous English tea, and then, in a strangely giddy mood, no doubt inspired by a lack of sleep, they found themselves wandering around the market stalls, tasting some of the Welsh cheeses on display, the biscuits and jams. Then Niraj caught a scent and went straight over to find where it was coming from. A vendor selling *seekh kebab*, grilled skewers of marinated, spiced ground lamb. Niraj immediately bought four, and they stood at a high table, sucking them down. Not just like his *nani* used to make, but pretty damn close. They almost forgot what time it was, or why they were here in the first place.

THE MEETING TOOK PLACE in a conference room adjacent to the CEO's office. Dark mahogany, luxurious leather, carpets so rich that Stuart wondered if he should take off his new shoes, ancient texts lining the walls, the proud founding fathers of one of the world's oldest and stodgiest institutions staring down at them. Stuart had never seen a conference room like this but for in the movies, and it reminded him of this question: What the hell were they doing here? How many conversations had he had with banks about cloud and distributed networking, only to receive those patronizing, masters-of-the-universe stares in return? These guys weren't going to do squat. They were going to act like they wanted to innovate, waste a lot of money purporting that they were innovating, and then find an excuse not to innovate anything.

Stuart and Niraj organized themselves into their seats, along with the head of bond trading, equity trading, and risk and compliance, and the head of IT. A minute later, the interim CEO sauntered in. Introductions, but all Stuart could focus on was the big, fat MIT ring on the CEO's finger, the brass rat, for those in the know. Stuart, who'd been rejected by MIT, couldn't help but stare. Gaudy, grandiose, and unnecessary, that ring. Still, on dark days, he wondered how his life would be different if he'd gone to MIT (not that he could have afforded it), where Richard Stallman, for many the father of open-source—as opposed to that Finnish snob Torvalds who kept trying to claim the title—began his illustrious career. Had he gone to MIT, would he perhaps have become this CIO person to his right, waxing on about the state of technology in finance (yawn)? Or would he be the Bond guy sitting across from him, looking overfed and bored? Some of the engineers Stuart had gone to Berkeley with had been recruited away by finance companies—math minds, computer scientists turned into modelers, arbitragers, risk takers. They moved across the country and lived in brownstones, summered in the Hamptons, took home a good million per year in salary, plus a bonus ten times that. It was a life Stuart could barely imagine, and not because he couldn't see himself lavishing it up with the best of them (and on occasion had), but in that life, he'd never have met Marie at the boring-as-hell telecom conference in Sacramento. That was what his life always came down to. That, and the fact that whenever he tried to work for someone, things inevitably went wrong. There was always a fallout. Except for those few times his boss had been a woman.

Stuart looked around the table. Not one woman. Sheila Dunn. A name that always came to mind when not one woman was at the table. No bullshit with Sheila. No drama. No politics. She'd started out as a secretary at Intel out of high school, taught herself how to code, and worked her way up to senior architect. She was managing an engineering department of three hundred by the time Chase Bank recruited her away. She ran its payments-platform project in partnership with Stuart's motley crew of engineers. After Chase, she went to Microsoft, then became the CTO of Bluewave, the leading Linux distro provider. Sheila was not only a brilliant technologist but a solid manager with a reputation for getting shit done. From client server to internet to cloud, she'd not been pushed out or beaten down. She'd persevered, quietly, unglamorously, and Stuart had become overwhelmed with an immense amount of pride for what she did. What all of them did. Amid all the unicorns and the hyperbole, all the press focusing on the few but not the many, it was easy to forget the Sheilas of the world, the Stuarts of the world, the ones out there keeping the nuts and bolts of technology churning, growing, changing, and evolving. Sheila was one of *them*. One of *them*, who had cracked the glass ceiling. She'd become CEO of Bluewave, earning the respect of shareholders and employees alike, and what had she gotten for her efforts? At forty-two, she was diagnosed with breast cancer. Within six months, she was dead.

"Stuart? Are you with us?"

He started wondering what was in the tea he'd been drinking all morning.

"Technology is moving fast, and the pace at which we are being left behind is growing exponentially," the interim CEO said. "Virtualization? Distributed computing? We can't even modify a firewall router without an operator having to walk over to the box and access it manually. It's ridiculous."

No shit, Stuart thought, pulling a tissue from his pocket. He hadn't gone to MIT, and he'd figured that out ten years ago. He wiped his brow, which was sweating, even though he was freezing in this room, which alternated between frigid and hot and stuffy. Or maybe it was the suit he was wearing. Was it starting to itch? He pulled at his tie. He thought he might be coming down with something.

Niraj said, "We are all just hanging on. No one really knows what they're doing. What we do know is that the future is data. Data that can give you visibility into what's going on with your network connections and, in your case, what's going on is this." He turned to Stuart to continue, as they'd practiced.

Stuart cleared his throat a few times. "Because of your no-cloud policy, rogue elements in your organization, those who don't have the patience to wait for IT to provision physical servers for their new projects, have taken it upon themselves to spin up virtual servers on their own and at will by establishing connections with Amazon Web Services, in order to do testing and development for whatever projects they might be working on."

A few people gave pointed looks to the CIO, who cleared his throat and asked, "I'm sorry, what projects are you talking about?"

"I think that's beside the point—"

"Shut them down," the CIO said, cutting Stuart off.

"It's not that simple," Stuart said.

"Why not?"

"Because they're pervasive and everywhere."

The silence grew profound.

"You've heard of skunkworks, a term developed by NASA and related to small groups of individuals focused on radical innovation. It's become a rather natural phenomenon in organizations, no matter the industry, no matter how strict or regulated the policies of that organization. Technology infrastructure being what it is today, thanks to open-source—yes, open-source—and cloud and now software-defined networking, it's simply too easy to experiment, to be innovative. To fail fast and fail a lot without anyone even knowing.

"It was through one of these rogue connections that your bug crawled, managing to infiltrate your core network and bring the system to its knees, and that's obviously a serious problem. And I'm sitting here looking at all your blank faces and seeing that you might be blindsided by what I'm telling you, that you might be thinking, *Who are these skunkworks fuckers? I'm going to rip their heads off,* but that's the last thing you want to do. Because the fact is that there is not just one or two of these rogue connections, but more like dozens—a parasite that has manifested and spread. You will not be able to stamp them out. That would mean stifling innovation, what these people feed off. You'll be swimming upstream. They'll win and you'll lose.

"What you need is much simpler than that. It's visibility and controls. Visibility into those connections and networks—who is accessing them, when and how, what ports are vulnerable and why—and controls to standardize the configuration of inbound and outbound traffic and shut down a connection, if necessary, in real time."

The IT guy opened his mouth to say something, but the Bond guy stopped him. "And you can do this?"

"We're the only people, frankly, who can," Niraj responded. "We're not theorists. We're not academics. We actually build this stuff. We've years of experience in building this stuff."

The Bond guy said, "Our guys can't build this stuff."

"And not only do we build it, we manage it, too. In fact, our team in Jaipur is getting ready to onboard two financial services clients who don't want to manage it themselves and for whom we've projected Five9 network uptime and a tenfold reduction in management costs, because when we manage the network services, we see the back end—what's working and what's not—and what's not working, we make better."

Stuart glanced at Niraj. *What two FS clients?* They barely had a facility in Jaipur, let alone clients. Sure, they had a few engineers there, a shell of an office, but without having yet closed the round, without funding, they would have no capabilities.

"We have a strict no-offshore policy," the interim CEO said.

Neither Stuart nor Niraj said anything. This was not news.

The interim CEO and the Bond guy conferred for some minutes. Then the interim CEO asked, "When can you bring your team over and get started?"

Niraj glanced at Stuart with a look that said, "Don't open your mouth."

At this point, Stuart wondered, if he did open his mouth, if the CEO might not just slap the million Vita was going to charge the Exchange for the project down on the table right then and there, because that was the way things had been going lately. They couldn't lose.

CHAPTER 15

THEY MET UP WITH JIM at a pub around the corner to debrief on the Exchange meeting. He looked the same—there was no mistaking the lanky, boyish frame; the wiry hair and glasses; the uniform of jeans, sneakers, a sweater of the finest cashmere. He must have been fiftysomething by now. They'd spoken via Skype a few times regarding the diagnostic results, Jim couldn't be directly involved because of a conflict of interest. Niraj ordered a plate of blood sausage, then got out his laptop and began walking Jim through Vita's cap table. They'd won the project to implement COMPASS software as a service (SaaS) at the Exchange, which the Exchange's engineers would operate on-site. Forget about COMPASS MNS—these guys were never going to put the keys to their crown jewels in the hands of Indians, which was just as well because Vita had no MNS capabilities in India yet; it barely even had a SaaS version of COMPASS yet. The team in Singapore had been heads down on the SaaS version, but without funding and more resources, it was slow going. Not to mention that they had no team to "bring over" to London. Everyone was booked consulting either at KT, SingTel, or Toyota, or internally on the platform build-out. If they had the funding in hand, they could hire an in-house recruiter to help sift through résumés at a faster pace, having almost already sapped their personal networks.

Jim watched Stuart and Niraj go back and forth on the subject for some minutes. "Where are you on raising the round?" he asked.

"We've got two weeks to close on a round of twelve million, for which we are three million short," Niraj said. Then he sat back. "We're thinking about talking to some VCs."

"VCs won't get COMPASS," Jim said.

Stuart looked at Niraj, as in, "That's what *I* said."

"Look, guys, here's what you need to know, what I didn't want to tell you until I saw how these guys responded to you." Jim sat back, then forward again, his eyes dialed in, knee bouncing. "The Exchange is in the market to buy a data research and analytics firm in the UK that can compete with Bloomberg. There is no growth in being just an exchange anymore; it's about owning the data. And once the Exchange acquires its Bloomberg, it's not going to know what to do with it. A research firm with the reach and scope of a Bloomberg means data centers all over the world and network access points in every country. Whether it be Singapore, Milan, Hong Kong, or Sydney, each satellite office is going to need access to a core network, and each one of those access points is going to need to be managed and monitored. And by the time this all happens, the Exchange will have already learned hard lessons about running COMPASS on-site, care of you guys, and it's going to practically throw its Bloomberg network over to you in India to manage. Imagine all that network data, streaming in from all over the world, at your disposal. And once you have that, well, then we'll talk about what your endgame is. In the meantime"— he stood up—"I'll have my accountant give you a call."

Stuart wasn't sure he'd intuited Jim right, and by the end of that day he would convince himself that he'd intuited him wrong. Not until Jim's accountant called the following morning before they boarded their flight would Stuart realize that he had intuited Jim right, but for now, all he could do was notice the missing ring on Jim's finger. Jim had gone to MIT with the interim CEO. "No brass rat?"

Jim glanced at his finger and smirked. "When you're in school, you wear the ring so the rat's ass points up at you, meaning the rat shits on you. After you graduate, you wear it pointed down, so that the rat can shit on the world." He swung his backpack over one shoulder. "And that's why I don't wear the ring. Give my regards to Marie." With that, he disappeared out the door and into the mist.

ON THE PLANE BACK from London, Niraj sent Stuart a Slack message from his seat in business class: "I thought we weren't going to broach MNS in the book, given that it's a marketing piece and we don't want to scare people off."

Marie had sent some recent manuscript pages for review, which Niraj got to do from the comfort of his last-minute upgrade, as opposed to Stuart, who'd been doing the same from his coach seat in back. "After that scene at KT with Hung Su Kim, I changed my mind. And now, after talking with Jim, I'm guessing you agree with me."

"Okay, fine, but do we need a whole chapter on women in tech?"

"Yes, we do."

"We're not ready for women."

"Please don't let anyone hear you say that. And, by the way, we have a woman and she's kicking ass."

"She's not a woman. She's LGBTQ."

"No, I believe she's technically a woman."

"See? We're not ready."

A minute went by.

"How is it up there?"

"The pinot is surprisingly excellent."

"This is really happening."

"Yes. It is."

"What makes us any different from the hundreds of

other network startups? We've got no product. We've sold them on a concept."

"We've got four top-tier clients, KT, SingTel, Toyota, and now the Exchange, currently building their IT strategies around that concept."

"We're consultants. We don't know shit about managing a platform."

"We know a lot of shit. We know as much shit as anyone. And guess what? Funding means you can hire that product manager you were after."

"By the way, Liam is out," Stuart typed.

"What do you mean 'out'?"

"Of India. He says it's a shithole and he won't go."

The flight attendant called for seat belts because of turbulence.

"Look, he's got a wife and they're about to adopt those Korean babies and they're going through all this rigmarole, and he can't go. Anyway, we've got traction with the engineers in Singapore. I say we keep the product team there, including Liam."

"We'll need COMPASS in three months."

"By the way, who are these two FS clients we have in India?"

Niraj didn't respond, and with that, the conversation ended. Stuart closed Slack, reclined his seat the inch that it would go, and opened the valuation cap table that Niraj had just sent him for the umpteenth time and that they would now, once it was updated, send to Jim's accountant. He spent the next few hours working with the projections, trying not to let his mind digress, once again, into the fact that this was *happening*. He stopped only when the turbulence grew untenable. Twenty minutes later, when the pilot still couldn't find a smooth altitude, Stuart began scrolling through movies as a distraction. He settled on *Ted*. Sure enough, it was so silly and dumb, it put him to sleep, though he didn't remember falling asleep, just that suddenly the plane was dropping. A smooth, steady, steep decline, the one always harbored in the dark recesses of one's mind, and here it was at last, his penultimate moment: The plane was going down. Fear, but mostly a profound sadness, enveloped him as he braced for the crash (at least, in some deeper, unconscious part of him he braced—his body didn't seem to be reacting). The descent went on for some time, an eternity, it seemed, and then, all at once, it was over and he was awake.

STUART AND NIRAJ HEARD the news when their plane landed in Singapore, when everyone's phones began going wild with texts from friends and loved ones. Terrorists had driven a van into pedestrians on the London Bridge and then gone on a stabbing rampage through the Borough Market. Where Stuart and Niraj had been wandering around only a day earlier, seven people were now dead. Niraj was visibly shaking as they stood in the line for customs. "We were right there," he said, still devouring the news on his phone. "That was the store where we bought the Welsh cheese."

Neither of them said anything for the next twenty minutes while they inched their way forward in the customs line and Stuart scrolled through Marie's dozen texts: "I am going crazy. Call me when you land."

The air outside was heavy, thick, disorienting. They made their way to the taxi line. "I'm never going to be able to go back now." Niraj, perspiring and out of breath, bored his eyes off into some distance. "From here. Us. What we're doing," he went on. "Vita has got to work, or I'm going to have nothing."

Stuart wasn't sure what Niraj meant—he had a conglomerate back in India waiting for him to run it—but he saw the wide fear in his partner's eyes. He might have been in shock. "It'll work," Stuart said, and he meant it with the whole of his being.

MARIE WAS THERE, HOLDING back tears, when Stuart opened the door. "I wasn't sure. I'd not heard from you. Your dad called."

Stuart hadn't even thought of his dad, whom he'd spoken to right before heading to London, having forgotten that he'd mentioned the trip to him. "What did he say?"

"I told him that you were on the plane as planned and—"

He pulled her into his arms, wordless. They stayed like that, man and woman, lovers, clinging in the foyer of a bodega in Singapore. Then Stuart pulled back and, clearing his throat, said that he was going to unpack. Marie followed him to the bedroom and sat on the bed, watching his movements. Unpacking was always the first thing he did when he returned from a business trip, before he even sat down, methodically, ritually, as if to wash everything clean away. Only when his suitcase was emptied and zipped up and stored away did he hand her the pen and say, "We won the project."

She nodded at the pen but couldn't look at him.

He knew what she was thinking, but he wasn't going to give up, or pause, even for a moment, just because some assholes had murdered seven people for no reason. "It only makes me want to fight harder, Marie."

"Oh, Stuart, fight for what?"

"We got the first three million," he said.

She blinked at him. "Please don't tell me it was Jim."

"Okay, I won't tell you."

Her eyes grew glossy.

"It'll be okay, Marie. Jim's a good guy. And he gets us in a way others don't. You know that more than anyone. He's going to be a silent investor. You won't even know he's there."

"Until you lose his money."

"I'm not going to lose his money. And thanks for the vote of confidence, by the way."

"I didn't mean it. It's just . . ."

"What?"

"Nothing. It's nothing." She couldn't say it. That she thought the stabbings were a bad omen.

"I said it'll be okay, Marie, and so it's going to be okay."

She nodded, then looked down at the pen. Felt the weight of it in her hand. Solid. Sturdy. If her father were alive, she'd give him the pen. He didn't like fine things, but she believed in her heart that he would like this pen. She took it with her to the kitchen (and from then on everywhere) and made hot tea with lemon because she felt as if she'd been infected with whatever had infected Stuart in London. A cold, yes, and so much more.

Stuart came in and got out the cups and added a shot of bourbon to his and, when she nodded at him, her cup, too. They stood there against the counter, holding the steaming cups in their hands. "Your father," she said suddenly.

"Oh, shit." Stuart almost spilled his tea setting his cup down on the counter while reaching for his cell.

His father answered right away, and they established that all was okay on Stuart's end, that his plane had taken off by the time of the attacks, that his father had been worried, that he wished Stuart had called him, that he'd not slept. It was some time before Stuart managed to redirect the discussion to his father's bad knee and the surgery he was now going to put off because the Pilates classes down at the Y were really helping to strengthen his hamstring. He went on about the exercises and the fancy machines and the ropes and bungees, all of which seemed to give him purpose, though he was driving the therapists nuts, he admitted, with all his questions and goofing around.

Stuart smiled for the first time since his plane had landed. "They're just doing their job, Dad."

There came the silence that sometimes happened with his father.

"How's Marie?" his father asked, finally.

"She's good. A little shook up. She says hi."

"Are you being good to her?"

He looked at Marie. "Am I being good to you?"

She gave him a blank stare.

"She says I'm being good to her." His voice cracked—it was all becoming too much, suddenly—and he told his father he'd call him tomorrow and got off the line.

CHAPTER 16
APRIL 2011—TWO MONTHS LATER

EVER SINCE THE HUNG SU KIM debacle, things at KT had not been the same. The KT people were more distant; there were fewer karaoke fests, fewer dinners together. But the KT CTO and Dr. Kwak were their friends, the original champions of their core open-source engine, Javelina, so it was to them that Vita went first to test COMPASS, which went fabulously until two errors occurred in the network application and Liam had to abort before the whole thing came crashing down, all while the Koreans sat around the conference table, scratching their heads and remembering Hung Su Kim's traitorous comment: "These guys don't know what they're doing."

Stuart was sure Hung Su Kim's dark gaze was what had brought the system to its knees. They were no less than shocked to see him in the room with his team of three, a number rumored to be growing. What they were doing there or working on was a mystery. Strategy-McKinsey crap, Stuart slur-texted Liam, who was seated next to him. After the meeting, Stuart tried to get hold of Niraj in India, where he and Smally were at work ramping up the offshore facilities, but Niraj was nowhere to be found, so Stuart called JS himself. JS already knew about the test. Stuart had to stop him: "Don't worry about the test. We'll fix it. I'm not concerned about that. What I'm concerned about is Hung Su Kim, and what he was doing in that room."

"It's very simple," JS responded, "Hung Su Kim works for me now."

Stuart frowned, waiting for JS to say more, perhaps explain, but JS said nothing and Stuart forced himself to keep it together. Keep your enemies close—maybe that was JS's strategy. What else could he possibly be doing with this guy?

"There is nothing for you to worry about, Stuart. Hung Su Kim's team's work at KT is uncompetitive with Vita's, not even complementary, and I assure you that your paths will barely cross."

"They just crossed." It came out as curt and foreboding, and while he knew he was overstepping, he'd had enough of this HSK thing.

"I believe you have other things to worry about, Stuart. We don't want KT to lose any more confidence."

He opened his mouth to say something in his defense, but he had nothing. They hung up, and Stuart had to take a few deep breaths, stamp down his pride, because in a way JS was right. Stuart had bigger issues at hand, specifically the glitches in COMPASS that hadn't been there three hours earlier when the team had performed their umpteenth dry run. He, Liam, and Dillan, the product manager Stuart had hired, stayed behind in the conference room and corralled the coders into a stand-up and worked through the bug for some time before it became apparent that there were deeper issues than just the code—Dillan being one of them. Dillan, who'd agreed to temporarily relocate to Singapore from Boulder, Colorado, had come in with the promise of discipline, transparency, and efficacy but had immediately been at odds with Liam, who was overworked and stressed. The team had been having turnover issues that Stuart had not been made aware of. Yelena, Vita's new CFO, had been inundating the engineers with requests for time sheets and expense reports and hours billed so that she could invoice clients.

Stuart sat Dillan down and explained the delicate balance required to protect the coders from administrative distractions so that they could do what they had been hired to do: code. Then he looked down and saw Dillan's shoes, after which he closed his eyes for many seconds to calm himself. Had he been wearing them in the meeting with KT, and if so, how had Stuart not noticed before? There was nothing that irritated Stuart more than those stupid, asinine body-glove shoes (other than perhaps cowboy boots). He wasted no time instructing Dillan, in no uncertain terms, to return to his hotel and change his footwear. They were not in Colorado, they were in Asia, where men wore suits and dress shoes to client meetings. Some uncomfortable back-and-forth about why, for medical reasons, Dillan was required to wear these body-glove shoes, led to a more intense confrontation in which Yelena, who besides being CFO also happened to be COO, called Stuart from Singapore to intercede on Dillan's behalf. Technically, Dillan reported to her, and she to Niraj, who finally returned Stuart's call.

"JS is a little pissed off," Niraj said. "What did you say to him?"

"Did you know Hung Su Kim was working for JS?"

"Yes. So what?"

"Why didn't you tell me?"

"Because I didn't think it had anything to do with anything." Stuart bit his tongue.

"JS is an investor. It makes no sense for him to sabotage things."

Stuart was beginning to wonder if anything made sense about working in this country unless you were Korean.

"Next time, call me first, and I'll take care of it."

"I did call you first. You weren't there." Stuart's tone was accusatory, and he instantly regretted it. These battles with Niraj were new and jarring, and Stuart wasn't used to them.

"JS is concerned we're going to miss the COMPASS deadline. What happened with the test?"

"We're trying to figure that out. The coders are experiencing a lot of noise. Can you ask Yelena to lay off for a bit?"

"If we don't bill clients, we don't make *revenue.*"

"All I'm saying is that there's a balance, and it hasn't been struck. I'm also starting to have concerns about Dillan."

"You have concerns about everyone, Stuart. We agreed that we wouldn't be able to grow unless you delegated. We're paying Dillan a lot of money. Let him do his job. And meanwhile, leave JS to me. I wish you hadn't jumped the gun and called him."

Stuart gritted his teeth. He wanted to accuse Niraj of not relaying the message to JS about Hung Su Kim as they had discussed, but he wasn't up for a battle right now. He needed to decompress, to separate himself from the code and think, and above all he needed to sleep. He would need sleep more than he knew in the coming weeks, which proved little different. Niraj continued spending most of his time in India while leaving the customer and operational reins to Yelena, and Dillan continued to poke and prod and deliver a plethora of fancy management reports that had little relevance to the task at hand.

So, when faced with another beta test crash two weeks after the first one, this time at SingTel, Stuart took Dillan into a room and promptly fired him, reminding himself that it was easier to ask for forgiveness later than to beg for permission now.

Or was it? Niraj called him an hour later, livid. "Is this because of the shoes?"

"Fuck those shoes."

"We don't have time to change course, Stuart."

"We're not changing course; we're adjusting how we drive."

"Beta tests at Toyota and the Exchange are up next. Not to mention the *launch.*"

Stuart took an audible breath, and then, speaking very slowly, said, "We are not going to launch a platform that doesn't work."

"How are you going to find another product manager at this stage?"

"I'm not going to hire another product manager." Stuart heard a horn through the phone. A scooter sputtering. He imagined Niraj choking on the exhaust. Stuart said, "Look, I made a mistake. I take full responsibility. What with the crunch to get the management team in place before the board meeting next month, trying to make a dent in the $12 million now burning a hole in our bank account, and in the ping-ponging between the Exchange and other clients, I made an incorrect assumption that a high-priced PM was the way to go. But I see now that that was a mistake. A mistake I am going to fix."

"How?"

"I'm going to take over the management of the engineering team."

"You realize that is the opposite of delegating."

"Decisions aren't static, Niraj. We must be flexible, adjust quickly to what's not working, and that's what I'm doing. I may be over forty, but I'm not a dinosaur. I'm changing course. I'm going to manage the team loosely, adopting a hybrid Agile-DevOps approach, a product development process based on hiring leaders, not managers. Using Agile, we don't need a PM; we need a scrum master who can take directions from me and facilitate the scrum team, aka the engineers. He'll be a peer, an advocate, not someone with a stick. He'll give the engineers daily guidance in the removal of obstacles. We're going to empower the team to self-organize, and the scrum master will be their servant, in a way. A servant-leader who will report to me, the product owner."

After a pause, Niraj asked, "What have you been smoking? Agile is just a cover for poor planning, and you know it."

Stuart ignored the comment he recalled having once uttered himself. "Look, I've already talked to Liam and the team about it and rallied them around the idea, and they're excited and reengaged. Now I just need you to tell the board we're extending the launch by one month."

Niraj said, "I'm not going back on my word."

"If a Formula One race car driver is approaching a turn at maximum speed, he needs to know how hard and at exactly what moment to brake so that he can reach the optimal speed as he comes out of the turn."

"What's your point?"

"Brakes make the car go faster."

The line went silent. The COMPASS glitches had stung. Someone had dropped the ball, and when it came to product, the buck stopped with Stuart. They'd never been ones to blame each other, yet that was exactly what they'd started doing, and Stuart had to pull up for a second and check himself. They had agreed that the funding would never change the values under which they'd agreed to run the company, one of which was that drama solved nothing. Getting shit done did. And yet something *had* changed. Between them. A slow, steady shift, a wave they couldn't push back—who had Stuart been trying to kid? No matter what anyone tried to tell you or promise you, funding always changed everything.

Niraj said, "Fine, hire a scrum master, whatever—we don't have time to dick around. I'll get you an extra month. Pick someone and go."

CHAPTER 17
MAY 2011—ONE MONTH LATER

COMPASS STARTED MAKING A turnaround. A week before Vita's board meeting, after successful tests at both Toyota and SingTel, the team returned to KT. This time, without Hung Su Kim in the room, the test went flawlessly. Afterward, KT took everyone out for soju bombs and karaoke, like old times—until the next morning, when Dr. Kwak called Stuart into his office and told him that the CIO had decided to pass on Phase III, the COMPASS SaaS implementation. He was not happy about it either, but his hands were tied. The CIO had decided they could build their own COMPASS.

Stuart wasn't stunned, given what had been going on at KT over the past few months, but Niraj was beside himself. As if physically hurt by the rejection, he had some words for his Korean friends. "Oh, sure, throw bodies at the problem, an army of them, as many as it takes, fast following being the modus operandi for South Korean enterprises, which is why their buildings collapse and their ferries sink and hundreds of people die unnecessarily. And by the way, there's no way JS is going to let this happen." But then Niraj called JS and—surprise, surprise—he let this happen.

What did he say? Stuart wanted to know.

Niraj seemed almost embarrassed to tell him. "He said to walk away. To let KT learn the hard way. In other words," Niraj added, "to let *us* learn the hard way."

Stuart frowned. "Learn what?"

"Two million in bookings up in smoke," Niraj responded. "That's what."

Neither of them needed to mention Vita's neglected sales pipeline, though the implication was there: What pipeline? To date, clients had sought out Vita, versus the other way around, and both Stuart and Niraj knew that this was no long-term sales strategy, but amid their various distractions they'd not gotten around to hiring a sales team. Now this: How to make up $2 million in Q2 sales bookings in less than three weeks' time, when the quarter ended? And how to break the news to the board? This, on top of the launch delay, was not how they'd wanted to start things off with their new investors.

On an emergency sales pipeline call with Yelena, the marketing team, and the consultants, they dove deep into the pipeline, updating the who, what, when, where, and how about each prospect on the list, digging deep into each of their own networks, stretching near and far; nothing was out of bounds. A quarter down the list, Stuart asked Niraj about the status of the two Indian COMPASS clients he'd referred to when they'd pitched the Exchange, wanting to get them officially on the list. It was an innocent question, a question that Stuart might have asked of anyone on the call, but what followed was a moment of dead silence that quickly grew uncomfortable. Stuart was about to move to the next prospect on the list, but then Niraj burst out into a sudden and uncharacteristic screaming tirade.

"Maybe our CTO should focus on the real issue here, which is why he dropped the ball on KT and we lost the follow-on work. Why don't you explain to the team why the fuck you let this happen?"

Stuart's laptop vibrated all the way from India, where Niraj had called in from. Yelena, who was seated next to Stuart, held Stuart's eyes for a long, disturbing moment, and then Stuart said to the group, "I think it's best to move to the next—"

Niraj dropped the line.

Stuart's heart began pounding in his chest, but he contained his emotions for the next hour or so that the call lasted. He didn't want to alarm the team. It wasn't until he hung up that he allowed himself to process what had happened, which was that his partner had just humiliated him, not to mention himself, the two of them, in front of their entire senior leadership team just because he was embarrassed to admit that those two MNS clients he'd been touting were vaporware, or such was the only rationale Stuart could think of for his partner's overly dramatic and very unprofessional behavior. And the more Stuart thought about it, the more incensed he became. He waited an hour to calm down and then called Niraj. Niraj did not pick up. Stuart left him a voice mail. Then an email. A Slack message. He got no response.

This progressed for three days. Niraj had some exchanges with Yelena about finances and the board package, and he called Liam and Biggy about some matters, but regarding Stuart and everything else he remained MIA. Not until it was time to fly to Tokyo for the board meeting did Stuart hear from Niraj, via Yelena. She'd become their go-between, the only adult in the room with two children, which was why Niraj had hired her in the first place. She dressed in Armani and wore stylish scarves and spoke four languages. She had a thick Russian accent even though she was a naturalized citizen, having immigrated to Ohio with her parents when she was thirteen, as part of the Russian Jewish migration. Unmarried and appearing to have no life outside work, she had various experiences consulting for startups and was living out of a rented Porsche SUV when Niraj ran into her at a cloud conference in London—could she get herself to Singapore? She was on a plane the next day. She was willing to travel, *wanted* to travel, to the far reaches of the world, if possible. Smart, organized, no-nonsense, and, most important, unafraid to work in a room filled with mostly men who often acted like boys.

She managed to convince Niraj that whatever his issue with Stuart was, the two needed to go to the board as a unified front. She arranged for them to meet at a café near Fumitaka-san's office the morning of the board meeting, agreeing to come along to keep the peace, but the peacekeeping turned out not to be necessary. Niraj had gotten over whatever bug had crawled up his ass. He was his usual self: coiffed, professional, a little heavy on the cologne, but above all even-tempered. He mentioned nothing of his absence, nor the outburst that had caused it, and, in the interest of time and on Yelena's advice, Stuart refrained from confronting him about it. He didn't want to set Niraj off before the board meeting. So Stuart just nodded and smiled, all the while thinking, *Jesus Christ, how the hell are we going to get through the next four hours?*

Fumitaka-san, Hideo-san, a translator, a lawyer, Yelena, Stuart, and Niraj sat around a dauntingly long, egg-shaped, slick black-lacquered conference table. The critical item for discussion was the launch delay, about which Niraj addressed all concerns, using Stuart's quote about needing brakes to go faster, a metaphor that Fumitaka-san favored greatly.

"We may have lost KT, but the COMPASS platform, thanks to Stuart's hands-on intervention, will soon be 'live' and operating in two continents: Europe and Asia."

Stuart cleared his throat. He preferred to use quotes around the word "live" because technically his COMPASS clients, including Toyota, SingTel, and the Exchange, would at first be going live with only a small portion of what the platform had to offer.

"Training is slow going," Stuart admitted when it was his turn to present, "even more so than expected. Our clients' engineers need a lot of help, and Liam has already offloaded much of the help-desk overload to the MNS team in India. In fact, the MNS team has been so inundated with client calls that Liam devised a mechanism to bypass the traditional Level 1, 2, and 3 problem resolution structure and, using automation and basic AI, was able to eliminate Level 1 and triage issues directly to Level 2, or even Level 3, something major Silicon Valley firms like Netflix, Facebook, and Google have already implemented successfully. Level 3 is where the big guns take over, the site reliability engineers (SREs), who maintain specialties in specific hardware vendors like Cisco, Juniper, and Palo Alto—not everyone is a Liam or Biggy, with expertise across all platforms—but with the automated problem isolation and routing mechanism it doesn't matter, because issues can flip between SREs in a heartbeat."

At the mention of FANGs, Fumitaka-san's and Hideo-san's faces conveyed an outwardly jovial appreciation that transcended the language barrier. They nodded and conferred and immediately set about approving all the various compensation packages Niraj and Stuart put on the table: the scrum master, the new VP of operations in India, two new product engineers, and even, uncharacteristically, Yelena's request for more options—all those Hermès scarves did not come cheap. And still Vita wasn't hiring fast enough. This led to a lengthy discussion of their burn rate, as well as a decision to hire a dedicated sales team. Yelena was speaking when Stuart noticed Niraj's eyes growing distant and glazed over. He'd gained more weight, Stuart thought. There was a shadow on his face, as if he'd not shaved that morning; either that or some other darkness had fallen upon him. At one point, Stuart thought that Niraj might even have fallen asleep, until suddenly he announced the signing of those two MNS clients in India whom he'd just about had a heart attack over three days prior. Again, heads nodded enthusiastically. Stuart, however, closed his eyes.

Niraj disappeared right after the meeting, and Yelena ran to catch a red-eye to London for a meeting at the Exchange. Stuart stayed behind to take a walk with Fumitaka-san at his insistence, which Stuart was happy to oblige. They could both use some air. The meeting had gone on for five hours. Down the back alley behind his office building was a row of dimly lit sake bars standing shuttered against the cold. They paused underneath a streetlight so Stuart could light a cigarette. Fumitaka-san did not smoke, and he seemed a little surprised that Stuart did, as was Stuart, who seemed to have forgotten himself for a moment. He didn't smoke unless under duress. Their coats were on, a dusting of snow on the ground. Stuart assumed he was going to get a deserved reprimand of some kind about the problems they'd had with COMPASS, or the issues with the sales pipeline, or the fact that their Japanese client base had not expanded beyond Toyota, which had been one of the contingencies for Fumitaka-san's company's investment.

"Are you taking care of yourself, Stuart?" Fumitaka-san asked softly, looking deeply into Stuart's eyes.

Stuart felt the weight of his body for a long moment. The funding had been in their account only three months, and yet it felt as if three years had passed. He was unsure how to respond.

Fumitaka-san waited calmly. His eyes said he could wait all night. They'd played golf together. He'd brought Stuart into his home to use his bathroom. Stuart was about to say something about Niraj, how he couldn't help feeling as if something was off with him, when Fumitaka-san said, "It looks like you've gained some weight, Stuart-san."

Stuart looked down at his stomach, then back up again.

"A man must take care of himself," Fumitaka-san said.

Stuart stamped out his cigarette.

"The Japanese may not know network infrastructure like you do, but we know that our bodies are our temples. Even the Romans knew it. *Mens sana in corpore sano*: 'a healthy mind in a healthy body.'"

Stuart, surprised to hear the Latin proverb, assured Fumitaka-san that his health was fine and that the few pounds he'd gained were simply a consequence of all his travel.

Fumitaka-san nodded, as if he understood all that mere humans had to tell themselves to survive.

They parted ways, but the encounter left Stuart in a state of foreboding. Niraj had put on a nice show for the board, as he had for Stuart with Yelena earlier at the café, but his erratic behavior could not go unaccounted for. Stuart did an abrupt turn, heading in the direction of where he knew Niraj would be, at the second-floor lounge of the five-star Conrad Hotel, located across the street from the three star Royal Park Hotel, where they were staying.

Stuart found Niraj at a table in the corner, sipping a double scotch and slouched before the illuminating screen of his laptop. When he saw Stuart, he nodded, as in, "Yes, you may approach."

Stuart took the chair across from Niraj, ordered a drink, and waited for it to arrive before asking, "Where were you? You were essentially MIA for three days."

"I had some personal business."

"We can't have another battle like that in front of the senior team."

"I know."

"It's bad for morale."

"I heard you."

"Have you spoken with JS?"

"He's been hard to get hold of."

"He needs to elect a board officer. Where are we on that?"

"Nowhere."

"Tell JS if he doesn't elect someone, we will."

"Okay."

"And I need to know who these two new MNS clients in India are."

"Some friends owed my dad some favors."

Niraj went back to what he'd been doing.

Stuart's scotch came, and he swallowed it while watching Niraj stare at his screen. He had some other things to go over with Niraj, but he had the instinct to call it a night. They'd survived the meeting. It was ten o'clock. He was beat. He told Niraj he was going to bed and that Niraj should do the same, that he didn't look so well. Niraj chortled at that, as in, "Go to bed? Ha," and then the waitress set down a plate of chicken wings, which Stuart instructed himself, after Fumitaka-san's lecture, not to reach for. He stood up. Niraj said he was going to stay and work awhile longer. Just before Stuart got on the elevator, he looked back and saw the waitress setting down another drink before Niraj. As he took in the sight of his partner, slumped to one side over his phone in the dim light, as if the weight of his body could no longer support itself upright, Stuart thought of the days when neither of them could gain weight even if they tried. Then the elevator opened and Stuart stepped in.

CHAPTER 18
AUGUST 2011

HAD THEY SEEN THE NEWS in the *Journal*? Jim called Stuart, wanting to know. They had not seen the news, but the news was this: The rumors were no longer rumors. The Exchange had, that morning, announced plans to buy Refinitiv, a data and analytics platform competitive with Bloomberg, for $26 billion. And here Vita was, sitting right there in the sweet spot with a platform to secure access to all that data in a distributed cloud environment that the new owners of Refinitiv didn't have. It wasn't a surprise three days later when the Exchange called Niraj, asking when it could send its senior management team over to India to tour Vita's MNS facilities and scope out what a Refinitiv MNS operation there might look like.

Stuart, Biggy, and Liam—yes Liam; Stuart would have no less than their A-plus team on this—hopped on a plane to Jaipur. A meet-and-greet with the network engineers, a simulation of the virtual environment. If all that went well, then negotiations. If all that went well, then, hopefully, a three-year, $5 million COMPASS MNS contract with Refinitiv. Fuck KT. Contrary to Stuart's initial skepticism about the two Indian clients Niraj claimed Vita had signed (why Stuart ever doubted Niraj at times remained a wonder that would make itself known only much later in this story), they did, in fact, materialize. They'd been operational on COMPASS MNS for two months now. Granted, they were small companies, one a tax accounting firm, the other a patent law firm. But managing actual, live networks, however small, had pushed the new VP of operations and the Indian team to get the infrastructure in place. The switches, routers, firewalls, Linux boxes—all the usual stuff—had been purchased, installed, and tested. But to support the size and depth of a Refinitiv, they'd expanded to thirteen Level 2 and 3 engineers on two floors of the Raghukul Tower that sprang up amid the beauty and bustle of the Pink City, as Jaipur was called because all its walls were washed in variations of the color.

When Smally and Niraj had done the search for an Indian office location, they'd found Delhi, their initial target, saturated and too competitive for engineering talent, and so they had come to Jaipur on a tip from a friend of a friend. Apparently, the land of opulent palaces and bazaars also happened to be a Tier 2 city for technology outsourcing. Their ten-story tower of glass on Khatipura Circle might have been orthogonal to the majestic allure of the Hawa Mahal, but the pinkish hue that spread throughout the sky at sunset was the most magnificent sight Stuart had ever seen. Plus, Jaipur was less polluted than Delhi or Mumbai, also less congested, not to mention that clients could stay at palace hotels, which were literally *palaces*, for next to nothing.

"One look at the flute-playing Lord Krishna inside the Walled City might be all it takes to convince Refinitiv that they're in God's hands," Stuart quipped to Yelena and Liam. They were stepping off the Raghukul Tower elevator onto the floor where Vita's new facilities were—their christening visit—and instantly had to halt at the stench of something rank.

Stuart looked at Yelena, who put a hand over her mouth. "No, you are not crazy," said the foul look in her eyes.

Liam's look: "I told you."

It was abominable, whatever it was.

The floor tiles were gleaming, the desks were polished, and the walls had new coats of paint with accents of bright yellow and red. The windows were spotless. The rolling chairs were still wrapped in plastic and squeak free. Even their thirteen Indian employees were combed and bathed and well dressed, more so than their American counterparts would have been for a day at the office in Silicon Valley. But had they not smelled it? Had they not *seen* it? Biggy, who'd walked off another elevator by then, took one whiff and turned around and walked back into it. It was shit. There was no other word to describe it. Stuart sat Smally down and broke the news without holding back. No. No. No. *No!* There was *no* way they could bring the Refinitiv people here and let them smell that shit, let alone see the bathrooms that Stuart had very quickly and horrifically discovered to be the source. It was a picture he would not get out of his mind for some time.

Stuart called Niraj in Delhi, where he'd been at the time on a family business matter. He barely knew where to begin. "How could—"

Niraj cut him off: "I'll take care of it."

"Did you even *see* the offices before Smally moved everyone into them? Or have you been in Delhi on personal business all this time? Did you simply trust Smally to do the right thing because Smally is trustworthy? Don't get me wrong—Smally *is* trustworthy. Only you made this one minor and apparently very cultural miscalculation. And no, Niraj, it's not only the fact that the toilets are holes in the ground; it's so, so much more than that. It brings a whole new meaning to the word 'shithole.'"

Niraj hung up on him.

Stuart, more calmly and with restraint, headed back into the conference room. "It's not like we have time to move offices, what with the Brits showing up in one week," he said to Smally, just before violently kicking over a trash can. "Not without compromising network service to our existing clients. If Vita was operating anywhere else, maybe, but in India, where infrastructure moves at a snail's pace? Speaking of which, has anyone tested the backup generator?" He looked directly at his VP of operations.

Sunil, from Chenni, was an affable, far too laid-back guy of about thirty, thin as a rail, and so tall that when he looked at Smally, as he did now, his chin hit his chest. Neither had an answer.

"Redundancy procedures?"

Sunil urged Stuart not to worry.

Not to worry? Not the answer he'd expected from his VP of ops. "News flash, guys: The electricity in India goes out frequently and very randomly, but then why am I telling you this?"

Liam refrained from any commentary after he went to test the generator and it blew up.

Stuart was supposed to meet Marie in Delhi that weekend but called and told her they would have to postpone. He had planned to take her to the Taj Mahal—he had seen the great structure many years earlier on a business trip and had vowed one day to return with her—but now he would spend the weekend with Sunil, Smally, and the team, fixing all the nontechnical issues that none of them had had the forethought to address. *Like the smell.*

Biggy came lumbering into the conference room just then, where they were all corralled once again because the *chaiwala* had come bearing tea from a plastic pot on a plastic tray, as he did every twenty minutes to the second, ad nauseam and without fail, to the point where Stuart had to finally ask Smally to tell the *chaiwala* thank you, but please stop. Just stop. But he did not stop. And so here they were, drinking tea out of tiny plastic cups, and Biggy comes in, smelling fresh like a daisy. He'd taken the back stairs up three flights to nine, where the Amex offices were, and had used their bathroom, and it was damn nice. So was the receptionist. "I bet we could sweet-talk her into letting us come up and use those bathrooms while Refinitiv is here."

"Meanwhile," Stuart added, "we'll get a cleaning crew to come clean ours and then close them off for use until we can get them renovated to Western standards. Sorry, guys; I know things have been zipping along here with our two little satisfied friends-and-family clients, but Refinitiv is the big league and this is the point where everything changes. We've one week to get readied, practiced, and in shape."

With that, they all went down to the cafeteria for lunch. Smally had warned them that the food was average, and they all got into a heated discussion about what they should feed the Brits; certainly, living in London, they were privy to Indian food, but Indian food in *India*? Nothing raw, for God's sake. No salads; fruit needed to be whole. One of the executives was Scottish. No, they at last decided that they would not bring the Brits to the cafeteria but would get lunch catered and make sure they offered Western options.

Niraj showed up two days later.

"Is everything all right?" Stuart wanted to know. It wasn't a question as much as the unspoken accusation, "Where the hell have you been?"

Niraj's response was to laugh like a deranged man.

Stuart eyed him strangely but pushed the issue no more. His partner had bags under his eyes and looked as pale as a ghost. Of all the times for their CEO to go off the rails. Just as COMPASS was finally coming together, thanks to a month's worth of hard, methodical coding and problem solving. And the Refinitiv MNS technical run-throughs were going well. Again, it was the nontechnical stuff that kept giving them problems, and he needed Niraj's leadership to fix them. For instance, the headsets didn't fit around the handful of turban-wearing Sikhs they had hired in the Tier 2 call center. And then, last night, Yelena had taken the liberty of calling the main office phone numbers of five Indian outsourcers to see how their phones were answered after-hours. A live receptionist, very professional, always. And then she'd called the Vita office after-hours. At nine, a security guard answered and said that everyone had gone home, which was not the answer a client in the middle of their own workday wanted to hear. The next day, Niraj figured out a twenty-four-seven schedule that included a night receptionist, thanks to Smally's little sister, who was willing to fill in until they found someone permanent.

They worked straight through Saturday. That night, they were all invited to a dinner party that a cousin or uncle or some such nebulous relation of Smally's and/or Niraj's was having in some swanky private villa overlooking the Walled City. It was ten o'clock, and the cleaning crew had just finished, and they were looking forward to this dinner, which they could only hope would include the most lavish Indian delicacies known to man. Their only unspoken wish was that they wouldn't arrive too late and miss the food. They all squeezed like cattle into the back of an open vehicle with no suspension and swallowed ample amounts of dust as their driver took them up a long and winding and very bumpy road to a sprawling pink hilltop villa lit with candles. They could hear music pumping and see dancing through its glass walls, clusters of handsome people smoking on balconies. A scene out of a Bollywood movie, of wealth and coolness. Open shirts and big fat watches came at them when they wandered inside. Bangles and the finest of fluttering scarves. Western attire, mostly. Lots of gold and fine silk. Volumes of amber liquid swirling around in crystal glasses. The tinkling of ice. Deep philosophical discussions. And no, they'd not missed "the dinner." In fact, there was no food of any kind anywhere in sight when they arrived, though Smally assured them that it would be coming as he led them to the bar, where a variety of single-malt scotches awaited them. Smally poured their glasses and then led them in and out of various rooms and parlors and secret cubbyholes where pockets of beautiful people asked them interesting and elusive questions. On empty stomachs, they quickly got buzzed. The Indian music, piping in from anywhere and everywhere, was hypnotizing. Stuart felt out of body, as in, "How did I get here, and where's the fucking food?"

"I'm starving," he said, as if no one knew.

Liam said, "This may make the whole trip to India worthwhile." He nodded up at the floating staircase that led from the foyer to a second-floor balcony, where Sunil, dressed in a bright purple silk shirt open to his chest, and a matching bandanna tied around his head, manned the DJ booth. He was sweating, bopping, intent, and focused.

They stood watching him for a minute. When Sunil saw them, he flashed a big smile, waved, and flipped on the song "We Are the Champions." Everybody went crazy.

Stuart looked at Liam, who yelled over the roar, "If he'd put the same focus into ops, we'd all be champions." Liam raised his glass up at Sunil.

"The problem with Sunil is that he's too nice," Stuart said, after the song ended and they could hear each other again. "The engineers take advantage of him. He'll be fine. He just needs guidance, direction. I'm going to have a talk with Niraj, because it needs to come from him."

"What needs to come from me?" Niraj was standing behind them.

Stuart turned around. "Our fearless leader. To what do we owe the honor?"

Niraj didn't like the implication, and perhaps Stuart shouldn't have said that, but he was tired, and hungry, and probably drunk. Niraj walked off.

Stuart, watching him go, "Was it something I said?"

They watched the dancers, who'd all convened on the terrace, now a large, bouncing roar. They danced with drinks in hand and in some cases balanced on their heads. These people could dance. Someone even managed to get Liam out there, and they were all teaching him how to dance like they were by mimicking screwing in lightbulbs with both hands. Stuart bummed a cigarette off someone, who lit it for him with a blow torch. Stuart did not like dancing—few of the team did—and now Laurie was out there, Biggy, Yelena. All the sultry, bangled ladies were showing them how to twist the lightbulbs into their imaginary sockets while grooving their hips. Indians made great doctors, engineers, professors, and philosophers, but above all they made the best dancers, and they knew it. Meanwhile, Stuart had backed himself off into a corner, wondering where all these people had come from and, better yet, where they would go when this was all over. His head was starting to spin. It was one o'clock.

Afraid someone was going to make him dance and hoping to find some food, he went wandering through a corridor and down a darkened hallway, where he came upon a closed door from which wafted sumptuous smells. He thought he might faint. He opened the door to find a bustling, sprawling kitchen. Piping-hot curries, skewers of roasted goat, and silver bowls of spicy biryani were spread across trays and platters and carts being rolled into a larger room farther on. He followed the trays, naturally, to discover that the buffet was only just now being set up and was not yet ready for patrons. In the center of all the bustle, a woman—their hostess, Stuart presumed—was having some words with a man in a chef's hat. She nodded and came toward Stuart, a glint in her eye, as the smoke from her cigarette trailed her. He did not want another cigarette, but he took the one she handed him anyway.

"I have been looking for you. I heard you were hungry, and I am so sorry, but you will have to get used to our crazy Indian ways. Niraj has told me so much about you."

Her head came up to his shoulders. He could see an inordinate amount of scalp through her uneven part, a dusting of purple ash, which brushed his chin as she leaned in for him to light her cigarette. The elegant white sheath she was wearing fell off one shoulder, and Stuart had to focus not to set it on fire.

Stuart would have been wrong to assume she was Niraj's cousin but felt, for whatever reason, and as he often did around seductive, not entirely unattractive women—okay, any woman, for that matter—that it was not his place to ask. He'd once asked a woman—a client he respected and admired greatly—when she was due, only to discover that she was not pregnant. That was when he stopped asking women any personal questions whatsoever.

She put her hand on his forearm as she explained that in India, dinner parties were more like dancing parties and the food wasn't put out until the dancing had climaxed, and it had been a long orgasm and so they were still waiting, but she would find him something to eat now. With a smoker's voice, she spoke in a throaty, self-deprecating manner, her pupils at full dilation. She would get him a plate of whatever he desired. No, he could wait, he said. It was just his head, he said. She had something for that, she said, but Stuart was no longer listening. He was gazing into the ash burning down on her cigarette, overwhelmed by a sudden stirring of desire.

He ate so much that night he was sick for two days.

On Tuesday, by the time Refinitiv came and went, Stuart had lost five pounds. The Amex bathrooms proved to be worth their weight in Biggy's flirting. Niraj, whom no one had heard from since the party, showed up just in time to wow Refinitiv with his "Why Vita?" pitch, a complement to

Stuart's "The Future of MNS" pitch—the Niraj and Stuart Show, as the team had begun to call their joint pitches because those were what had brought them all to where they were now. This lunacy.

CHAPTER 19
AUGUST 2011

WHEN STUART HAD SAID that he would be in India for an extended stay, Marie's response was "When should I come?" Once she had found herself so far away from home, only the desire to go further was left. So when Professor Meena suggested that Marie, on her way to Delhi, stop off in Mumbai to meet her for the AnitaB.org conference, the largest of its kind for women in technology and whose lively atmosphere and speakers she thought Marie might enjoy, Marie did not hesitate.

Professor Meena picked Marie up at the Taj Hotel at seven in the morning, and they set out for the Renaissance conference facilities, a two-hour drive from Mumbai. Marie had been working with Professor Meena on the book edits for a good month by now, via email and Skype, and she looked in person exactly as she did on Skype, dressed in a red-and-gold sari, a string of brown beads around her neck, a bindi in the center of her forehead, dark shades perched atop a mess of peppery hair pulled back hastily in a bun.

She'd been perfunctory about the manuscript edits, and Marie appreciated her approach. "This is wrong" was one of her kinder comments. Every so often, she might make a sweeping thematic suggestion, like today. Before their driver had even managed to navigate out of Colaba Causeway, Professor Meena admitted that she'd been confused about the purpose of the managed-services chapter Marie had just submitted. "If, as you say, the book's objectives are to teach, train, and inspire network engineers and their managers to get on board with the virtual revolution, why would you suddenly, there in the end, say, 'Scratch all that—in fact, we're going to give away your jobs to all those hardworking, underpaid Indians'?"

A hand rapped on Marie's window, interrupting the professor and startling Marie. Their car had been idling in a long line of assorted vehicles stuck at a red light in a perpetually clogged intersection. Marie looked at the window, and while a variety of beggars and merchants milled around, she could detect no source of the knock. She looked back at Professor Meena, and then the rap hit the window again. This time when Marie looked at the window, a dark and very chafed hand without a body attached to it, seemingly, was waving at her. Marie looked at Professor Meena, who gave no indication that anything was amiss. A toddler, surely, Marie thought, too short to be fully seen; there were only thousands of them crawling around the streets half-naked, either alone or attended to by another, older toddler. Marie peeked over the edge of the car door to find not a toddler but an older man with no legs grinning widely up at her. She gasped but then caught herself and hoped Professor Meena had not seen. She was embarrassed by her frightened reaction, especially since the smile on the man's face couldn't have been more earnest and welcoming. If only the car would inch along a bit more quickly, but no, it would not, at which point Professor Meena repeated her question: "I don't understand the purpose of the MNS chapter."

Marie, after catching her breath, said, "Managed network services is Vita's end goal. It's why Stuart and Niraj are in Jaipur presently, to prepare operations for their first big offshore contract. I've encouraged Stuart to include an MNS chapter, because we agreed from the start to tell the truth."

"Then I must tell you the truth," Professor Meena said.

The car sputtered to a start again, swerved sharply, jostled. Marie respected Professor Meena. She had been a linguistics professor at the University in Bangalore, loved language in all its forms, and had lectured there for many years, before leaving to raise her three children. When she returned to the workforce years later, the university had no positions, so she taught herself programming and then worked as a software engineer for Dell. She eventually returned to school and earned a postgraduate degree from IIM-B in business analytics. After stints at Cisco Asia and WIPRO, she settled into this niche of technical writing because it allowed her to work from home and be present for her three adult children, one of whom had a disability and still needed her. She would be a grandmother soon.

"I appreciate whatever wisdom you can offer," Marie said.

"While outsourcing was the inspiration for India's new middle class, it is not true what people say, that India will be the next China of consumerism, that Indian outsourcing is moving our countrymen and women out of poverty. You see all these billboards for Starbucks, Netflix, and Amazon?"

Marie didn't respond. She didn't think it was a question. Those billboards were everywhere. Not to mention that she'd had a Starbucks that morning from the kiosk in her hotel.

"While these brand-name American companies have come here to sell us their products, the fact remains that few of us will be sipping Frappuccinos or subscribing to Netflix. For only the top ten percent of Indian earners does an iPhone cost less than half a year's salary. And a subscription to Netflix is the equivalent of leasing a car for the people in your country." She paused to say something in Hindi to their driver and then continued, "Technically, sure, some of us have 'arrived.' We've surpassed our forefathers; we own a phone, a car, a watch, a TV. But we're complacent. We're not learning. Or innovating. We leave that to our clients—the Americans."

Marie was about to respond, but then the driver said something. Professor Meena and he conversed for a moment before he took a sudden right turn into a mustard field and proceeded to drive straight through it. Professor Meena explained that he was going to take a shortcut to avoid the congestion, as if driving through a mustard field were the most normal of things. Marie couldn't see a road, or anything anywhere but sweeping shades of yellow. It would have been spectacular if it hadn't been entirely bizarre. Ten or so breathless minutes like this, and they hit the road—literally, their car caught air—and were bumping along. It was two lanes, but they were speeding now, and it wasn't long before the signs of congested city life were replaced with wasteland, mostly, mixed every so often with an abandoned, half-decayed concrete structure, and Marie could at last respond to Professor Meena's comments.

"Vita's MNS operation is about cost arbitrage—sure, I will not deny that. But they are not here body shopping. They are hiring these men and women to be high-value software engineers, experts in cloud and virtual networks, because while COMPASS is technology driven, it needs people behind the wheel—smart people; trained people; proactive, problem-solving people willing and open to learn. They can't be complacent. They have to think because their clients can't."

"Then Vita is the exception to the rule. And even if it's true what you say, pretty soon COMPASS will be fully automated, and then where will that leave those highly trained Indian engineers?"

"Where will it leave everybody?" Marie added flatly.

"Anyway, in a few years, it won't matter. Wage inflation in India is going through the roof. Soon you'll be moving off to another location, where labor is cheaper."

Their driver screeched to a stop so suddenly that Marie had to brace her hand on the seat back in front of her with all her might. A long line of cars appeared before them; they weren't the only ones with this shortcut idea.

Professor Meena sighed. "The fact of the matter is that even after two decades of dramatic growth, thanks to outsourcing and the like, most of our country remains dark and lives in poverty."

Ten minutes passed, and they did not move. Twenty minutes. Thirty. Professor Meena remained nonplussed, but then her phone beeped and she frowned down at it. It was a long moment before she looked up again and said, "Social media is killing the people in our country."

"It's killing people everywhere."

"I'm not talking theoretically. Literally, this moment, a woman, a woman my age, a grandmother, was killed, thanks to WhatsApp." She showed Marie her phone with the picture. "People are sending posts on WhatsApp under aliases, purporting that children are being kidnapped off Indian streets. They're posting fake videos of men on scooters swiping up three-year-old toddlers in front of their families, and now vigilantes have taken to the streets, raging and going after anyone they suspect of being one of these"—she used air quotes—"kidnappers."

"It makes no sense. Why do such a thing?"

"Because they can. We've allowed them to. That's the whole problem. We are not thinking these things through." She huffed and shook her head and bit the inside of her lip. "You see what happens when we leave the coding to men?" She sat back and faced forward again. Her eyes were steely. "I wonder, if the programmers behind the WhatsApp algorithms had been women, might these women have considered the implications of their social media program in greater depth and from different perspectives? Might this not be happening?"

"I guess we'll never know."

She looked hard at Marie and said, "Don't you see? It's our lives on the line, and we can't risk not trying everything."

"I concluded, a long time ago, that the only way to change things is to blow up the world and start over."

"The Hindu god Shiva believes that life is a continuous cycle of starting over. That nobody should forget the void from which they came or get too comfortable with all the things they've built up around them. Shiva destroys worlds so that they can be reborn."

"So, *that's* who's been doing it."

Professor Meena laughed, uncharacteristically. "Speaking of Shiva," she said, "have you plans to see the cave carvings of him on Elephanta Island? You must go. There are ferries that leave directly from the Gateway outside your hotel."

"I will go tomorrow. I have the day to sightsee before I meet Stuart in Delhi."

Professor Meena looked past Marie and out the window. It had been more than half an hour that they'd not moved, and now people were abandoning their cars and walking ahead to see what was going on. Professor Meena spoke to the driver, and he got out and did the same. "I hope we will not be further delayed. I would really like for you to hear Anita B. speak. She talks about the importance of recruiting girls into technology while they are still in the early stages of forming themselves. She says they need to learn to be brave, not perfect. To open their mouths and speak, rather than hold everything in for fear of being wrong. She is very inspiring, Anita B. She may even convince you, Marie."

"I am beyond being the target of anyone's conviction."

"You don't strike me as someone who gives up."

Marie looked out the window. The road was a parking lot as far as the eye could see. A trickle of sweat rolled down her spine. With the ignition off, the car was a hotbox.

Professor Meena suggested they get out and stretch their

legs, not that there was anywhere to go. Between the two opposing traffic lanes was a three-foot cement divider, and on their right, a sharp ravine. Professor Meena pulled a bottle of water from a small cooler the driver had on the passenger seat. She offered one to Marie, who stared at the lid, not wrapped in plastic, and shook her head no, saying something about not wanting to have to go to the bathroom, which was why she'd not had any water to drink before they left and why her throat was parched now. Also, she was starting to get concerned about where their driver was. "Do you think he has abandoned us?" She laughed nervously.

Professor Meena said that she would be right back, and then she too disappeared into the swarms of people wandering up and down the roadside. Music played from some of the cars' radios. People were staring at Marie. A skeletal, sari-dressed woman carrying a baby and followed by a gang of small children seemed on a mission to get to Marie. She came up close with her baby, smiling beautifully and speaking to the boy next to her, who was trying to communicate with Marie in indecipherable English.

"She wants you to hold her baby," Professor Meena said, having just returned. "She believes it is good luck for a white woman to hold her baby."

Marie took the baby and held her. The baby did not cry; she stared at Marie with big brown eyes. She had double piercings in her ears and nose. She was a beautiful baby. Marie wondered what would happen to her as she passed the baby back, while the woman kept nodding at Marie in deep appreciation and gratitude (for what?) and Professor Meena urged the group who had come to see the white woman to return to their car or *tuk-tuk* or bus or motor scooter, or whatever contraption they had come from.

Their driver returned. He told Professor Meena, who told Marie, that a very unfortunate situation was occurring.

Today, a guru from Gujarat, a region just to the north of Mumbai, had come to preach to his followers, who had all followed him down here, and then he had gone home and now they were all following him back.

"But what does this mean?" Marie asked. They had now been stuck on this road for more than an hour.

Professor Meena said that she was very sorry but that this was not untypical. There was no forewarning for these things, and there was nothing to do but wait.

Two hours? Three? Worse? Marie again thought about having to use the bathroom. There was clearly no place to go except for that crumbling structure in the distance, and there certainly wasn't a bathroom there. She shaded her eyes to see around her. The sun was beating down, and she'd brought no hat.

"You should drink some water so you don't dehydrate."

Marie nodded and took the bottle but did not drink from it.

Professor Meena took Marie in search of shade, but there was none to be had, except for behind the bus some distance ahead, all of whose patrons were crowded around its back. They found a spot by the open bus door and sat on the step. At some point, the bus driver pulled out a bottle of whiskey and Marie took a sip.

"I am afraid we will miss the conference," Professor Meena said. "At this point, our best bet, once we get moving again, will be to find a break in the divider and turn around and go back."

Two more hours passed, the sun reached its peak, and they did not move. Marie could barely swallow. Then, suddenly, people were jumping back into their cars, so the two women ran back to theirs and woke up their driver, and soon they were moving, too. But it was three o'clock by now. They drove until an opening came in the ravine, and their driver made a sudden left, then a right turn, then a bumpy right transition across the break in the divider, and headed back to Mumbai.

It was dusk by the time they at last arrived at the Taj, its sprawling opulence making Marie feel suddenly ashamed of herself, for feeling the need to stay there. Professor Meena was very apologetic about their ill-fated drive but said that she had appreciated all their conversations. She was disappointed that Marie could not meet Anita B. but hoped that someday she would.

When Marie got to her room, she could barely open the door. Dehydration, desperation to pee, the whole ordeal—which might have been terrifying; she wasn't sure—was all catching up with her. She was shaking so hard that her hands couldn't work the lock with the old-fashioned key. At last inside, she relieved herself in the bathroom, her head propped in her hand, for an inordinately long time. Afterward, from the window of her turreted room, ensconced in velvet, she stood staring down at the Gateway, alive with all its revelry, feeling immediately isolated. The light was fading, the Arabian Sea on fire with purples and golds.

CHAPTER 20
AUGUST 2011

"STUART!" MARIE GRABBED HIS arm. She'd caught their driver nodding off, and this wasn't the first time.

"How far are we now?" Stuart leaned in and shouted over the muffler.

They were almost at the rest stop, the driver assured them, as he'd been assuring them for the past two hours of what was now going on a four-hour journey. They would soon be there and they could "rest" (meaning use the toilet, or more likely a hole in the ground, which, aside from incidents like at the Raghukul Office Tower, one quickly came to terms with living in Asia, often even finding the experience more sanitary than a western toilet because nothing was touched, given you had the leg strength and flexibility to squat, that was) before they began the final leg toward their destination. After her plane from Mumbai to Delhi had been delayed four hours because of fog, all Marie had wanted to do, upon crawling into the car's backseat, covered in beads that were supposed to be comfortable, was lose her mind to slumber, but, after seeing the driver nod off, she knew she could not sleep. If she did, who was going to keep Stuart from sleeping, and if Stuart slept, who was going to keep the driver awake? So Marie talked to Stuart and Stuart talked to the driver as their car moved forward, along torn-up roads, in a procession of charred vehicles, street beggars, urchins, and emaciated animals, passing crumbling buildings, facades covered in scaffolding, fires burning off in the distance, and children, masses of them, eyes wide and wanting.

"Perhaps we should have flown," Marie said.

Stuart did not smile. It had been a long two weeks in Jaipur. They'd wowed the Brits and were already in contract negotiations, but he couldn't think about any of that now.

Marie pulled Stuart's hand away from his mouth. He'd been chewing his thumb down to the bone. She was about to ask the source of his torment . . .

"You don't want to know," he said.

"I want to know."

"The bathrooms, Marie. It had to do with the bathrooms." And various other things he wasn't ready to tell her.

He was right. She didn't want to know.

They fell silent, the cabbage fields moving now, and it wasn't long before they forgot their mission to stay awake.

Rest. Just these few minutes. Escape his thoughts. If that was even possible. And it felt so nice. So utterly . . .

"You're sleeping, Stuart."

His eyes opened, even though he hadn't instructed them to. Beyond Marie, out the window, a camel decorated to carry a prince or a maharaja walked along the side of the road with no one riding him.

Marie said that she'd tell Stuart a story to keep him awake— something that had happened to her back in Mumbai—but only if he promised not to be mad at her.

Why would he ever want to hear a story with a preface like that? No. he didn't want to hear about anything that would no doubt include negligence on her part. He'd no patience for negligence. Traveling in these countries required discipline. Focus. And more and more, she seemed to have neither. He had wanted Marie to come straight to Jaipur to meet him, versus going to Mumbai alone—there had been terrorist attacks on the Taj Hotel in the not-so-distant past—but who was he to say? She did as she pleased. It had always been like this, and it would always be like this. It was the reason they weren't married. At some point, she'd stopped believing in paper transactions, so he'd stopped asking. They'd joined most of their accounts at that point anyway, and he'd begun putting her on all his legal documents, including the Vita ownership agreement. He didn't need a marriage license to tell him what felt right. To take responsibility even if she wouldn't.

"At Professor Meena's suggestion, I left the hotel on a mission to see the temple carvings of the Hindu god Shiva, but there were no boats going to Elephanta Island that day, because of high tides at the Gateway landing." She turned at him. "Is it me, or is it impossible to get anywhere in this country?" He did not answer. "Anyway, I went walking along the Colaba Causeway instead, and as I made my way through the dizzying variety of colorful sidewalk stalls, plus the odd snake charmer and performing monkey, a little boy began to follow me, as they do, about six years old, frayed shorts and no shoes. This one was particularly tenacious. I tried everything just short of handing him my entire wallet, but I could not get rid of him. He would not take my money. It went on and on like this for a few hours. He trotted five paces behind, ahead, or beside me, making sure I didn't fall into potholes or get run over by a scooter or knocked over by the odd cow. If I even hinted at eyeing an item at a stall, he immediately began bargaining for me, and I would quickly shake my head no, as would he, which meant yes, as if he understood everything there ever was to know about me. I finally escaped back to my hotel, where he said, in five different ways, that he would be there waiting for me when I returned." She looked at Stuart. "'Right here. Waiting.'"

He nodded, as in, "I get it."

"Sure enough, the next morning when I again set out for Elephanta Island, he was there, waiting. Those dark lashes and brown moon eyes. 'Lady, lady, I take you where you want to go.' I stood there, feeling every instinct I'd ever had tumble down around me, and then, forgetting about Shiva, I walked off with this boy attached to my side, as if he and I had always been this way. But still, wherever we were going, I wanted the transaction to be up front, and so once again I paused and held out coins. He pushed them back into my wallet. Where did I wish to go? I chose a temple nearby that I had read about, and he set about getting me there. He cleared my path, and I moved into the open spaces. When we found the temple, he showed me how to place an offering. How to bow and clap. Then we made our way back. I felt bolder. I even stopped at a few stalls and let him barter me a scarf. A handbag. Still, he would accept no coins. I kept trying. I knew it was coming, the big ask—what would it be? Meanwhile, I felt myself smiling inside. He was ironic, as if he knew I knew he knew, this mutual knowledge that I would not win in the end. I would catch him examining me out of the sides of his eyes, and he vice versa, and it was in those moments that a connection passed between us so great it hurt. I was very confused.

"A few hours passed, and suddenly I found that we had traveled off the beaten path to a vacant lot, where a decaying stucco structure sat. We stood under the brutal white sun, grime clinging to every inch of me, staring at the structure, which I soon realized was our final and ultimate destination. He was pointing for me to go in there, alone, but I did not want to. He remained adamant, pushed and prodded me and gestured in a variety of ways, but I could not go in there. It was a store of some kind, the crooked sign tried to indicate, though from where I stood I could see no food for sale, only tall, thin men in dark, dingy shadows. I tried to give him the money again so that he could go in there and get what he needed. He wouldn't take it. He kept pointing at the structure. I finally put a wad of cash into his hand and turned and fled and did not look back for some time—until it occurred to me that I didn't know where I was. It took me an hour to find my way in darkness back to the hotel, where inside its gold-leaf turrets and red velvet walls I remained cowering until the next morning, when it was time to go to the airport. I did not see the boy, because my head was down, but I am sure he was there."

Some moments passed.

"He wanted you to buy rice for his family," the driver surprised them both by saying.

"But why not just take the money and buy it himself?" Marie asked.

"Because the network will take the money," he said.

She looked at Stuart, who said, "The network that owns him."

A slow burn. "I'm an idiot," she said.

"You're not an idiot," Stuart replied.

"I should have bought him the rice."

"Don't worry about it."

Don't worry about it? She was sure she'd never forget about it. Oh, how she loathed herself for being so afraid. Afraid of going into that store.

Their car smacked into the car in front of them. Marie was too startled to scream. Stuart grabbed her hand while the driver sat there as if nothing had happened, until the car in front of them drove on and so did he. Marie's eyes held Stuart's. "Make no mistake," she seemed to say. "That just happened."

At the rest stop, she and Stuart shared a cigarette. When she had met Stuart, he'd had the habit of smoking during coding sprees, but he'd long since quit. She'd barely smoked three cigarettes in her life, but when he returned with their espressos and a pack of Camel Lights, she held out her trembling hand for one. What was strange was that he handed it over to her with no question. That was when she knew they had passed beyond all reason. It was one thing for him to kill himself, but not her. They stood at a tall table inside a dark tomb of ancient and dusted-over deity statues for sale, their hands shaking as they brought the bitter, lukewarm liquid to their lips via tiny paper cups and inhaled smoke into their lungs.

"Where have we come to?" she asked.

He lit a new cigarette with the old. "Here," he said. "We've come here."

Some moments passed while they each contemplated that. Then Stuart exhaled a long pull of smoke. "I think something's going on with Niraj's father."

He stamped out his cigarette, with more vigor than necessary, she noticed.

"I'm not sure what it is. All I know is that Niraj has been distracted lately, acting strange."

She stared at him, not wanting to look alarmed. "Maybe it's India. Now that he's so close to his family, maybe they're putting pressure on him."

He didn't say anything.

"You know, you could just ask him. That's what friends do. They ask."

"We're not that kind of friends."

"Are we still doing that?"

"I met his fiancée," Stuart said, after a moment.

"She actually exists."

"She does."

"What was she like?"

"Not like I expected."

"What did you expect?"

"I don't know. But not that."

They crawled back into their vehicle of death. Their driver, his name was Raji, was lively and fully awake on the second part of their journey. He was an economist, he told them, like his father before him, and his father before him. There had never been another path for him besides academia. So here he was, with his three advanced degrees from the University of Mumbai, and barely able to find work as a teacher. He must have seen the looks on their faces through the rearview. "You wonder why I peddle these driving tours, but you must not. Today I will earn equal to one month's teacher's salary. Plus, I meet people from all over. Interesting people. People like you."

Marie mumbled some humble gesture that in the end sounded stupid.

Raji went on to describe his nephew, which was where the long lineage of academia in his family would end, he had decided. Raji was raising this nephew for his brother, who was dead. He was smart; Raji was sending him to the technology university. He was doing everything he could to give this boy an education in technology so that one day he could leave his country and go to the States, where opportunities abounded.

Marie wondered if the driver wanted money from them— whether they should be giving this man money for this nephew who wanted to go to the States, or if the network would take the money they gave him, too. Or maybe what the driver was subtly asking them was if they would take this nephew back with them to the States because that was the only way it could be done, by stripping people away from their families, one by one.

They arrived at their hotel, haggard and rubbery and feeling as if some unknown fate had befallen them. It was eleven at night. They'd splurged for a room with a view of the Taj Mahal, but all they could see at this hour from their balcony was its faint silhouette in the foggy blackness. They drank scotch and stared out at it until the alcohol turned the sky purple and the silhouette was gone.

The next morning, they woke up early and as excited as either of them could remember, and there it was, the magnificent mausoleum, as sleepy and fogged over as their minds. Below them sprawled the hotel's grand, expansive pool and its tiered gardens. In the distance, on the burned hills on either side of the great wonder built by a man for the love of a woman, squatted members of the body politic, here and there, by the roadside, specks from this distance but not too far away for Stuart and Marie to see that their pants were down. It took Marie a while to adjust to what she was seeing, a site that rose up in her mind beyond all belief—the Taj at once ruins, the world all our toilet.

CHAPTER 21
NOVEMBER 2011—THREE MONTHS LATER

"THIS IS REALLY INTERESTING, Marie," the Dane said, on a lounge by the pool, reading a copy of the book.

"To you and the three others who bought it."

"I like what Stuart said about you in the acknowledgments section: 'ghost author'—you sound so mysterious. When's the book tour?"

"We used a small press and have little budget for PR. No book tour."

The Dane sat up from her lounge suddenly. "You know what you need?"

Marie could only imagine.

"A book-signing party. Giorgio and I will throw it for you both. It'll be grand. So many people will come, and it'll be a great way to get the word out."

"Vita has hired a new chief marketing officer who's got some plans to give away the book at cloud technology conferences."

"Sounds exciting."

"Doesn't it?" Marie fake-yawned.

"UC Berkeley is going to do a cover spread in its alumni magazine. Whatever you do, don't look at the reviews on Amazon. Stuart's got a few haters, and they've decided to make their voices heard."

The Dane lay back down. "Yeah, who am I kidding? Giorgio and I know no one in Singapore. Who would I even invite besides you? Anyway, don't listen to those assholes.

Let it go. It's done. You did your best. Think of it like your baby, the baby you didn't have, and now that baby is all grown up and you have to let her go."

It had been more than a year since Marie had started working on the book for Stuart, long enough for her to be experiencing postpartum depression, but she hated that cliché. There was no void she needed to fill because she couldn't have a child. Once she'd gotten over the instinct for a child, it was gone, never to have been there in the first place, manufactured inside her like everything else, seemingly— nothing but data, process, analysis, and information that she continually manipulated in her mind into some story. She was a machine not so unlike the machines that Stuart spent his every waking hour programming to do whatever he wanted them to do.

Marie dove into the pool and swam fifty laps.

Afterward, she clung to the side, catching her breath.

"Feel better?"

"Yes."

"What are you going to do, now that your baby is out there getting shat upon?"

Marie, pulling herself out of the pool, said, "I was thinking of taking a Java programming course."

After a pause: "Seriously?"

"I'm just curious if I could do it."

"And what if you can?"

Marie thought about it for a moment. "Then maybe I'll change the world."

The Dane laughed, a hearty, wonderful laugh that became infectious. The two of them. It went on for some time.

"Seriously," Marie said when things calmed down. "My trip to India, particularly my time with Professor Meena, has left me teetering, strangely, on the brink of some great hope." She paused to stay a quiver in her voice. "Rich or poor, old or young, the Indians looked at me as if they really saw something. Like I'd existed in a past life or something. I've never experienced that before, this feeling that I'm so much more than who I am."

A moment passed.

"Maybe I should go to India," the Dane said. Marie looked at the Dane and said that she didn't think India was for her. The Dane said that Marie was probably right, followed by "Enough about you; let's talk about me. Do you think I should leave him?" It was a question the Dane had pondered out loud before, in a tone Marie could never quite read as serious or kidding.

"What about my money?"

"Your money will be fine," the Dane replied. "Giorgio will make you a ton of money. Your money is irrelevant to this discussion."

"So then leave him," Marie said.

"Yes. That's what I'll do." They'd arrived here before too, only for the Dane to turn around and say, "If only it were possible. If only I had a place to go. If only . . ." She cleared her throat, taking Marie by surprise this time. The Dane wasn't one to get emotional. "If not for the kids." She was a strong, hard woman, but she had to look away now, as her eyes welled and she spoke to some dark harbor in her soul. "I'll never leave the kids."

"No," Marie said. "You won't."

A moment passed. The Dane said, "Marriage is an illness, you said."

"Someone said."

"Who?"

A pale light fluttered through the bougainvillea. A warm breeze. Life was strange, Marie thought. So far away was she from that conversation, and yet . . . "It was some time ago. I went to visit my stepmother a few years after my father died,

feeling some pressure about marriage. Stuart had been bringing it up again, and so I asked her about it, if she thought it
was real, and, after thinking about it a moment, she said that
marriage was an illness. You see, she began, her first husband
had been diagnosed with a heart condition. They were in
their early twenties, and she was pregnant with her fourth
child. She didn't know what she was doing in terms of how
to be a mother. Then, one day, her husband fell over in the
backyard. He went on to suffer from a heart condition that
kept him laid up most of the time. He was not a pleasant
sick person. He was the kind of man who liked to live, to
do things. She did the best she could, but this seemed to go
on for a long time. And then he died, at the hospital, when
she had stepped out of the room.

"We were drinking margaritas at the time, my stepmother
and I, at a Mexican restaurant that my father had come to love,
even though the entire time I had known him he hated Mexican
food, foreign food of any kind. Anyway, my stepmother and
I sipped our drinks and then she went on, in answer to my
question. She said that my father had depression. For twenty
years, she lived with his depression, day in and day out. And
then he died because she was not watching out for him as she
perhaps should have been. I said, 'Don't say that. You gave
his life so much meaning.' She said, 'I was going to leave him,
but then it occurred to me I had nowhere to go.' I said, 'You
were going to leave him?' She said, 'Oh, honey,' and reached
for my hand."

WHEN MARIE GOT HOME, Stuart was there, waiting for her
with a martini. "You know who liked the book?" he said,
handing her the chilled glass.

"Who?"

"Sanjay."

"Who's Sanjay?"

"You met Sanjay. He's a junior architect. Wears the turban?"

"Oh, him."

"He absolutely loved it. He says he's going to recommend it to all his friends."

"You know soon they'll have computers to write books," she said, and then she swallowed her olive.

CHAPTER 22
FEBRUARY 2012—THREE MONTHS LATER

ONCE REFINITIV WAS RUNNING large as Vita's champion MNS client, more and more data analytics providers began coming at them in droves. Over the next six months, MNS India grew faster than anyone expected, so much so that WIPRO and IBM, two companies with massive outsourcing facilities in India, began snooping around. Vita was onboarding more and more clients, training more and more Level 2 and 3 engineers, amassing more and more data. Everyone was wildly busy, the board was satisfied, and there was no reason to be moody and distant, which was how Niraj had been behaving, more and more, since they'd signed Refinitiv, in almost perfect disproportion to everything positive that was happening. While Stuart was on the road, bouncing between Singapore, India, and their various consulting clients, Niraj curtailed his travel. Staying hunkered down, he conducted most business from his apartment in Singapore. He'd been missing stand-ups and conference calls. When Niraj did show up, Stuart often smelled liquor on his breath.

Then, all of a sudden, he was gone.

Stuart had just returned to Singapore after a week spent in obscurity, buried underground in one of Toyota's backup data centers, located a few miles outside Osaka. He'd thought Niraj had been in London during that time for a global trading summit that the Exchange had invited him to, but then Yelena informed Stuart on Friday that Niraj hadn't shown up at the conference. She'd been able to cover for Niraj, but she now urged Stuart to get to London straightaway, because things were going down at the Exchange that needed, if not the CEO's attention, then Stuart's.

But where was Niraj? Stuart corralled the Dream Team on Skype to discover that no one had heard from Niraj in a week. A week! Everyone had thought everyone else had been in contact with him. Had he mentioned a vacation? Ha—neither Stuart nor Niraj had taken so much as a day off in three years, and when Niraj had gone off the grid recently, it had never been more than two days before an email or Slack message showed up from him, barking at someone for something they'd done wrong.

Yelena called Smally. Smally would know where Niraj was. But then they discovered that Smally hadn't shown up at the Jaipur MNS facilities since yesterday. Stuart left multiple messages for both Niraj and Smally asking them to call him ASAP, and the next day, when Stuart had still not heard back, he had the instinct to call JS. JS was friends with Niraj in a way Stuart was not, but he was also an investor, and Stuart didn't want to throw the board into a panic.

Yelena wanted to know if they should call the police.

Stuart instructed her to get hold of Niraj's fiancée. Stuart had a vague recollection of having been drunkenly texted her number but quickly put that out of his mind. She had flirted heavily with him that night of the "dinner" party, and it had been such a long time since . . . well . . . and he had found himself rather flattered by the attention and playing along. It wasn't until sometime later in the evening that he'd learned she was Niraj's fiancée, at which point Stuart went off and found a rather large bathroom, where, after a sudden explosion from his bowels—he had eaten fast and furiously—he fell asleep on the floor. Yelena found him at sunrise, after much searching, and they all crawled back into that open-aired contraption and rumbled their way back down the hill.

YELENA HEADED TO JAIPUR TO find Smally while Stuart flew to London to head off whatever crisis Yelena had unsurfaced at the Exchange. He wore the fine suit Niraj had made him buy that day just before seven people were stabbed on the London Bridge—out of solidarity, defiance, or foreboding, he did not know—preparing to act business as usual and as if all their lives hadn't possibly just turned upside down. Still no word from Niraj, but Stuart had no time for dark thoughts—Yelena's intuition to send him here had been right. He arrived at the Exchange to discover that Jim's rat-shits-on-you-MIT-ring-wearing buddy, the Exchange's interim CEO, Vita's key stakeholder, had been replaced by a full-time CEO, who, because he was the interim CEO's rival, brought in his own CTO, who brought in his own consultants to do a viability assessment of all the interim CEO's projects, his first instinct being to blow up every one of them, including the COMPASS implementation.

Stuart immediately called Jim, who was matter-of-fact about the news because it didn't impact the Refinitiv contract, and that was the contract that mattered. The Exchange's contract was a means to that end and therefore dispensable—its engineers weren't ever going to "get" COMPASS enough to derive any real value from it. Jim told Stuart to stay focused on what mattered—India—and the critical mass of data Vita was amassing there, and then Stuart found himself getting involved in one of Jim's elusively cerebral discourses about data. Before Stuart knew it, an hour had passed and they'd not discussed one word of the problem directly at hand, which was how Stuart should go about winning over the Exchange's new CEO, because, while Jim considered that person dispensable, Stuart did not. One point three million dollars of revenues were at stake, he was about to remind Jim, but then Jim got another call and had to get off. He wished Stuart luck and hung up.

Stuart stared at his phone. He had twenty-four hours—now twenty-three—to prepare his case to the new CEO for why their $1.3 million project should continue. He didn't even have time to get infuriated at Niraj for going AWOL; instead, he worked straight through the night, developing the PowerPoint slides and vetting them over Skype with Yelena, Liam, Biggy, and Franco, reconnaissance that left Stuart feeling only more confident about the work they were doing at the Exchange. Regardless of what Jim had said, it mattered, if only for its import in the financial industry as a whole.

By the time the sun rose—had there ever been sun in London before this moment?—Stuart knew in his heart and soul that the work was good, important. That was always what drove him, and it was with that thought that he marched through the revolving lobby door of the Exchange, through all the bells and whistles of the ever-shrinking trading floor, past the towering scions, ready to nail this meeting with the new CEO, only to discover that he was in fact meeting not with the CEO but with the CEO's gatekeeper.

An unnervingly quiet Austrian gentleman, ex-Accenture, mid-thirties. In a small conference room overlooking that dreaded clock, he sat leaning back for the entirety of Stuart's spiel, pressing his fingers together in contemplation, nodding at times—yes, he got it, yes, he did; what Stuart was saying all made logical sense, and as a pragmatic individual, he had to say that he agreed with Stuart wholeheartedly. There was no other direction for the Exchange besides COMPASS at this point. This pause in the action to reassess was simply a matter of quality assurance, checks and balances, protocol and procedure. Stuart left the meeting relieved.

The following day, he walked tall into the executive office of the CEO, who promptly thanked Stuart and his team for their time and service but asked that they please remove themselves from the premises within twenty-four hours. There was some blank space here while Stuart remained frozen in his seat, wondering if the new CEO meant he was also to leave his office at this very moment. Meanwhile, the reality was catching up with him. Had he missed something? Eighteen months of grueling, groundbreaking work waved off like the nuisance of a fly, and why? Because of a grudge. A fucking grudge. (A year from now, after the new CEO with the ax to grind got the ax himself for securities fraud related to Refinitiv, the Exchange would try to bring back the COMPASS project, but it would never be resurrected on the scale of its original charter; its fate was to linger on, on the fringe, in perpetuity, the way Stuart, in dark moments, often felt about his career.)

"And by the way," the CEO added, "we're selling Refinitiv."

"But you just acquired Refinitiv."

"Change of strategic focus is all I will say."

Even men weren't safe from the whims of *men*. Vindictive, bombastic fucks. Kill them all.

Stuart got to his feet, expressed his sympathies, and walked out.

CHAPTER 23
FEBRUARY 2012

"I'M CRAVING A LEMON SODA," the Dane said.

They were standing on the shore of East Coast Park, staring out at the placid water on which shone the reflections of the glass skyscrapers towering behind them, stretching far out and beyond, where the seas blended into other seas, everything shimmering in the morning sun.

Marie checked her watch. "We should probably get started."

Some other swimmers were already well into their practice runs, their microscopic arms crawling along the water's surface a ways out, a long, steady glide that seemed to be getting them nowhere. The Dane grabbed the oar and dragged the plastic canoe into the green-and-gold water. The little boy climbed in, eyes wide with excitement, while the little girl, who couldn't swim, stayed back with the nanny, tears in her eyes. The Dane pushed off, and Marie dove in. She took up pace beside the canoe, which took some moments to get organized, what with all the splashing between the boy and the Dane and Marie getting her bearings and setting her mark. Then the Dane rowed and Marie trailed alongside the boy, who dragged his hand through the water. She found her rhythm. It had been years since she'd swum out in the open, but it didn't take long for her to settle back into her stride, inside the warm, watery womb of her origin. All of them liquid beings, she thought, sliding through the surface of the water, watching her arms slip in and out, the oars, the scissoring, the boy's fingers, the laughter, the girl's tears somewhere in the distance, all of them moving in a rhythm she couldn't feel, as if they'd been transported through time, so far away and yet here, as they could have been anywhere.

Afterward, they sat on the shore, hugging their knees and staring out at the sea from which they'd just come. The girl had curled up in the Dane's arms. A slight breeze blew the soft strands of her cotton-colored hair. She squirmed and nuzzled until she found a desirable position.

"What exactly are we training for?" the Dane asked. Marie's eyes rested upon the girl. She didn't know, she said, but whatever it was, they should be ready.

As it turned out, Marie wasn't going to be changing the world with her coding anytime soon. She thought back to the past four weeks, which she'd spent obsessing over JavaScript during the days while Stuart was at work or, more often, traveling. Studying the guides, perusing the chat rooms, watching hundreds of YouTube videos, consumed and obsessed and lost to the world, like when she'd been writing the book, only with the book she could fake it. In this case, either the program worked or it didn't, its answer the truth, rather than the nefarious, bloated, bullshit answers she was used to formulating. She'd been planning on surprising Stuart, who had no idea she'd started learning how to code. She'd found a funny little marriage app on one of the practice sites and had attempted to re-create it with a twist. The thing was, she did re-create it. It had been far from easy; at best, the project had been meticulous, tedious, painful, and, in the end, exhilarating when she'd gotten it to work. At times, she'd thought it impossible. At times, she'd envisioned her laptop crashing through the window. She was ridiculous. This was ridiculous. Staying up all night like this, and for what? Stuart was only going to laugh at her, or pity her, or, worst case, want to hire her. By morning, she'd come to the gripping realization that coding had brought her right back to where she'd started, to that part of herself she'd grown to despise, that obsessive-compulsive, competitive nature of hers: it was better to kill yourself figuring something out than to let someone think that you couldn't.

The Dane wanted to see the app. Marie got out her iPhone. The Dane clicked the link, and up popped "Will you marry me?" There were two possible responses: yes and no. The Dane tried pressing "yes," but when she did, the button moved to a different part of the screen. She tried it again, and the button moved again. It kept moving each time she tried pressing "yes." The Dane looked up at her. "I don't get it."

"The 'no' works," Marie said.

"He can't say yes?"

Marie shrugged.

"You're funny."

"Ha ha."

"What did Stuart think?"

"I never showed it to him."

After a stunned pause, the Dane asked, "Why?"

"I don't know. I guess"—Marie sighed—"as much as I want him to know that I can do it, I don't want him to know that I don't want to do it."

CHAPTER 24
MARCH 2012

"*SHE'S* A HOOT," YELENA assured Stuart, with a chortle of her own. She'd just returned from India, where she'd managed to speak with the fiancée, if only by phone. "But then, you've interacted with her, so you already know." She looked dead at Stuart. "I mean, could you understand her? I certainly as hell could not. It was almost as if . . . well, as if she was on drugs or something. Or just drugged. I'm not sure she had a full grasp of Niraj's situation—something about a wedding amid bankruptcy proceedings—let alone her own faculties, based on my few phone conversations with her. At times, she seemed to be speaking gibberish."

His face remained expressionless. Yelena seemed to be taking great pleasure in telling him all this.

"I also spent time with the SREs and was able to acquire the phone number of Smally's little sister, the one who had worked as the night receptionist in Jaipur for those months before we hired someone full-time. We met at the Coffee Café near the Raghukul Tower. Smally has gone back to Bangalore, is what she told me. He has a cousin who lives there, and he doesn't appear to be returning to Jaipur anytime soon." She showed Stuart a link on Smally's Facebook page, her go-to source for critical information: an article published that morning on the front page of the *Times of India*. The founder and chairman of one of India's largest auto-parts manufacturing companies—also known as the Car Horn

King—was being taken down for tax evasion and money laundering. There was a picture of the man: midseventies, mustache, a head full of peppery hair, and that mountainous nose. Niraj's father.

"Car Horn King?" Yelena seemed to think that was cute.

According to the article, the first product Niraj's father ever produced was a car horn for the early Hindustan ambassador. The government had recently raided all the Car Horn King's homes and offices, and he was now awaiting trial. There had been threats against the family, harassment. Stuart shook his head. As fucked up as it was, at least Niraj's behavior these past months made sense now; all this time, the Indian tax regime had been hounding his father, he'd been going through a torturous criminal investigation, and Niraj had not said a word. According to the article, Niraj's brother was being charged with fraud, too. Stuart hadn't even known Niraj had a brother.

Stuart left Niraj another voice mail, explaining that he'd read the news—that he hoped Niraj and his family were doing all right. He did not mention the loss of the Exchange as a client; though if Niraj was still checking email, he would know shortly. The purpose of Stuart's voice mail was not Vita but to show Niraj his support. "Take whatever time you need," Stuart said, "and let us know if there's anything we can do." A year since the series A, they were up to forty-two employees and had offices in Singapore, India, and Tokyo (if you counted the tiny closet they were borrowing from Fumitaka-san's company) and a burn rate of close to $350,000 a month, but take all the time you need, Niraj!

The reality was, they had no time. The shock of that hit Stuart—this could change everything. He'd yet to inform the board about losing the Exchange, and now, on top of that, he'd have to inform them about this situation with their CEO. It made no sense for Niraj not to at least have called

Stuart. He knew they weren't friends in the traditional sense, but after everything they'd been through together, Stuart deserved more than this, and he got angry all over again.

THAT EVENING, MARIE RETURNED home to find Stuart staring absently at the thick, furry leaves of a ficus tree exploding in one corner of the living room.

"The Dane thought we needed plants," Marie said.

He pushed his palm against his forehead, as if he could rub out all that was going on in his brain, which now included, as Stuart was leaving the office, a call from Liam: "Is Niraj coming back?" Stuart had specifically asked Yelena to keep the news under wraps until he could talk to the Dream Team himself, and now . . . "And if he's not coming back, what happens to us?"

Stuart had wanted to remind Liam that he'd worked for Stuart long before he'd worked for Niraj, and, though Liam and Niraj had bonded over these past few years, specifically on everything anti-Brit, that it was Stuart who kept Liam fed and happy. Stuart and COMPASS, that was, the platform they had built from grit and guts. Fuck Niraj, Stuart wanted to say. Niraj could go to hell for not warning him about what was going on. For putting the company at risk.

"We're in the middle of the due diligence phase of our adoption," Liam had reminded Stuart, as if he needed to be reminded that it was often a choice people made, to torture themselves . . . Stuart stopped his mind from spiraling. He was not in a good mood.

"By the way," Liam had added. "I was wondering if you could write a character reference." There was a pause; it was a rather orthogonal direction in their conversation, not to mention the fact that Stuart barely knew Liam beyond his technical prowess and penchant for dry wit and shots of bad tequila. "Or perhaps you could have Marie write it for you, since she's the writer in the family."

"I can write the letter myself, thank you," he had responded. "Just tell me what you want me to say, and I'll say it."

Now, Stuart's hand was still pressing his forehead. "Did you tell the Dane why plants were a bad idea?"

He dropped his hand and looked so profoundly at Marie that she took a step backward. Killing plants had been her thing before they'd moved to Singapore, and she let out a long, slow exhale reminding herself that this was her job in this moment, to absorb as much of the brunt for everything that was going wrong, as much as she could bear. "Go to Delhi," she said.

"I'm not going to Delhi."

A moment passed.

"Don't look at me like that, Marie."

"Like what?"

"I don't have time to go chasing down Niraj. He knows I know. He can reach out to me."

"Now you sound like a three-year-old."

"What am I supposed to do?"

The plant leaves trembled. She suppressed any further remark, lest the vein now bulging down the center of his forehead split his head in two. When the telecom firm she'd worked for had gone bankrupt all those years ago, a security guard had escorted Marie out of the building with only her emptied-out briefcase and purse. No laptop, no papers, nothing. She came home and sat on the couch, shaking visibly for two days straight. Stuart came and sat by her and said all those very kind and logical things to get her to move beyond it—it wasn't her, it was them, etc. Come to bed, he would say, returning every hour on the hour until dawn approached and she finally said, low and animalistic, "Just let me do this." There was nothing she could do for him either.

"Are you hungry?" she asked.

Above all, he was starving. And yet how could he possibly eat? He grabbed an open bottle of wine and took it with a glass to the living room, where two wicker chairs and their accompanying ottomans sat side by side. He took a seat in one, Marie in the other, and he gazed down at the early-twentieth-century Agra rug. Niraj had bartered the Indian proprietor down to $3,000 from $10,000 in a dank and musty store far out of the way of where they'd been headed at the time, on the outskirts of Delhi. It was a deal one did not pass up, Niraj had assured Stuart. There was another one of its kind lavishing their bedroom—a gift to himself after Vita had been funded—and it was into those ancient threads that Stuart now gazed, thinking of all his past failures, biting his cuticles until they bled.

Part of him just wanted to play golf.

"What you need to do, Stuart, is act like a CEO."

He looked at her.

"What makes you think you can't do this without him?" And then, upon further thought, she added, "Or is it that you don't want to?"

All of the above.

"He's been gone four weeks, Stuart. I'm not sure what you're waiting for."

CHAPTER 25
MARCH 2012

HE'D BEEN WAITING FOR NIRAJ to come back—this was the answer to Marie's question. But the reality was that Marie was right: Stuart needed to address the possibility that Niraj wasn't coming back, and, as such, he had fiduciary responsibilities. He needed to get a handle, quickly, on how Niraj's absence affected the future of Vita, its clients, and its investors. They'd booked $5 million in revenue this past year and had committed to doubling that the next, and now, given the loss of the Exchange, Stuart's first line of duty was to ensure that Vita could cover those loses. He would have to let some of the consultants go. He'd have to craft the right message to their employees and be ready to speak at an all-hands to stamp down rumors. That message would be that Niraj was on personal leave. Stuart would explain nothing further. He'd had Yelena confirm with their lawyer that the Indian government had no claims on Vita's assets, with respect to the seed funding from Niraj's father; the preferred shares were in Niraj's name. Niraj's words came to Stuart's mind, the ones he'd whispered that day he and Stuart had landed in Singapore and gotten word of the terrorist attacks on the London Bridge. *"Vita has got to work, or I'm going to have nothing."* It was as if Niraj's father had willed his son the seed capital as a parting gift, knowing what was about to happen.

On an emergency call with the board, Stuart was elected acting CEO, and, that same day, he had Liam remove Niraj's email and system access. "Are you sure?" Liam had asked, just before pressing the enter key. Stuart was sure.

He and Liam then divided up Niraj's emails, Stuart responding to the ones client- or partner-related, and Liam to those tech- or vendor-related. They put Yelena in charge of clients, and they would need to send someone to Jaipur to replace Smally. But who? Smally was not someone you could replace. Stuart sent over Biggy, who had developed an affinity for India, aka the Amex receptionist, to provide guidance to Sunil until they could figure out a permanent situation. Then Stuart sat down and took a hard look at the three-year strategy he and Niraj had mapped out for Vita. On an emergency board call with Fumitaka-san and Hideo-san, they'd discussed finding another Niraj, at least temporarily, someone who could serve clients at a strategic consulting level, but now, suddenly, it occurred to Stuart that maybe they didn't need another Niraj. The strategy as it stood projected that in three years Vita's revenues would be 80 percent recurring, which meant that clients paid for COMPASS on a subscription basis, based on certain usage metrics, whether they were using COMPASS on their own premises in a SaaS model, or offshoring their network to Vita's MNS group in India.

The remaining 20 percent of revenues would be nonrecurring, aka one-off consulting projects, such as the scoping, design, and implementation of systems. The ratio was presently the opposite: 20 percent recurring and 80 percent consulting. And yet, Stuart noticed only now, Niraj had more consultants in Vita's recruiting pipeline than Level 2 and 3 engineers, which was strange. It should have been the opposite. And then another thought occurred to Stuart: Why three years? With no Exchange and no Niraj, why not shut down consulting now? Because it would send them directly into the red, that was why not now, Stuart argued with Niraj in his head. Vita had always been profitable and would always be profitable. That had been their guiding tenet from the beginning.

"What are you waiting for?" was Jim's response when Stuart called to run this idea by him.

"I've not gone crazy like all those other Valley lunatics?"

"Welcome to the big leagues, Stuart."

After Stuart hung up, he got a strange and fateful feeling, one that had been cropping up in his psyche lately, even before Niraj left, which was that they were circling around to that place from which they'd hoped to escape— as if they could have escaped it in the first place. The big leagues. In other words, what Jim was saying, and Marie, to some extent, was that without Niraj, there was nothing stopping Stuart but Stuart, and his reluctance to Go Big. For the first time, it was just him. No guru. No partner. No sidekick. No boss. So he got to work, with Yelena's help, developing a more aggressive three-year COMPASS MNS strategy that included expanding to other offshoring locations in Ireland—a proposal Stuart had put forth to Niraj a year ago, to no avail, that would dig deeply into the $8 million in remaining funding they'd yet to spend, put them at 100 percent recurring revenues after year one, and send Vita into a spiraling operating loss.

He then got on a plane because he wanted to look each of his investors in the eye when he told them that their money remained in good hands.

He started with JS because his tentacles stretched far and wide. The only problem was that, since Niraj had gone rogue, JS hadn't returned Stuart's calls and/or they'd "missed" each other in an exchange of voice mails. JS had been traveling. He made excuses. Stuart showed up uninvited at his office in Gangnam, where he waited for an hour—a strange, eerie, and possibly sick feeling seeping into his stomach—before being shown in.

He'd never met JS in his office, only in obscure, nameless, underground lounges with bottles on hand, and he didn't think it a good sign. Stuart sat down on the Italian leather couch across from JS, seated at his maple desk. Around him, in the large corner office that overlooked the Han River, various art pieces were strategically placed. Commemorative wine and champagne magnums; pictures of JS with famous golfers; framed copies of magazine articles—Top Distributor of the Year, Cisco Partner of the Year, Oracle Partner of the Year—highlighting industry wins, which in Asia could make or break a business. JS, who owned a variety of firms, positioned them in such a manner as to take advantage of his standing in Korean society. Status was everything, and this office was a testament to that.

JS came over and sat in a matching leather chair closer to Stuart.

Stuart cleared his throat and proceeded to tell JS that he'd come to him today to propose a more aggressive recurring-revenue strategy for Vita, given the loss of the Exchange and the present situation with Niraj. Stuart paused here to give JS the opportunity to elaborate on Niraj's situation, about which Stuart knew squat, Niraj and JS being old business-school buddies, after all, but JS did no such elaboration, and Stuart continued. "The fact is, our consulting practice has been slowing down and will no doubt continue to do so without Niraj breathing life into it. The time is now. Both COMPASS SaaS and the offshore MNS model have been proven with customers like Toyota and Refinitiv. Specifically, offshore MNS is where the margins are, as well as the growth. Hell, even WIPRO expressed interest if Vita were to think of selling itself."

JS's eyes lit up ever so slightly—Stuart's intention. He'd told no one about his discussion with WIPRO because he had no interest in selling. Vita wasn't ready. And he had no plans to bring it up now, but he was desperate for a sign, a reaction, anything that might demonstrate that JS still believed in all this.

"Ha!" Stuart quickly added. "We aren't even close to where we need to be to think of selling. We need to invest in offshore MNS, keep it thriving, growing, expanding. We have to trust it, the COMPASS platform, and ourselves." He could feel his heart pounding.

"The Exchange was a blow, certainly," JS said.

"It was political," Stuart assured JS, nothing other than a change in executive management. It had happened to Stuart more than once in his career: out with the old and in with the new—a big fat sucking sound. It was a blow, yes, but also a wake-up call. If they were targeting MNS, they needed to get there faster, they needed to redirect all their resources and manpower, and that meant winding down consulting earlier than planned. The operating losses would be strategic. They were flipping the switch now, and he needed JS onboard.

A thoughtful moment passed as JS considered all that Stuart had said—or seemed to. Who the hell knew what was going on underneath that quaffed, chiseled, all-seeing demeanor, other than the fact that he knew everything already? That he'd not already pondered exactly this?

At last he blinked, slowly, gave a nod of sorts, and said, "Take six months. Prove the MNS numbers, then come back to Fumitaka-san's executive board with a pitch to raise a series B, presuming that is what you are here planting the seeds for."

Stuart sat perfectly still, lest JS break out in wild laughter and say, "Just kidding."

No wild laughter came, just Hung Su Kim, now walking through the door, which could perhaps have been the same thing.

JS excused himself to speak with Hung Su Kim for a few minutes.

Stuart, watching them, wondered if this was some kind of stunt.

Hung Su Kim left, and JS said that he had a rather important request of Stuart. He wanted Stuart to be on the advisory board of a new company he had founded and appointed Hung Su Kim to run, a consulting company focused on network and cloud security.

A few stunned moments passed, in which Stuart reminded himself to be very careful about how he played this. So this was the reason for all those Hung Su Kim sightings at KT at the same time the Vita team was being edged out. JS was jumping into the hole Stuart and Niraj had dug and that he was never going to let them fill. Why? Because Stuart and Niraj weren't Korean. Stuart hated himself for thinking that, and he cursed Niraj for not being here to hear his friend JS admit outright that he'd been stealing their consulting business right out from under them all this time. "Isn't having me on the board a conflict of interest?"

"Now that you're no longer in the consulting business, I don't believe it is."

Stuart bit his tongue so as not to fall over in wild laughter. Fine, JS could ignore the conflict of interest, but did he not know that Stuart would have nothing to do with a company Hung Su Kim was involved in? Besides the fact that Hung Su Kim knew nothing about building cloud networks, let alone secure ones! Where he had wondered before, Stuart was certain now that Niraj had never told JS about their run-in with Hung Su Kim. And if Niraj *had* glossed over it, Stuart felt it his duty to clear the matter up now so there would be no more confusion. He was very careful to remain unemotional, not to let his anger get the better of him, as he explained to JS the issues they had had with Hung Su Kim, and that because of those issues and Hung Su Kim's behavior, Stuart could never work with Hung Su Kim again, and he suggested JS consider the same.

Again, JS made as if to take into deep consideration all that Stuart had said, with an expression that didn't change as Stuart proceeded to turn down the offer to serve on the advisory board of JS's new company. Stuart meant no disrespect. He wanted only to be fully open and honest with JS, who had always been a valuable supporter and asset to Vita. Inside, he was battling off Niraj's oft-quoted words "keep your enemies close" because that was what JS had become in this moment. How about "fuck your enemies"? Stuart would have nothing to do with HSK, ever, even if it meant no quid pro quo, no more Toyotas or KTs; such was presumably the message in JS's ever more pervasive and deepening steely gaze. Quid pro quo? *Sorry, Niraj, maybe this is the moment I screw everything up, but I won't do it.* Stuart felt sick suddenly, as if he might vomit all over the exquisite Asian artifacts. He needed to leave. This office. This country. But before he did, he blurted out, "Have you heard from him?"

JS's eyes receded ever so slightly, as if Stuart had stepped across the line into the demilitarized zone, but what did it matter now?

"Niraj," Stuart said, in case JS had already laid his friend to rest. "The threats to his family are escalating. Should I be worried for his safety?"

JS, adjusting his seat position, his tie, said, "I cannot elaborate about Niraj."

But you will.

JS glanced at his Franck Muller. At Stuart. Then at something in the distance. "What I will say is that I am neither surprised nor alarmed by what is happening to Niraj's family. Counter to popular belief, the terrorists in India are not the Pakistani but the tax authorities." He then mumbled something indecipherably disparaging, if not outright and uncharacteristically vicious, something about the filth and disgust in India, about the way in which third-world countries operated and how one could only imagine the fate of such people. "In any event," JS said, returning to his cool, even nature, "in terms of Niraj himself, there is no cause for alarm." And then, somewhat ironically, an alarm went off—a faint, high-pitched sound that emanated from, well, everywhere, it seemed. Stuart sat very still, waiting for the alarm to turn off, but it did not. Across from him, JS continued talking as he had before, even as two jets roared so close to the window behind him that the panes rattled.

Stuart felt the vibrations in his bones. "Should I be alarmed?"

JS looked at Stuart as if he were being juvenile.

A woman's voice was giving instructions in Korean over the loudspeaker.

"Is there something I should be doing?"

"It's a test," JS said.

Stuart had read that morning in the *New York Times* about a military standoff between North and South Korea that had been coming to a head. The secretary of state had gone so far as to say that they were on the brink of war.

"Your media will turn it into hyperbole, but to us it is just another day. Nothing will happen. But you will not be able to leave now."

Stuart wasn't sure he had heard JS right. *Not leave?* All he wanted to do was get the hell out of there.

"You will notice, if you stand at the window and look down at the streets, they are bare."

Stuart understood this as a request, and anyway, having experienced far too many frustrating hours stuck in Seoul's unending traffic, he knew this was something he wanted to see. He got up and went to the window. An eerie silence. Vacuous. Where had everyone gone, and so quickly? JS was not kidding. Not a soul. Even the Hannam Bridge, typically bumper to bumper, was ghostly.

"If you are going to the airport, no one will take you."

Stuart checked his watch. His flight to Tokyo was in two hours. "For how long must I wait?"

"One never exactly knows."

Stuart remained where he was, staring down at the gray, sprawling smolder, then moved his gaze upward to the pewter-green mountains in the near distance, beyond which was that dreaded DMZ that Stuart had never felt inspired to visit, no matter how many flyers were slipped under their corporate-apartment door, offering tours to the border. You could crawl through a tunnel right up to the edge, apparently, to a thick wooden door, on the other side of which the world was starving.

CHAPTER 26
APRIL 2012

QUID PRO QUO OR NOT, JS had given Stuart his word—six months to prove his all-recurring-revenue strategy—and, after having also sold Fumitaka-san and Hideo-san on the new plan, Stuart got to work executing it.

He wound down the consulting projects gracefully (the timing was such that Vita could simply let the contracts end). He let go of most of the consultants (but for Laurie and a few key others) and replaced them with Level 2 and 3 MNS engineers in India. The scrum master and COMPASS platform team remained status quo in Singapore under Liam, whom Stuart appointed interim CTO. He sent Yelena and Franco to Dublin to scope out engineering talent, ideally to buy, not build. They had no Niraj or Smally in Dublin. They had a few referrals and contacts but knew not one Irishman, if you didn't count Padraig Harrington, whom Stuart had once watched win the Open back in the days when he was offered tickets to such things. He doubted that Paddy would remember him.

A portion of the sales team was laid off, the others retrained to be SaaS and MNS-centric. In three months, Vita dropped from forty-two employees to thirty and was officially in the red.

And the world didn't end.

The Exchange sold Refinitiv, as it had threatened, but it didn't turn out to be such a threat. The acquirer bought it precisely *because* of its offshored MNS network; as it turned out, they wanted to extend the services to accommodate their own network operations, which made Refinitiv's look paltry. Vita rented more space to accommodate the L2 and L3 network engineers, expanded its global cloud footprint to support the growth, and, as a by-product, developed IP to securely provision and manage the cloud services from a single control panel. Stuart gave Professor Meena an offer she couldn't refuse to replace Sunil, who left to pursue DJing full-time, and with her came a treasure trove of network-engineering résumés, all of them women. With Refinitiv's acquirer came partners and customers, most from Europe and Australia, who helped to further extend the Vita MNS offering worldwide.

COMPASS SaaS sales were more problematic. For three years, marquee clients like Toyota and SingTel had been coming to Vita unsolicited, but no more. One would have thought they'd have cemented their mark here in Asia, but in reality they'd barely cracked the surface. A wall went up. The tide pulled back, thanks to JS. Every time Stuart thought about his meeting with JS, he had to exhale slow, calming air from his lungs in an attempt to subdue the revenge streak he'd been born with, thanks to his father and all those imaginary bullies out to get his son. Fuck your enemies. No. As CEO, he was beyond all that now. Cool, confident, he would stay the course he'd chosen and not run back to consulting revenues for the easy buck. This downturn in SaaS sales was a wave they'd have to ride out.

Meanwhile, for the first time since they'd signed on with Vita, the Dream Team got raises and bonuses. Nothing major—a 15 percent raise, plus twenty grand each, peanuts to what those guys in Silicon Valley were getting, but it was better than nothing. Retention was critical at this stage. They'd been working their asses off for two and a half years now. How long could he realistically expect them to stay without a payoff?

One thing was for sure: he didn't like being CEO. He was sure he was no good at it, even though he would never utter that out loud, least of all to Marie, who remained blind in her belief that he was far more capable in ways he simply was not. It was a circular problem that went back to the origins of man; he was pretty sure it was he who had made himself appear as such, capable of all. It was his nature as an engineer; there was an answer to every problem if you just stayed the course and figured it out. But now, more and more, he felt the need to remind her, when she asked him a question, "You know, Marie, I don't know everything." And then, when her eyes turned doe-like, he'd add delicately, "You can figure it out yourself, you know." How had he let it get to this?

Three months later, after Yelena and Franco's exhaustive search, they settled on a Dublin-based company to purchase as part of their effort to extend their offshoring reach. It was owned and run by two twin brothers and consisted of eight thickly accented network engineers, all of whom were smart, all of whom "got it," according to Franco, who'd met with each of them individually. The brothers were asking for $4 million, and since they were bringing in revenues at breakeven, Yelena suggested that, so as not to deplete Vita's cash, they issue more Vita shares and dilute the company to fund the acquisition. Meanwhile, with a ramped-up $500K monthly burn rate to cover, they needed to get going on raising the series B. Stuart convinced Fumitaka-san to get him a spot at his Japanese conglomerate's executive board's upcoming investor meeting, and he and Yelena crafted the PowerPoint pitch deck.

They'd be asking for $10 million at a pre-money valuation of $60 million. This, raised together with the acquisition money, would dilute the valuation of Vita 16 percent. The problem was, in month three of Stuart's go-big-or-go-home plan, they'd proven little other than that they were still deeply in the red. And now this problem with their receivables had come to his attention. Clients not paying their bills—there always were some rogue payers out there, but to the tune of $350K? Also, the MNS margins still weren't where they needed to be. Professor Meena was working to improve processes in Jaipur; they were making progress, but not fast enough. All were problems with which Stuart could not consume himself presently, as much as he wanted to. He instructed Yelena to get to the bottom of the receivables issue, packed his best suit, and flew to Tokyo.

He had fifteen minutes to make his spiel in front of a dozen dark-suited men, including Fumitaka-san and JS, plus three dark-suited women, including the translator, all of them seated around that same dauntingly long conference table where they held Vita's board meetings. The table appeared to have shrunk since Stuart's last visit—or perhaps it was he who'd grown bigger. Stuart's was one of ten pitches the group would hear that day. Oddly, he wasn't nervous. He felt confident about the research his team had done, the knowledge and experience that twenty years in network computing had given him—was it at last all coming together? He was prepared to be honest about what he had seen over the course of Vita's life, and he knew the biggest issue the board would want addressed was Vita's management team's ability to execute without Niraj. Stuart answered the question before they could ask it.

"For Vita to be successful, we must execute on the technology platforms flawlessly. Getting the platforms to market as quickly as possible is critical, and the technical and managerial leadership at Vita is unequaled in our space. Furthermore, we project that the growth in sales from our existing customer base will allow us to reach profitability in eighteen months, but only if we have the platforms in place and ready to be deployed within a specified time frame. Extending existing relationships is much easier than finding new clients—and I have the right level of executive relationships to make this happen. The time to build is now."

He left the room while they conferred. Ten minutes later, they called him back in to tell him that they had summarily rejected his pitch.

Even Fumitaka-san was surprised by his board's hard no. To assure Stuart of this, he took Stuart out for dinner that night at his favorite restaurant, which offered blowfish, the most sought-after and dangerous delicacy known to man. Fumitaka-san, who had coached and counseled Stuart and never once given up on him, seated across from him in the small booth, assured him, "I did what I could. It's not that my partners don't believe in you or your capabilities. Their problem is much simpler: the MNS numbers still aren't big enough."

Big. The game Stuart had pretended all along not to be playing, he'd lost. "I'm starting to wonder if they were ever going to be big enough."

Fumitaka-san poured Stuart more sake.

Stuart poured Fumitaka-san more sake, which he shot down.

"The fact of the matter, Stuart-san, is that Vita has not penetrated our Asian client base as much as we had hoped." His face was already beet red from drink.

"I don't think you really expected us to."

Fumitaka-san did not indicate this to be a wrong assumption, so Stuart continued.

"I thought you, JS, and Hideo-san invested in Vita because of the growth potential of MNS. But I understand now that you invested because you wanted knowledge. To be trained. You wanted to start your own companies with your own people using our know-how and technical capabilities and IP."

"You must not take it personally," Fumitaka-san said.

"But I *do* take it personally," Stuart said, stamping down the sliver of doubt that lived with him now, about how things might be proceeding differently if Niraj were here, still running the show.

"You came to Asia to prove your idea, yourselves, and you have."

Some moments passed in which neither of them drank.

"What happens now?" Stuart asked.

Fumitaka-san cleared his throat. "We want you—we being JS, Hideo-san, and I—to go back to WIPRO and see what they're willing to offer for Vita."

Stuart, who had just picked up his sake cup, set it down.

"We believe that MNS will soon be a commodity like everything else and that it will be better to get out now, while Vita still has cash in the bank and isn't desperate."

The waiter set down the much-anticipated plate of blowfish between them. Stuart stared at what it had come to, the end of the line in his and Fumitaka's game of chicken: exotic dishes the Asian could dare the American to eat. Since Fumitaka-san had first watched Stuart suck down the innards of that chicken at the golf club—the look on Fumitaka-san's face—he'd taken Stuart for increasingly more daring meals. Grilled eel that was still moving as it sizzled on the hot plate before them, grilled pig and cow innards, live squid and shrimp, the toasted sperm sack of the blowfish. What would Stuart's threshold be? When would he say no? Stuart made a vow to himself never to say no, even to the dog he'd eaten in Korea, though he'd not told that to Marie and never would. He'd take the dog to his grave. And now he was down in the bowels of a Ginza subway station at a seven-table restaurant with chefs who'd trained thirty years to receive their license to serve what now lay on the round plate between Stuart and Fumitaka-san—thinly sliced, translucent, presented in a circular pattern around various herbs neatly arranged in the middle. Take three pieces of the raw fish with your chopsticks, place a small amount of herbs on the fish, roll the pieces together, dip in ponzu, pray

"Look, Stuart-san. Take a few days off and think about it."

Stuart nodded at the fish.

"Give it some thought. Step away from all this. Get perspective. We'll regroup when you get back."

Stuart had perspective, he wanted to say. Instead, he picked up his chopsticks and slipped into them three—not two or four or one but three—slices of raw blowfish, thinking, *What's the worst that can happen?* He was already dead.

CHAPTER 27
JULY 2012

WHEN MARIE RETURNED TO the bodega at four o'clock, she found Stuart lying on the Agra rug, staring up at the ceiling. She could only imagine what he was thinking. He'd spent the past few days in India touring WIPRO through the Vita Jaipur facilities. It was all under the radar. Hush-hush. The very beginnings of talks.

Marie went into the kitchen, where a bag of swag lay spilled on the counter. She examined the contents, startling at the sound of Stuart blowing his nose behind her, as if he'd waited until the exact moment of her return to make the wretched sound that she'd never, in fifteen years, gotten used to. As if the entirety of the world's problems could be pushed out two little nostrils.

She came and stood over him. He was sliding the tissue back into his pocket.

It was only then that she noticed a drone in pieces in one corner, the remote lying dead by his side. She pictured it crashing against the wall. Normally he might have waited to demonstrate the drone in front of her. He was always returning home with swag of some kind, and theirs had become a ritual. He'd extract things from the bag ceremoniously, one by one, his eyes sparkling with delight, hers dulled in feigned boredom. How many gray hoodies can one have? Flashlight pens?

She peered down at him, he up at her.

And yes, she loved the fact that they could go all this time without words. Without pretending to be in some kind of mood they weren't, which was probably why they were always relieved to see each other after even the smallest absence.

She knelt beside him and took a sip from the tumbler he was balancing on his chest. "You sound terrible. Should I get your inhaler?"

He sat up, retrieved another tissue from his front pocket, and blew his nose again. The worst part about Tokyo might not even have been the meeting with Fumitaka-san's board or the blowfish that miraculously hadn't killed him, but rather the conference he'd had to attend afterward in Osaka. Niraj had committed to speaking at the conference before he'd disappeared, and it was too late to renege, so Stuart had decided to take his place. The last thing Stuart wanted to do was give Vita's spiel—what even *was* their spiel now? He managed to get through the speech, even got a drone for his efforts. But it had been sweltering in Osaka, wet and sticky, and the conference facility freezing. His sinuses were a disaster, and then his inhaler went out. All those wide-eyed believers. Stuart couldn't get off that stage soon enough.

"My prescription is out," he told Marie.

"I'll get it refilled. Leave it with me."

There had been a time when he'd loathed her attending to his menial tasks. Now, he reached into his pocket, handed her his inhaler, and dropped back down.

"The Dane said we could use her condo in Thailand. I checked flights. We can leave Friday."

He didn't say anything.

She lay down next to him. "It'll be good to get away."

"Book the flights."

She slid her head onto his shoulder. "When's the last time we lay on a beach?"

Her head rose, fell, with his breath.

"By the way," he said. "You're not going to like this, but I made the mistake of mentioning our anniversary to Yelena, and she wants to take us to dinner tonight."

It took Marie a moment to make the connection. "Oh, Stuart, why would you tell her about that?"

"It just came out."

The anniversary of their first date. He'd never once forgotten it.

"I owe her something. We grinded all day and yet made little progress in figuring out our receivables situation, other than that it's worse than I thought. Tomorrow, we'll spend the day slogging through collections and payments, our financials, and getting all our client and partner agreements ready for whatever comes next."

"And what does come next?"

"WIPRO does their due diligence. Or we look for other buyers. Or I search elsewhere for a series B."

"You can't ride this thing out without more funding?"

He made some kind of noise.

"I thought you said you had three million in cash left."

"At a monthly burn of five hundred K, do the math, Marie." She did the math.

"Without the ability to grow revenue, which we can't do without funding, we'll be out of cash in six months."

Six months seemed like an eternity to her.

"Maybe by then we could reach a breakeven, but that means Vita would become a lifestyle business, and no one's interested in a lifestyle business—certainly not our investors."

"I might be interested in a lifestyle business."

"I'm not going to work my ass off, grinding it out year after year after year. That's not why I started this thing."

She sat up, suddenly frustrated at the futility. *Why did you start this thing?* "I can't imagine going to dinner tonight."

"Cena. Eight o'clock."

"I thought Cena was our place."

"Apparently, it's hers, too. At one point we got so fed up with what we were doing that we started talking about food. Yelena loves talking about food. I mentioned a craving for pasta carbonara, and she said, 'Cena!' Before I knew what had happened, she was on the phone, making a reservation."

Marie blew air out through her lips. Now was not the time to abandon him. Yelena had become Stuart's go-to person. She had stuck by Stuart when the shit went down with Niraj. "Okay, fine."

Cena, on the banks of the river, was where the expat Italians hung out, amid the antics of the chef-owner, Carlo, who, along with serving and waiting and hosting, broke out into opera at will. Carlo had run the place for nearly thirty years, having fled Sicily to hide away here and make this sumptuous food for those craving the old world. The three of them sat at a candlelit table in a back corner of the open-aired restaurant, under the slow whirl of a ceiling fan. Yelena's face had a sheen of moisture as she pulled out her iPhone and showed them another *Times of India* article that she'd just been alerted to. She didn't want to spoil their dinner, she said, but she thought Stuart should know.

"Car Horn King Found Dead," the headline read.

No one spoke for a few minutes while Stuart speed-read the article for the pertinent facts. Then he passed the phone to Marie, who quickly did the same.

A week ago, a fisherman had found the body of Niraj's father floating near the shoreline of the coastal city of Mangaluru, in southern India, where he had gone for a few days of vacation, to get away from the investigation and the trial. He'd asked his driver to drop him off at a bridge on the waterfront, telling him that he wanted to walk and to pick him up on the other side. He got out and made a call, according to the driver. But he never showed up on the other side.

Marie felt as if she were sinking.

There was an ongoing investigation, but the presumption was suicide. Niraj's father had left a letter to his board, apparently, but the article didn't say what was in it.

"His company employs thirty thousand people."

"The stock fell twenty percent today."

"Jesus."

"It gets weirder and weirder."

"Poor Niraj."

So it went between the two women, while Stuart glanced around desperately for their waiter and that bottle of Barolo Yelena had graciously ordered for them. He didn't know how much more he could stand of all this. He insisted they change the subject, and Yelena agreed that yes, this was not why she had brought them here. They poured the wine, and she showed them pictures of her new dog and the house she was hoping to buy in Hampstead Heath. Stuart ordered the carbonara, Yelena the fritto misto and ravioli, and Marie, who could barely think of eating, the crudo, but before any of that, some antipasti, and then Yelena announced that she was leaving Vita.

Marie almost spat out her olive. She didn't dare look at Stuart while Yelena went on to explain that she'd been wanting to get back into finance for some time now and the offer she'd been coveting had at last come through. It was one she couldn't refuse. *Hence the house in Hampstead Heath.* Guiltless, unapologetic, she looked point blank at Stuart and said that without further funding, Stuart couldn't afford her anymore. Didn't he see? She was doing him a favor.

Afterward, outside, they watched Yelena slip tipsily into a cab, and Marie turned to Stuart and said, "Happy anniversary."

CHAPTER 28
JULY 2012

A CLAP SPLIT THE lingering silence, a flash of light breaking open the sky. Stuart and Marie were in the Bangkok airport, waiting for their connection. Out the window, a black and ominous cloud frothed and churned. "Maybe we should get a car to Hua Hin instead," Marie said. "I can't stand the thought of that puddle jumper." With that came a rumbling from above, buckets of rain just waiting to be tipped over. "It's going to come down. And I'm not flying in that thing when it's coming down."

"The three-hour drive to Hua Hin will be monstrous. Remember India? Trust me," Stuart said. "It'll pass through soon enough."

It did not pass through soon enough. Even the pilot couldn't hide his concern, going stone-cold mute the last ten minutes of the flight after he'd been a chatty Kathy the first twenty. He turned off the autopilot and flew the plane down manually, the cabin banging and skidding along the fog and mist, rain pelting against the window, those ridiculous windshield wipers batting frantically back and forth, only making it worse.

Standing in the dank and rinky-dink Hua Hin terminal, Marie cried and Stuart held her. "I'm sorry," he kept saying. "We should have driven. I should have listened to you—"

"Why didn't you?"

He exhaled. Now that the squall was gone, everything felt at once quiet and lush. Alive. But for her tears. He'd wanted to get here, that was why. Away from there.

"Sometimes I wonder if you do this to punish me."

He couldn't speak when she got like this. Everything inside him went blank.

"Fine, die—see if I care—but you're not taking me down with you." She stomped off.

He sat down on a bench and waited for her to come back. She always came back, after she'd settled down. And now she was back. "It's not worth it," she said, plopping down next to him.

"What's not worth it?"

"I don't know how you're still standing."

"I'm sitting."

"You're miserable."

Not entirely.

"God, I can't wait until this is all over. How close are you on the WIPRO offer?"

"Marie," he said sternly, "I told you. After the trip I'll discuss it, but not now. I need to disconnect. And you promised me."

She sucked on her lips. She had promised him.

A *tuk-tuk* sputtered up. He stood up and told her to get in.

ON THE EDGE OF THE SEA, in a three-bedroom penthouse attached to a resort that the Dane and her husband rarely used, Stuart turned off his cell phone and lay in a hammock for two straight days, staring out at the Gulf of Siam, not thinking. He needed to disconnect. No book, no magazine, nothing but the white-hot sky and the lapping shore and the trickles of sweat rolling down his belly, Marie lost at sea somewhere, having swum out to the far reaches of the earth. "There's nothing to be sorry about," she had said that afternoon, even though he knew different. Sex had never been their problem. He'd had looming bankruptcies before, and the sex had survived. But that morning, she'd gone to the bathroom to clean herself and had not come out for some time.

He managed to extract himself from the hammock, his third and final day of total escape, and ambled to the shore, where he stood with his hand against the glare, looking for her. He waded slowly out in the murky water that refused to rise above his chest. No matter how far he ventured, the ground was always there, with its invisible prickling crabs. He floated on his back.

Marie shot up from the water, looking around. How far had she gotten?

At lunch, he talked idly: One day, they would live in Pamplona. He'd become fluent in Spanish. He'd write a novel. They were eating scalding *tom kha gai* at a cardboard shack near the shore. He wouldn't allow her to talk about Vita. "A novel about what?" she asked, and he opened his arms to indicate all that was around him and that needed no explanation. Living in Asia, they'd become used to a certain style of life, a lofty kind of apartness, an abundance of wealth that went beyond money.

And yet that night, before their three-hour drive back to Bangkok, they chose the ridiculously overpriced and totally unnecessary—what with all the sumptuous street food available—resort restaurant. Their car would pick them up in a few hours, and the proximity of the restaurant lessened the weight of their impending departure. It was a repose from the frugality of their existence, albeit a kingly kind of frugality, one of the reasons it would be difficult to leave Asia, something they'd not discussed, even though it, too, was out there. If the company sold, where would they live? Would they return home? What was home any longer?

Admittedly, and perhaps poetically, the restaurant was rather sublime, the warm wind brushing through the palms all around them. A half dozen or so tables, white-clothed, candlelit, were spread around the edges of a pool in which floated white lilies. Far too romantic, ridiculously and perfectly romantic, setting alight their skin and their senses. The hush of too many adolescent Thai waiters standing at attention. In the distance, over the thatched bungalows, the moonlit sea.

After he'd signed the check, they went to the ocean-front bar. They were the only ones there, the only ones in the entire condo complex, it seemed, though that probably wasn't true. Marie could see people in the softly lit windows of the glass tower that rose above the jungle in the short distance beyond. It was the off-season, but to her it made no difference. High season, off-season, it seemed like these resort places in Southeast Asia were always empty. Or something felt empty, anyway, the wind making that hollow sound through the leaves. Marie told Stuart this now, about the lack of people, and, spotting a young couple wandering through the eaves toward the bar, he chided her for speaking too soon. He watched them, all tangled up in each other's bodies, wondering how it was possible to walk like that. They barely separated even as they slid onto stools on the other side of the bar.

There was a time, Marie thought, her eyes not leaving the couple, when she might have scoffed at them, as she sensed Stuart doing now. But these days, she found herself observing young couples in a way she hadn't before, back when they'd remained invisible to her, back when no one knew love the way she did.

British, Stuart guessed. Worse, Australian.

Twenty-five? Thirty? Eighteen? Oh, she could no longer tell ages. And if they weren't in love, they thought they were. Wasn't that enough?

"You're supposed to be looking at me," he said.

She looked at him. "It's time, Stuart," she said. "To talk about Vita. I know you don't want to—"

"Can we at least wait for our drinks?"

The bartender brought them two single malts.

Stuart gazed into the far distance. "Last Friday, I spent an hour on the phone with Liam, calming him down. He and his wife had just brought the babies home. They've begun the trial period. They'll be monitored, scrutinized by the Korean adoption police. He's overwhelmed with diapers, formula, his mother-in-law; he said he wasn't sure he should take the CTO position, what with the new priorities. Ah, the dreaded priorities! Childcare, college, a mortgage, not to mention that one of the babies was born with a cleft lip. She needs an operation and possibly more operations after that. He said he'd have to curtail his travel. Blah blah blah. And the crazy thing is that I told him to calm down. That he should do whatever he needed to do. That Vita has his back. But the reality is, I don't know what that means anymore." He swallowed his drink. "I didn't tell you this before, Marie, because I knew you'd . . ."

When he paused, she said, "That I'd what, chuck a spaz?" She looked away, despising herself.

"Two times revenues, Marie—that's what those cheap bastards threw out as a preliminary offer for Vita. I can't sell for two times revenue. I won't. Sure, our investors will make back their money, with minimal returns, and you and I will be lucky to take home a little more than we put in, but as far as the Dream Team is concerned, their options will barely be worth a few thousand dollars. You might as well pluck out my fingernails one by one."

"They knew the risks, Stuart. We all did." She looked at him. "It's not like you didn't do everything you could have. You presented Fumitaka-san's board with a sound option to save their investment, and they turned it down. With WIPRO, your employees will at least get jobs, benefits—"

"WIPRO, Marie, is the place engineers go to die."

And just like that it was back, the miserableness. After two days of repose. She looked around at the lush emptiness all around them. That morning, they'd lain side by side on the scorched sand, she covered head to toe so as not to burn, he covered with nothing, wanting to blister. They didn't need much, she thought. "We'll go to Pamplona. We can live off a little cash there."

"Oh, Marie, we're not going to live in Pamplona."

"We'll start over. We've done it before."

"Start over with what?"

She chewed the inside of her cheek until it bled.

"Not to mention the golden handcuffs. I'll be forced to stay at WIPRO for at least two years to hit earn-out numbers before any of that 'little cash' materializes."

Pamplona. For one moment, she'd allowed herself to dream. "Not really golden handcuffs then, are they?" she said. "More like bronze handcuffs."

"Or just handcuffs."

She swallowed her drink.

"Aw, hell, maybe you're right, Marie."

She stared at him sidelong. "Did you just say I was right?"

"Maybe WIPRO *is* the place for Liam, for all of us. A couple years. A person can do anything for a couple of years."

She slid her arm underneath his, their skin and sweat melding, a molten pot. "It won't be like this forever." It came out hollow, even if it was true, something they both knew—that, if nothing else, with time things passed. Everything passed. She looked at him through the layers of knowing, then up and into the stars glowing faintly between the clouds, before settling her gaze upon the inward tilt of the bar's thatched roof, allowing herself this little respite, until she saw there, clinging to the eave, a gecko much larger than the ones she'd become accustomed to seeing around their bodega and that she'd long since stopped screaming at. This one had big red splotches and orange eyes bulging out of a head seemingly twice the size of its body.

"I think we should move," she said.

He followed her gaze and made a point not to move or flinch once he saw what had alarmed her. He knew instantly what it was—harmless, for the most part, but not a typical sighting.

"That does not look right," she said.

"Ignore it," he said. And then, just then, it fell from the ceiling and landed on Stuart's arm. It was so disconcertingly unexpected that Marie didn't even scream.

"Not a gecko, a *tokay*, the kind with the vicious bite," the bartender, coming over while carving a pineapple rind, warned, though at this point Stuart didn't need to be warned—the beast, the size of Stuart's forearm, had clamped on for dear life.

"They say it's good luck," the bartender added.

Stuart remained frozen, staring at the jaws clenching into his flesh as if the sight were detached from him—as if this were happening to someone else's arm.

"He won't let go." The Aussie sauntered over and told them the news.

With that the pain came searing through Stuart's arm, up his neck and throat, which was collapsing on him. "It's all right, Marie, it's all right!"

As if she'd said it wasn't. "It doesn't look all right."

He reached into his pocket for his breathalyzer, put it to his mouth, and sucked.

"They're going to have to cut it off," the Aussie told his girlfriend, who had joined him.

"His arm?"

"His head."

The girlfriend's face exploded in horror.

"Hand me your knife," Marie instructed the bartender, her voice dead calm. From where this dead calmness came, she did not know. Perhaps she wanted to show this young couple what a relationship came down to in the end: the resurrection of one's inner warrior. This was Stuart, weakened and vulnerable and looking ready to faint, and she couldn't bear it.

The bartender set a bottle of whiskey on the counter.

"At least use the eighteen-year-old," Stuart chided meekly. Beads of sweat had formed on his forehead, his face felt drained of blood, and his stomach was lurching. He was no good with pain, blood, or any form of it. If this had happened to Marie, he might well have fainted, something she knew, and *please don't look at me like that, Marie!*

The bartender splashed the alcohol over the *tokay*'s head and mouth, and it dribbled and pooled on Stuart's arm and the bar counter. Stuart closed his eyes as the fire entered the wound and then spread through his limbs. When he opened his eyes again, the *tokay* hadn't so much as blinked, but then, how could it, with no eyelids?

Marie gave the bartender one last look, but all she got in return was one of those all-seeing Thai smiles that could have meant anything.

She made a slice in the *tokay*'s neck, just deep enough not to cut clean through to Stuart's arm. The beast let go, only to then clamp down harder. Stuart clutched his chest. Then the world went quiet as they all watched, with no small amount of fascination, the beast's blood oozing from the wound. Waiting, all of them, until slowly the red splotches grew fainter, the skin slacker, grayer. It was hard to tell when it was actually dead.

"The poor thing," the girl said.

The bartender helped Marie extract the teeth from Stuart's arm, carefully, one by one, while Stuart took swigs of whiskey straight from the bottle. On his arm were two concentric circles of teeth marks smeared with blood. Stuart poured whiskey onto the wound and then took another swig.

"It's swelling," Marie said, standing up. "We should go to the hospital."

He took another swig and stayed put.

"Stuart." She'd assumed he'd agree. Stuart was nothing if not meticulous about taking precautions against bacterial infections. They never drank water from a tap in Asia, even to brush their teeth, for instance, and they scrutinized even the slightest bug bite or scratch. Three years in Asia, and neither of them had ever been seriously ill.

"If it was carrying bacteria, the whiskey has killed it by now."

The bartender brought over a bucket filled with ice water, and Stuart sank his fist into it until his forearm was submerged. A chill flooded his brain as the water morphed to pink and the whiskey dulled his senses. Soon his arm was numb. Perhaps the worst was over.

The Aussies went back to their drinks, and the bartender was off serving another couple. "Stuart," Marie began again, the *tokay* lying defiled in a pool of its own blood.

He waved her off, as if suddenly he were this big beast of a man who fought lions in the wild, instead of a software engineer with his head in the clouds. Whatever he was, there was one thing he was not, and that was frivolous, and it was frivolous not to go straight to the hospital to see if he needed a shot. "I said we're not going, Marie."

She shut her mouth. He was doing it again. The opposite-of-whatever-she-said thing. "Fine, whatever. Since when have I ever been able to persuade you to do anything?"

He couldn't deny her this truth. And yet, ironically, hadn't he done everything for her? She'd only ever been adamant that he pursued his dream, even more so after she'd stopped pursuing hers. And he had. Still was. For her, for him, for them, for their future. He'd brought her here. He'd shown her the world.

The bartender cleared away the *tokay* but left the bottle.

Stuart's body felt like it was leaving him. "Fuck it," he snapped, startling Marie.

She looked at him. He didn't look right. He was pale; his eyes, normally deep amber, were suddenly gray-blue and iridescent. It was the drink. She should get him home, she thought, out of this place that was no place at all, to see a doctor for a shot, but she was not about to bring that up again. At this point, all she wanted to do was get on with the inevitable, whatever that was, one step at a time, but he wasn't ready. He was hunkered down and not about to move.

"Fuck it," he snapped again, with a calm so eerie he was starting to frighten her.

She stood up. "We should go, Stuart."

Nothing. He remained staring into the bucket as if he could see the reflection of his bloodstained soul. "Part of me just wants to stay the course, burn through the cash, and drive the company into bankruptcy so that JS will get nothing."

She didn't know whether to laugh or cry or simply roll her eyes, so she frowned, hard, into the eyes of whoever this man before her had become. "But you won't do that."

"Watch me," his eyes said.

A moment of white space passed between them.

Stuart pulled his arm out of the ice and examined the wound, red, swollen, and welted, though it didn't seem to be getting worse. Marie attempted to dry it with a napkin, but he pulled away, took the cloth from her, and patted the wound himself. She watched him, as if from a great distance. When he stood up, he half stumbled. She wrapped an arm around his waist, and now it was they who were two pieces of a puzzle fitted together as they walked back to their condo in utter darkness, at times knocking hips or stopping to feel with their feet the path ahead for blind crevices or steps, going slowly, holding on to each other.

CHAPTER 29
ONE WEEK LATER

MARIE SNORED AFTER TOO much wine, softly, delicately, but disturbingly nonetheless. It kept Stuart up, that and the dull throbbing in his forearm. He'd irritated the *tokay* bite by pounding on his keyboard for the past few hours, working on a ridiculously overpriced counteroffer to match the ridiculously underpriced offer for Vita that those cheap WIPRO bastards had made—numbers that had now taken possession of his sleep. Every time he closed his eyes, he saw them, until the numbers became fuzzy and everything else became clear—like a lot of things that had become clear since Thailand.

First, the $340,000 in missing receivables. It had taken the tunnel-vision mind of a middle-aged, balding, visor-wearing accountant from RentACFO.com whom Stuart had hired to replace Yelena short-term (for a fifth of her salary) to figure out that the receivables were missing because those clients had not been billed. Accounting 101: no invoice, no payment. What the hell had Yelena been doing? Stuart forced himself not to obsess about that. She'd been socked in in Dublin while also managing clients with Niraj gone, but still, if she'd needed help, she should have asked. But then, what did it matter? What mattered was that they invoice those clients, get their payments in pronto.

This bump in cash would provide some justification for the counteroffer that Stuart was about to deliver to WIPRO and that would lead to a host of fruitless negotiations—his way of stalling. WIPRO wasn't going to budge; nor was Stuart, who'd made up his mind to go bankrupt before he'd sell at that offer price. Still, he'd plow forward with WIPRO, if only to keep the board off his back. Due diligence, going through Vita's life span of client contracts, partner agreements, financial statements, employee history reports, and tax filings, all the things he needed to have in order for any kind of company exit to occur.

He grabbed his forearm, and Marie moaned, as if for him. They'd been back from Thailand one week, and he'd not told her about the persistent throbbing. But that sound . . . He looked down at her. A kind of high-pitched, fluttering noise, as if she were singing from the bottom of an ocean. Maybe he should wake her. Oh, hell, he had no idea what to do about Marie half the time—the hollow weeping, the ferocious sneezes, the convulsing hiccups, the wheezing cough, her hum, her sigh, her scream, her groan, certainly her moan, but this? He got up and went to hunt for something for the pain.

Vicodin. He found the bottle in Marie's medicine cabinet. Empty, dammit. He'd told her to save the pills for when one of them was in real pain, like now. He slammed the medicine cabinet shut and immediately regretted it. For all the snoring and moaning, Marie was a light sleeper. At once she was at the bathroom door. "What's wrong?"

"Nothing," he said. "Go back to bed."

"Is it the arm?"

"I . . ." He forgot what he was going to say.

"Stuart?"

"Yes?"

"Please stop this."

He looked at her. "Stop what?"

She didn't open her mouth—*this ridiculous WIPRO counter, your insistence on blowing up this deal*—lest he reach inside it and rip out her tongue.

"I just couldn't sleep, that's all. You were snoring."

"I was snoring?"

"Singing, actually."

"Singing?"

"Yes, singing."

"I don't remember dreaming."

"Well, you were."

"That's weird. What was I singing?"

"How would I know?"

"Hum it for me."

"I'm not going to hum it for you."

She didn't like being so vulnerable, for him to hear the things that came from her dreams. "Oh, Jesus, Stuart." She came to him. He'd unwrapped his bandage to apply more ointment, and Marie let out a gasp.

"Don't say anything," he said.

She put her hand over her mouth.

"I've made an appointment for tomorrow."

"We're going now." She went to the closet and got dressed.

BEFORE HER, AN EXPANSE of the bluest ocean. DANGER-
OUS SURF, the sign said. SWIMMING NOT RECOMMENDED.
Someone there, in the background. No swimming? She
scoffed at the sign and marched out to stand before the deep,
building swells, the wild abandon of her lost being rising
from somewhere deep, her feet sinking farther and farther
into the submerged sand, the retreating waves tugging at her
legs. At last she did fall down, stunned by the cold water
rushing over her breasts. A boy's hand reached out for her,
she recognized his glossy, imploring eyes. "Hello," she said,
at the same moment a security guard came and scooted him
outside, all the water and earth and her rushing out with him.

"Marie?"

She opened her eyes.

"What is it, Marie?" Stuart was staring down at her.

She sat up with alarm and blinked in the fluorescent light, the yellow-stained walls of the emergency room waiting area, the stench of formaldehyde. Out the window, the boy was gone. "It's all right." She sat up. "I'm all right."

Stuart's arm had a fresh bandage on it. "I'm done. We can go."

"That's it?"

No, that wasn't it, but he didn't say that out loud, didn't need to. She could tell by the look on his face. "What? What else?"

His eyes receded, as if he were seeing her from far away. "He wants me to see a specialist."

"Specialist? Why?"

"Because I'm over forty, that's why."

"And?"

"And my blood pressure is high."

There was a pause.

"How high?"

"High enough that he wants me to come in."

"Oh, Jesus, have you been smoking?"

"It's all right."

"When will you see him?"

"Tomorrow."

"That soon?"

"He doesn't think I should wait."

THE PULMONARY SPECIALIST found nothing—Stuart's blood pressure reading had been a false positive. And yet Marie seemed almost unnerved, if not disappointed. She insisted he get a full workup done. She called various doctors and scheduled appointments for his heart, his thyroid, his cholesterol. And, for that matter, he might as well get a colonoscopy. "I'm not fifty yet," he reminded her. She was disheartened to learn that the next available procedure was eight weeks out. Colonoscopies were in high demand, apparently. Meanwhile, the colonoscopy prep kit sat prominently on their bathroom counter, as if they might at last get to the very bottom of something.

"Bankruptcy," she said. "And how does that play out, again?"

They were in the waiting room of the ear, nose, and throat doctor, the result of which appointment, like that of all the other doctors' appointments, would be that Stuart was in perfect health—a truth he already knew in his marrow. No matter what Marie wanted to believe, Stuart was in full control of his faculties. If that *tokay* hadn't destroyed him, nothing would. "The same way it played out before," he responded finally.

Before. A million years ago, as if it were yesterday, Marie thought. And it always left them in the same place. "We should have adopted," she said.

Stuart didn't say anything. She wouldn't want him to. The nurse called his name, and he went in for his examination. When he returned, Marie was gone. Not literally, but he knew the look, her eyes dialed in on some long-lost thought, her face slackened, a state of being he might have staved off had he perhaps responded to her comment about adoption, instead of choosing not to.

As they were leaving, he asked playfully, "What are you scheming about now?" The idea was that she would smirk, or at least throw him a bone, but she only looked at him like he wasn't there.

And so it went.

She grew quiet over subsequent days, devoid of sarcasm. Limiting conversation to the necessities. Nothing was funny anymore. He didn't like it when she got like this. Pulling away. She was all he had.

"You never know—maybe WIPRO will accept our balls-out counteroffer and we'll be millionaires again." He made the mistake of guffawing after saying this.

She only stared at him.

"I love you," he said.

He found himself saying it more often.

"I really miss you," he texted when they were apart.

The hazel stood out in her eyes and her face remained lifeless, as if any expression whatsoever might be the end of her. She'd gone somewhere, but he knew it wasn't any place she wanted to be. Wherever she was, it was killing her.

"You won't leave me, will you?" he'd ask, his voice curling up at the end, because it was a question she'd never once given him a straight answer to, so she certainly wasn't going to give him one now.

"Where are you going?" he might moan, half-asleep, in the dead of night if she got up to go the bathroom. Normally she'd respond with something like "Paris," but now all she said was, "The bathroom."

It was the missing sardonic humor that was unbearable.

He pulled her into an embrace often and anywhere, in sporadic, random moments—the laundry room, for instance, the walk-in closet—privately and utterly alone.

The sex returned, more desperate than tender. She helped him strip off her top, and he yanked her to the edge of the bed.

CHAPTER 30
SEPTEMBER 2012

IT WAS COLD.

Marie was in San Francisco, a city she had lived in most of her life, yet she'd not thought to bring a coat. She reminded herself to breathe.

They met at a restaurant on the side of Nob Hill near the iconic Bank of America building, where the firm's offices were located. There were white tablecloths, lots of jeans and blazers, some sneakers, and not one hoodie—this was the financial district, not South Park or SOMA—and a few suits, including Irene's. Marie spotted the pale pink fuzz and fur, the comfortable shoes—her old boss had always dressed in a soft and fluffy way that belied her razor-sharp intellect.

The hug was awkward. Marie was much taller than Irene, and they'd never hugged before.

The waiter came over, and Irene, like Churchill, ordered champagne and got right down to business. "Tell me why I'm here."

It was Marie who had asked for this meeting, and one didn't play with Irene; one needed a spiel with Irene, and it didn't go like this: "My sugar daddy is about to drive his company into bankruptcy, and my money, the little of it I had saved from my illustrious career, is under the management of a misogynistic hedgie. Basically, Irene, what I need is money by way of a job." No, that was not how Marie's spiel would go. The spiel would go like this: "I'm ready to sink my teeth into work again, Irene. It's time and I'm ready." She would deliver it without one flinch or fidget or falter or hesitation. Marie could have passed a lie detector test—that was how good she was at telling people the things they wanted to hear.

Irene nodded, scrutinizing Marie, as she always had, from her perch, the one Marie stepped up to. She'd always felt high with Irene. She felt high now. Woozy, even. Maybe this wasn't a ruse. Maybe she could do this.

Irene probed Marie about the new banking laws, the regulatory changes in the Federal Communications Act, what she thought about SoftBank's investments in financial services, and Marie told her. She told her because she had studied exactly these things.

Irene was not unimpressed by Marie's answers.

"Whatever I don't know, I'll learn. I'm not afraid of hard work."

"My senior managers range in age from twenty-nine to thirty-six."

"I'll be working for people younger than I am. That's a given."

"At first."

"I don't care how old they are if they're smart." That part was true.

"They're putting women up for partner in droves, but they're going to want to know you're committed; otherwise, they won't be interested."

"I wouldn't be sitting here if I weren't all in."

Irene talked about a project at Verizon. Another at AT&T. All the cleanup going on after the mortgage debacle. Then she said that she'd call HR and have them set up meetings for Marie with her team for tomorrow. "How long are you in town?"

"For as long as necessary."

"Where are you on relocating?"

"I'm wherever you want me to be. My assumption is that I'll be on the road most of the time anyway and that it doesn't matter where I live."

"We're in a talent battle with Silicon Valley that we can't win. It'll give you an advantage if you move here. Are you looking at other firms?"

"I came to you first."

That pleased Irene. That Marie had not gone to the Dazzler, the rising, hotshot partner Marie had once worked for at the same time she had worked for Irene. "You've heard about him, then?" Irene asked.

Marie glanced down at her menu.

"He's moved around," Irene continued, "but he's now back at the firm, which is crazy. Though I imagine, with all that's going on, that will change soon."

Marie felt Irene's eyes on her.

Irene picked up her menu and said that it was only a matter of time now, with respect to the Dazzler, which should have made Marie, of all people, happy. Irene put down the menu. Her eyes were back on Marie, waiting for her to say something about Chicago, Marie surmised, stunned even though this was what she'd anticipated. Either Marie copped to Chicago, or no job. Either she blew the whistle on the Dazzler, or no partner track. Irene wanted to take down the Dazzler, still, even now, for blocking her partnership way back when.

Marie said to Irene that it had been ten years and that she didn't see the point. Irene said nothing was too late, not anymore, for this kind of thing. Marie said that she was still unsure if it had been "this kind of thing," and Irene said that others had come forth about the Dazzler and so should Marie.

"It wasn't the Dazzler who harassed me," Marie said, her eyes gone dead, for she had thought she could do it, for Stuart, if nothing else, but apparently she couldn't. Lie anymore.

Irene shrank backward, ever so slightly. This woman who never shrank. Not the Dazzler? It was the CEO, Marie told her, the Dazzler's biggest client, and therefore Marie's, too. Irene's eyes narrowed. The Dazzler may have had a penchant for all-nighters in his hotel room, and, yes, some of those times he had slipped into his robe, but Marie had never been alone and he had never touched her or done anything inappropriate, in her mind.

Irene's eyes showed no emotion whatsoever.

Their client, the CEO, was another story. Marie told Irene about the calls and the late-night knocks on her hotel room door, his hand on her knee, the work dinners that only Marie was invited to, the presents, the Dom and caviar, though Marie had let nothing physical happen. She'd listened to him—that was all. He was lonely—that was all. He had asked Marie to read the manuscript of a novel he was working on, and she had. It was about a woman he'd fallen in love with in Spain. He was not in love with his wife, and Marie was feeling sorry for him was what it came down to. And perhaps the Dazzler knew, knew Marie had this hold over the CEO, and so he encouraged her dinners, and that made Marie feel empowered, important. They needed the CEO to champion their proposals, their organizational changes, to agree to firing three hundred people, and so maybe it worked in reverse. Maybe the CEO and Marie were using each other. Who knew where he was now? Probably back in Spain, where he'd been stationed before Chicago. He adored Spain.

Irene was silent. By now, Marie had probably said too much. "The sad part is that neither of us won. The project was a failure. They sent us all home. I thought they were going to fire me. But then they promoted me."

"And that's why you left the firm?"

"No. Not really. Maybe. I don't know."

Irene nodded.

"The Dazzler could have used me as a scapegoat, but he didn't."

Irene looked at Marie, figuring her out. That she was no good for this. Never had been.

Marie left lunch having eaten nothing and feeling numb. When she reached the corner of California and Montgomery, she paused, not knowing where to go or what to do. She had a few friends from business school she could have called to meet for a drink. Though, as she recalled, they'd moved out of the city to raise children in rich suburbs. Still, they would have wanted her to call. They would have made the trip in to meet her, to reminisce, but what was all that now?

Clouds hovered low. She turned up the collar on her thin blazer and started walking down California Street. A bus pulled up randomly—and not one of the gleaming white buses that chauffeured tech workers to Google or Facebook, the ones that floated up and down the hills, making their discreet stops, no flags or logos because they didn't need any. This was the city bus, the one Marie had sleepwalked onto every day at dawn back when she was working at the firm. In fact, she wondered if this might be the exact same bus. She got on just as it started to rain, and the bus lurched up the hill, puffing and gasping.

Out the window, trash flew and commuters fought with umbrellas. Homeless abounded, seeking shelter in entryways. She had been so happy to abandon these hills, had not once in almost three years looked back. And yet here she was, fated to be back because one must face one's demons, so Professor Meena had said to Marie on that dreaded car ride. Professor Meena had been terrified of having to present her testimony to the high court about Mumbai's inadequate handicapped facilities the following day, but she wasn't going to let that stop her. Her son deserved more, and she was not going to back down from this battle. Tears flooded Marie's eyes. Water rushed down the streets.

When Marie got back to her hotel down on the wharf, she threw on her swimsuit and sweats, walked down to Aquatic Park, and bought a wetsuit. She stripped down, pulled the suit on, and dove in. The water's temperature took her breath away, and for a moment her heartbeat too, before it began again, wildly at first, but she knew to remain steady, all body and breath and movement. The water was choppy this time of day, and she had to work to find her stride, stroke by stroke, and as she did her mind grew steadier, determined, one eye on her mark, the other on the tankers and ferries. When she was younger, she might have crossed, but not today. Today the prison island would do. She had the stamina in her now. She'd been training for this. Two miles to Alcatraz, two miles back, not trying to escape. Because now she knew there was no escape.

CHAPTER 31
SEPTEMBER 2012

"IT WAS JUST SOMETHING I needed to do. It's over now."

The Dane wanted to know if Marie had seen any friends.

"No."

"Family?"

"No."

The Dane waited for Marie to elaborate, but no elaboration came.

"You must have really respected this woman."

Marie said, "When I first met Irene, she was pregnant, but none of us knew it until after she'd had the baby—she was not a thin woman. She'd been flying from New York to Ohio for a client meeting when she went into labor. The plane landed, she had the baby, and she still made the meeting the next day. We hit it off immediately, even though I looked Irene's opposite and was anything but deadly, like she was—more of the diligent, heads-down type. A thinker, analytical. Irene asked for my opinions. No, she demanded them. I told her what I thought, and she listened.

"At the time, I'd also been working with one of the rising partners at the firm, whom I like to call the Dazzler. While the Dazzler patronized Irene, my bone-dry, no-drama style had gotten his attention. Plus, I knew my place. When push came to shove, I backed down. I deferred. Irene did not. She would not back down. Didn't have to, because she was usually right. I would watch the Dazzler roll his eyes when Irene turned the other way. I didn't understand it. Irene was persistent, smart, yet few partners wanted to work with her. She was friendly and personable, and with her penchant for champagne, she could even be fun at times. She took me under her wing, saw something in me—this was after the telecom debacle, and I was desperate for a reboot and Irene seemed on a mission to give me one. She didn't understand why I put up with the Dazzler's antics, like the three in the morning calls to scrap and rewrite a presentation scheduled for that morning, all-nighters spent in his hotel room, working on a proposal. I did sometimes sense envy in Irene's cautions—the hotshot partner wasn't calling her at three. He would say, 'Jump,' and I would say, 'How high?' It wasn't uncommon for me to get on a plane with only a few hours' notice.

"'You could say no,' Irene told me once, and I thought, *She'll never understand*. Irene was in full control of her faculties. She knew who she was and what she had to offer. She didn't need to succumb, to obsess, like I did.

"Irene's partner quest went on and on, until it became gruelingly apparent that the firm's board didn't want her to be partner. Or a contingent of them, the male contingent, which was all of them, had rallied against her, so she began to assure me. I didn't believe her. I didn't see the Dazzler in that way, or other male partners I had worked with, the Stutterer being one of them—none of those men had held his stuttering against him. Part of me wondered if Irene was being high-maintenance. Causing problems. Complaining too much. And now I'm sitting here, trying to remember a time at work that I ever complained about anything. It was always about the work. I needed these men for the work. To prove my worth. Because the work was good. The work was edgy."

She paused to replenish the air in her lungs.

"I guess I went to San Francisco to look Irene in the eyes and see what would happen with this woman who had never once relented, still and always in the thick of it. No gaps or breaks. No sabbaticals. No languorous, existential drifting, no following her husband across the world to Asia. No ghostwriting a book for two men who couldn't write it themselves. Nope, no living like a ghost for Irene. Nothing. Just that nice, shrewd, not entirely unsmiling face staring back at me. Hard work had been good to her; fighting the battle had kept her alive and youthful."

"I still don't understand why you went all the way there."

"I went there because we need the money. I want Stuart to have options when the time comes. But in the end, I couldn't do it. I'm weak and a coward. I could have given her what she wanted, but I didn't. Maybe I never had any intention of giving it."

The Dane nodded.

"Maybe I just wanted closure. Maybe Irene reminds me of my mother and I wanted to see her one last time before I said goodbye to her forever."

The Dane looked at Marie sidelong. "That's deep."

"It is." And then she laughed, unexpectedly.

"Look, Marie, if you want a job, I'll give you a job. Just don't leave again."

"I don't want a job; I want an adventure." It felt good to be silly. It had been a while.

"Seriously, I've been thinking about this. Isabella needs to learn how to swim. You could teach her."

Marie looked at the Dane. It was a rather orthogonal request. *Teach?*

"I would pay you handsomely."

"I couldn't take your money."

"So, you'll do it?"

After an uncertain pause, Marie said, "I don't know much about it."

"You're a fabulous swimmer."

"Teaching, I mean."

"All I know is, you'll be better at it than I am."

This girl, Isabella, who would speak only Italian to Marie, was so petrified of the water that she wouldn't put even her little pinky toe into it. This part, the Dane had left out. That and the cussing. *Che cazzo!* She had a foul mouth, the Dane finally admitted, though Marie wouldn't have known the difference. *Fa freddo!* The first day, the girl scraped her shins so badly on the side of the pool as she clambered out that Marie had to apply bandages and apologize profusely to the Dane. When Marie got home that night, Stuart asked her what the hell had happened to her arms. She looked down at the bloody scratches and said, "It's a jungle out there."

CHAPTER 32
SEPTEMBER 2012

STUART KEPT ASKING HER if she'd heard back from the firm. "Any day now," she would say. Or, "They're setting up meetings." What she wanted to say was that she couldn't do it, but she couldn't get the words to form. It was what he expected her to say, she knew, just as she knew what he'd say, in response.

"It's okay—you don't have to go back to work."

"It's not okay," she'd say.

They both knew it was not okay. Three days she'd been home, and her rolling suitcase still lay open and barely unpacked on their bedroom floor. "Maybe try something else," he'd say, "another firm," and she'd think, *He's not getting it.* When you've been with someone long enough, you can anticipate exactly how any conversation will go, so the point of having the conversation at all becomes lost.

"I saw Niraj," he said, "while you were in Frisco."

The problem with this theory on conversations is that inevitably one of them will not go how you anticipated. Just when you think he can't surprise you any longer, that's exactly what he does. "What?" she said, as if she were going deaf.

"You were right, Marie. You're always right. I should have gone to see him before. Something happened to him. I'm not sure what, exactly, something related to all the stress; plus, as you know, he's never exactly been the picture of health. He wouldn't go into it, just said he'd been ill and unable to travel."

"Slow down, Stuart. Can you back up? How did you find him?"

"Professor Meena found an address for one of Niraj's father's winter homes in Bangalore. I flew there from Jaipur. After touring WIPRO through the facilities for the umpteenth time, I went and knocked on the front door."

She blinked at him. *Your just telling me this now?*

"Well, I didn't actually knock on the front door. More like buzzed at the gated entrance, behind which lay a long and winding road carved out of a thicket of jungle where monkeys swung from trees. Press were camped out in front, and other assorted black vehicles. A few minutes later, I was met by a young girl of about ten who took my hand and led me through the gate and into a side door, along dark halls, until we reached a library of some sort, with ancient and dusty books lining the walls and where three elderly, sari-clad women sat on ancient chairs side by side, with solemn looks on their faces. Niraj, wearing a white kurta, stepped out of the shadows to greet me. He seemed relieved to see me, more so than I would have thought, and I felt immediately at ease. I wasn't sure, exactly, what I'd thought I'd find. He introduced me, rather formally, to his mother and his two aunts, who stood and bowed. The *chaiwala* brought in tea on an ornate silver platter, and Niraj's mother expressed how much she had heard about me and had wanted to meet me. She was sorry it was under these circumstances. How was my journey? she wanted to know. I must be very tired, I should plan on staying the night, or for as long as I needed. I was welcome in their home. She said that the Indian government had been out to get her husband for some time, and that she has vowed to fight for his honor and that of her family. Some things happen for a reason, and in this case, it was the return of their youngest son, Niraj, from a long absence. Her eyes were weighted with sparkles as she looked at Niraj and said, 'Soon we will have a wedding. A wedding to cover all this darkness with light.'

"Niraj kept his head bowed in deference. When tea was over, he took me onto the back patio, where a dog lay on her side, looking sucked dead by the pups strewn about her swollen nipples."

It took a minute for him to continue.

"His mother was in denial, Niraj explained to me. His brother was going to jail, the government had frozen their assets, and there would be no marriage. He said that his mother put on a good face but was in a state of great shock and depression. And that's when he told me that he himself had been ill and unable to travel, but that according to his doctors he was making a full recovery. 'Good,' I told him. 'We need you back, Niraj. I can't do this without you.'"

After a pause, Marie said, "You actually said that?"

"I wasn't expecting those words to come from my mouth, not after the way he acted before he left. I just felt such great relief at seeing him again that I blurted it out. I told him that my being CEO was interim, and that if he came back and was up to it, we could see how things went; he could ease into it."

"But, Stuart—"

"Do you want to hear the story or not?" he asked.

She sucked on her lips.

"There's more," he said.

"I'm going to sit down," she said.

"Remember that letter? The one Niraj's father left for the board before he . . ." Stuart cleared his throat. "You know . . ."

"I know."

"His mother has never seen it. Niraj fears it might be too much for her, but he made a point of going and getting it and showing it to me. His hands were trembling as he unfolded it. In the letter, his father wrote that he'd been under a lot of harassment from tax authorities, as well as his equity investors, that there had been threats to his life, and that while he'd no intention of cheating anybody, he took sole responsibility for his mistakes and the law should hold him and only him accountable. He'd failed as an entrepreneur, but his family was innocent."

Stuart fell silent while Marie processed all that he had said.

"Niraj said that while his father had quit, I was no quitter."

Marie, for her part, had no intention of making a correlation between Stuart and Niraj's father.

"Don't you see, Marie? Niraj and I, that's what we've always told each other, since the beginning: We aren't in this for the money; we're in it to build something."

"You mean *only* the money," she threw in. "Come on, Stuart."

His nostrils flared; she bit her tongue.

"At this point," he continued, "I asked Niraj if I could have a drink, and he called for someone who brought out a bottle, though he himself had stopped drinking. It was then that I noticed how much weight he'd lost. He showed me his nicotine patch, and so I waved the bottle away and the girl brought us some bottled water. I couldn't imagine bringing up Vita, the reason I had come. It seemed so trivial compared with what Niraj was going through. But then he asked me how Vita was going. He'd heard about the Exchange. I shrugged. The Exchange seemed so long ago. And then I started talking. I must have gone on for an hour about WIPRO, Yelena bailing, the *tokay* bite, the handcuffs—not golden or even bronze—while Niraj listened."

"What did he say?"

"He said the *tokay* bite was good luck."

Marie closed her eyes. Stuart still wore a bandage and was on a mild antibiotic, but those concentric teeth marks would be etched in her mind forever.

"Niraj said I should do what was in my gut. I told him I didn't want to sell but that the investors had my hands tied and that as far as JS was concerned, we were personas non grata. He insisted I not give up, said something will turn up because that's how things always work out for me, the man with the golden touch. And I'll admit here that I sensed a touch of bitterness in his tone when he said that. I told him that maybe it was that way once, a long time ago, but that that time is long past."

Marie was starting to wonder if she was even in the room anymore—if it weren't just those two.

"Niraj told me six more weeks before the doctor would clear him to fly."

"Once again, Stuart, clear him of what?"

"I don't know, and anyway, does it matter?"

"Uh, maybe."

"He's making a full recovery, that's what matters, and I told him that was good and reiterated that we need him to come back."

"That's what I don't understand, Stuart. Come back to what? At this rate, you're going bankrupt, and, unless I heard you wrong, that seems to be your intention. To have JS get nothing. What is it, exactly, that Niraj is coming back to?"

"I knew you wouldn't understand."

"Stuart—"

"I can't sell, Marie!"

She stepped backward, but the wall was there and she banged into it, and then his phone rang. He made no move to get it.

It kept ringing.

CHAPTER 33
OCTOBER 2012

MARIE FOUND A SWIM GURU in New Jersey, Ingrid, and exchanged emails with her. Ingrid said that traditional methods for teaching swimming did not work for people with an extreme fear of water. Ingrid's approach was based on being present. It shouldn't be a battle with the girl, Ingrid wrote; it should be a conversation. Ingrid also suggested a group class so that the girl would know that she was not alone, that others were afraid, too. It was important that the girl feel in control through every step of the process. You can teach someone the mechanics of swimming, but if they do not feel in control, they might panic in deep water, Ingrid wrote. If they are not in control, they aren't safe.

Try to get under the cause of her fear.

Explain to her what water is.

Get her to understand what it means to be fully present. Do you understand what it means to be fully present?

Marie evaded the question. This wasn't about her.

If you do something you don't really want to do, Ingrid wrote, you are fighting yourself, you are somewhere else, you're thinking only about getting it over with.

If she becomes scared, you need to stop and go back to a step that's not scary. The process should be gentle. Go slowly. This is not about breaking her.

My mother threw me in, Marie wrote Ingrid at one point. I was three. "Swim," she said.

It should be fun, Ingrid wrote back.

Has it ever been fun for me? Marie wondered.

We learn naturally and easily when we have fun. Pushing hinders learning.

Has my whole life been a lie?

For two weeks, the girl sat three feet back from the edge of the pool and stretched her feet far enough that they dangled over but didn't touch the water. The third week, she finally scooted close enough to tap the bottom of her feet against the surface, until, slowly, she sank them down onto the step where Marie had been waiting and stood. "Breathe. Relax."

The girl's eyes were bulging, her body as rigid as a board. One hand gripped the rail. Marie took her other hand and brought her down to the second step, then the third, then finally the bottom, where the water came to her thighs. She jumped out and grabbed her towel and said it was time to go.

Still, it was something, Marie thought, feeling slightly altered.

On the following day, the girl waded back and forth in the shallow end, holding the edge, and then Marie said it was time to put on goggles. Marie got on her knees, put her face in the water, and blew bubbles. "You can even make a song," she said. The girl did not follow suit, but it was okay. She wasn't ready. When at last she tried, at once she gasped and stood and stared at her legs in the water as if they were disconnected from her body.

On a subsequent day, the girl waded from one end of the shallow end to the other without holding the edge, her expression morphing from surprise to wonder, as if the sky had opened up and spilled down a bucket of sunshine. Then someone appeared, as if out of nowhere, to use the pool, and the girl leaped for the steps and scrambled to get out, scraping her thigh this time.

"You're good at this," the Dane said, applying disinfectant and ointment to the wound.

To the girl's great relief, she and Marie couldn't come back to the pool for a few weeks. They retreated to the bath, where Marie held the nozzle over the girl's head, the girl holding her breath as the water engulfed her.

CHAPTER 34
OCTOBER 2012

"HE COULD BE CALLING about the babies," Marie said.

"What, they're colicky and I'm going to know what to do?"

"Aren't you, like, the godfather or something?" She held his eyes firmly until he picked up the call.

"I've got it," Liam said.

"Got what?"

"The source of the hack."

Stuart had to think for a minute. He felt as if a year had passed in three months, another in the past week, so much had been going on.

"That NEWTV security engineer you passed off to me. He gave us access to the data, and we've been doing some trolling of our own."

"We?"

"Biggy and Franco. It only took us a day or so."

The fog began to clear. A network engineer at NEWTV, one of the fastest-growing cable providers in the United States, had called Stuart three days earlier at the suggestion of a friend of Stuart's, whose name he would not disclose. NEWTV had experienced a security breach in its network that morning, and this friend insisted that only Stuart and his team could get at the source. Stuart almost hung up on the guy. He had no time for subterfuge, given all the other subterfuge, and anyway, whoever this friend was, Stuart had no time to be doing favors for friends. He passed the call off to Liam and forgot about it.

Apparently, as Liam now described it, the hack involved the premature release of the season two finale of one of the hottest cable TV dramas before its official air date. This had not been news to the Dream Team, who had a Slack channel devoted to each Dungeons and Dragons subplot and had already seen the aforementioned version by the time Stuart got the call. The sector was in an uproar, as was Marie, who had not been privy to the prereleased finale and inadvertently heard about the surprise ending before she'd seen the episode. Both NEWTV and the cable company that produced the show, not to mention Marie, wanted answers.

Liam said, "Want to take a look?"

Stuart flipped open his laptop, which was never out of arm's reach, and dug his way into the trail of crumbs Liam had left for him in the code. It didn't take long to get up to speed, thanks to Franco, who had slapped together some quick automation tools to mine NEWTV's data. They'd all agreed, for some time now and at Professor Meena's urging, that they needed a data-mining expert in-house as their own petabytes of client data grew unwieldy. But they'd never gotten around to it, and now they were in a hiring freeze. Still, as crude a tool as Franco's was, they'd been able to figure out how the hacker broke into NEWTV's network, which was—hold the crescendo here—through a misconfigured firewall. Basically, one of NEWTV's network engineers had fat-fingered a configuration. It was a stupid, silly mistake that Stuart had seen happen time and again.

As they'd found at the Exchange, a lot of network engineering issues came down to process: enterprises configuring networks by hand, employing little automation, operating with gross inconsistencies, firewalls managed in silos across the organization. Problems that the DevOps module of COMPASS was built to solve. But the worst part was, buried in the dark depths of NEWTV's network, Stuart discovered the Cowboy's shitty software-defined network module running. He had to pull back from his machine and regroup for a moment, palm his eyes, which, when he was finished, blurred on a vision of Marie—many hours had passed, apparently— telling him that he should come to bed, that he was too old for this. There it was again, his age, this ever-closer-to-theend business.

Something else was going on, Stuart was sure. But what? He leaned so far back in his chair, he almost tipped backward.

"Don't hurt yourself," Marie said.

"Jim," Stuart said, as it struck him. He swiveled forward abruptly, his face at the screen. "Jim said it from the start— it's about the data."

There was no point asking him what he was talking about. He was already gone, full of abandon, as if everything were new and fresh and for the taking. The loss of trusted clients, the back stab from JS, the board's rejection, the tragedy with Niraj, Yelena and the receivables, WIPRO, the *tokay*—all that was forgotten. As were sales pipelines, burn rates, product margins. It was about the code now. It was always about the code. She watched him a bit longer. They might as well be at their beginning, back when she used to love this about him. She still loved this about him. But they were getting older. This was getting old. She went back to bed and tossed and turned and couldn't fall back to sleep. Visions of Pamplona, Hemingway, the bullfighters. Those poor, fated beasts.

HIS PALMS WERE SWEATING. There was more to this breach. He was sure of it. He worked with the team through the night, trolling not only NEWTV's network data but the network data of all of Vita's existing MNS clients, looking for clues; simulating the breach; breaking it apart step by step; reengineering it forward, backward, sideways. He'd

known Vita was sitting on a lot of network data, as Jim
kept reminding him, but he was not fully cognizant of *how
much* data. And maybe that was what Jim had been trying
to tell him all along. A treasure trove of data was essentially
what they had. And as the hours passed, he began to see
patterns in the topology of that data, what it looked like
from different purviews, how the trolls were trying to get
in—it was amazing how many people liked to fuck around
with corporate networks just for kicks. Patterns they'd not
known to look for before . . . and then there it was. All at
once. Stuart sat back. It was bad. He sat forward. Ran the
routine again. Same result. He sat back again. Some moments
passed. Then he sent Liam a slack message.

> Stuart: "Did you see this?"
> Liam: "Yes."
> Stuart: "Does NEWTV know?"
> Liam: "Nobody knows."
> Stuart: "We need to call someone. And, Liam,
> keep this internal."

STUART WAS STILL AT HIS computer at dawn the next morning. He didn't notice Marie leave, even though she'd walked
back and forth three times, pretending she'd forgotten something. At the first hue of gray light, she took a taxi to East
Coast Park and swam inside the buoys for an hour in an early
rain that had come out of nowhere. Back and forth, back and
forth, with a handful of other swimmers for whom hard rain
meant only one thing: training against the elements, for when
you swam out in the open, nature was in control and anything could happen. Marie had always swum through weather,
pushed through it as if she were in control. In the end, it was the
reason she'd never be able to compete at a high level, according

to her coach, because she was never in control, weather or no weather. To be in full control, one needed to be present, and Marie had only ever swum to escape. She pulled up and gasped suddenly, looking around her, raindrops stabbing at her face.

IT WAS SIX IN THE evening in El Segundo, and Liam and Stuart were having trouble getting in touch with anyone at NEWTV. The VP of network security was not responding to texts, and forget about maneuvering through NEWTV's AVR system. They finally just called the main office line. A security guard answered, and they told him that they needed to talk to the person in charge. As in *the* person. The CEO or COO or CFO or CTO—a C in the acronym was preferred. The guard finally put Stuart through to an on-duty cloud engineer (or so he thought), the only guy who was working late. Stuart immediately recognized the thick Boston accent.

"Jack?" As in Boston Jack. As in *open-source* Jack.

"Who's this?"

"Stuart."

"Stuart?"

"How many Stuarts do you know?"

The line went silent.

"I thought you were dead," Stuart said finally.

"I might as well be."

"You're the friend?"

"They don't listen to me that much here, but I still have some pull. It took you a while."

"You've got a problem on your hands, Jack."

"I know."

Stuart had a million questions for Jack, like what the hell he was doing in California when he only ever spoke about how much he hated the place, but he focused on the issue at hand. Ten minutes later, the CTIO—not to be confused with

CIO or CTO, but some new combination of the two—was calling Stuart from her daughter's soccer game. Stuart spoke with her for twenty minutes. After he hung up, he Slacked the team to start packing—they were flying to El Segundo.

Just like that, the man with the golden touch was headed home.

Well, not home, but close enough. They were leaving Kansas, folks, for the Land of the Free, and something tactile reached deep inside Stuart: *Maybe this is your bridge back.* He got up and paced to the bedroom, which was when it occurred to him that Marie was gone. What day was it? He left the bodega with his phone, tracking her on Find My Friends. She was at the Shangri-La. He found the pool. He was pretty sure it was the wrong pool. He texted her, but she didn't answer. He came upon a gate that was locked—a gate she had mentioned to him some time ago. When? Where had they been? He recalled dumplings, slippery and steaming, and his stomach growled with a hunger he'd not had in some time. No TRESPASSING, the sign said. He thought of crawling over the gate, as she had. Had she? He turned around and spotted a bench near a little bridge connecting two lily ponds. He went over and lay down on it and fell asleep to the sound of water trickling somewhere beneath him.

BY MONDAY, NEWS OF the one million NEWTV customers whose data had been compromised hit the global wire. But thanks to Stuart, Jack, and the Dream Team, NEWTV was able to get ahead of the whirlwind and do damage control. It had already informed its customers via email and hired a PR firm to spin the messaging. Sure enough, Vita's clients, like Toyota and SingTel, and even traitors, like the Exchange and KT, wanted to know where they stood in terms of vulnerability. Suddenly, Dr. Kwak was calling. *Ask fucking Hung*

Su Kim, Stuart spat back to Kwak in his head. *If you're on COMPASS, you're covered; if you're not, you're fucked*, he wanted to say. Instead, he had Professor Meena send all Vita's clients, old and new, more copies of what he now preferred to call Marie's book to distribute to their teams, telling them he'd be happy to get on a plane and speak to them about it.

CHAPTER 35
OCTOBER 2012

WHEN STUART STEPPED OUT of LAX, his hair fell straight. That made it noticeably thinner in certain spots, which had apparently been masked during his time in Asia, where the humidity had made it appear full and wavy. Notwithstanding that, the cool ocean air felt like a rebirth. He drove in his rental with all the windows down. He'd not been back to the States in three years. Had he even missed it? His hair had not, apparently. And were those waves he heard crashing or his mind adjusting to some long-lost rhythm? Who had ever even heard of El Segundo?

The NEWTV offices were in a suburban strip mall, a U-shaped cluster of five-story stucco buildings surrounded by a gigantic Whole Foods, Barnes & Noble, an 18-plex AMC movie theater, Houston's, California Pizza Kitchen, Wolfgang Puck, and a parking lot the size of a football field. Inside, the offices were old-school but for the flat TV screens everywhere showcasing all the great cable NEWTV had laid throughout the world and that would soon become obsolete. Rooms with actual doors and cubicles. No beer stations. No dogs running around, Stuart noted, as he was given a badge and sent down a staircase to the basement. He'd arrived a day ahead of the others so that he could meet with Jack one-on-one before Vita made its presentation to the CTIO. Stuart and his team had uncovered the source of the hack and saved NEWTV's asses, and for that the CTIO was giving them a seat at the table.

An office with no window. Jack had always liked it dark. The laugh was familiar—it had a gasping quality. He was seated behind his desk, swiveled to face the flat-screen, his feet on the credenza. Lucy and Ethel were frantically stuffing chocolates into their clothes and mouths to keep up with the speeding conveyor belt.

"This episode always reminds me of *Duck Soup*," Stuart said, watching over Jack's shoulder.

Jack laughed. He'd been the one to indoctrinate Stuart in the Marx brothers. They must have watched *Duck Soup* a dozen times together. Stuart had to gather himself for a moment as he glanced around and wondered how it was that Jack had found himself here, of all places, in these very average yet comfortable nine-to-five digs, wearing a wilted white dress shirt and corporate slacks, the ponytail gone. "I thought you hated California."

Jack shrugged. "One makes concessions."

"One doesn't make concessions. You taught me that."

"You don't have kids, I take it."

"Nope."

"I've got two."

Stuart nodded. Then he saw Marie's book on the otherwise empty metal desk. Jack picked it up, flipped it open to a random page. "Didn't *I* say this?"

"Probably."

Jack nodded at the page admiringly.

"You married her, I presume. That Stanford swimmer you were all gaga about."

"Something like marriage, anyway," Stuart said, his mind trying to process the presence of that book. Here. In the hands of Jack. "How the hell did you stumble upon that?"

"One of my guys left it in the bathroom. It's how I found you."

"Funny guy," Stuart said, though he wasn't laughing. He was still staring at the book, as if it were an aberration, a life he and Marie had created but that didn't belong to them anymore. It had its own destiny now. Stuart turned and studied a schism of tiny cracks on the blank wall, collecting himself. "Nice view," he said finally.

"It's not for everybody." Jack threw the book back down on the desk. It landed with a thud.

Stuart exhaled and turned back around. There was no other way to say it other than to just say it. "Look, Jack, we're going to tell the CTIO tomorrow that in an ideal world, she would blow up what they've developed to date and start over."

Jack smiled fleetingly.

"The platform they're using is not scalable. It's inefficient and porous, it cracks easily, and that's only the start of their problems."

"She won't go for it, now that the merger is in play."

AriaNet, the behemoth, stalwart telecom that no one wanted to work for—the buyout had become public a week ago.

"They've got to get the NEWTV platform to a point where it can support the influx of the AriaNet subscriber base," he said. "We're talking over one hundred million new accounts by year end, which makes the network breach even more problematic, given that AriaNet bought NEWTV in large part because of the scalability and security of our platform. She's under a lot of pressure. The SEC is on everyone's asses. The technology could make or break the deal. But that's not even the biggest problem. The biggest problem is the Super Bowl coming up next February, four months from now, the date on which an estimated fifty million subscribers, many from the AriaNet acquisition, will simultaneously log in to the new NEWTV-AriaNet platform to watch the game, a platform built specifically to support wild surges in bandwidth without collapsing. This is what they've sold themselves on, their ability to do this. And right now they can't do squat."

"Like I said, she has no choice but to blow it up and start over."

"The VP of security is out, and my ass is next in line."

"But why is your ass on the line?"

"Someone's got to take the fall for the breach."

"Why not the Cowboy?"

"He's got her ear. He and his twenty thousand Twitter followers."

"I wish you'd come to me sooner."

"Like I said, where the hell was I going to find you?"

Stuart hated to see Jack so vulnerable, and he wanted to help him, to show this CTIO who it was she had under her roof—one of the legendary, early pioneers of open-source software. Had everyone forgotten? Had Jack forgotten? The guy who revolutionized how software was consumed, the software that made the FANGs possible and landed Jack . . . where?

"My daughter is on the surf team. At five every morning, we drive down to Manhattan Beach so she can ride the waves for an hour before school."

Stuart looked past Jack, as if through the concrete he could see the water and Jack and his daughter in it, a puffy white cloud scudding across the sky.

"It's not such a bad life."

Stuart stood up, went to the whiteboard, and wrote "COMPASS." "Three months, one week, three days, and counting until the Super Bowl. Fine—as you say, it's unrealistic to think we can rip out the existing infrastructure and start over, so we've got to figure out how to layer COMPASS into the existing infrastructure in time for the big game, in a way that will lay the foundation for revamping the long-term network design afterward. We have to iterate, and if we deploy COMPASS with enough modifications to the existing network, including removing the Cowboy's shitty SDN platform, I believe we can do it. It's what happens beyond February that matters, and that's something I want to talk to you about, Jack." Stuart paused and looked around, as if others might be in earshot.

Jack looked around, too, implying that down here, there were no others.

"If this isn't a sign, running into you like this, Jack, I don't know what is"—a sign about his cybersecurity idea, Stuart was about to say—but Jack interrupted.

"Your arm is bleeding," he said.

Stuart looked down. A spot of blood had seeped through his dress shirt. "War wound," Stuart said, waving it off. "Probably scratched it open in my sleep. You have time to grab a drink?"

At eight, after a couple of beers with Jack and a long discussion about data, Stuart went back to his hotel, crawled into bed on an empty stomach, and dreamed that he was climbing a glacier somewhere in the Alps—maybe Mont Blanc, maybe the Matterhorn, definitely Italy—but he never seemed to make it beyond 2,500 meters. He kept asking passersby whether he'd moved up the mountain or not; then he'd be floating above the glacier, but never in the right direction. All the while, he'd see people climbing effortlessly to the top of the ridge, gondolas streaming by, up and down the mountain, some filled with passengers, some empty. He was never able to hitch a ride.

He woke at dawn the next morning, strapped on running shoes, drove down to Manhattan Beach, and set out for a jog along the Strand, where the mansions loomed and white sand stretched for miles. A silvery sheen was seeping onto the horizon, waves rising toward a fading moon, a handful of early risers walking their dogs. He was sweating after only a few blocks, getting his stride. It had been a dream of his and Marie's to one day live steps from an ocean where she could swim every day. It had always been only a matter of time, they'd assured each other. Fifteen years' worth of assuring each other, and now? Had they gone too far this time to ever come home?

At the end of the pier, shaking and out of breath, he braced his forearms on the railing and looked out at the deep, welling infinity. The seagulls cawed. He turned and began to walk back but stopped and looked out over the pier's south railing to watch the surfers, wondering if Jack's daughter was among them. It was amazing they didn't crash into the pier, Stuart thought, along with the waves they were riding. Then, as if hearing his thought, one of them rode a wave right underneath where Stuart stood, through the pillars, to come out on the other side, presumably, where Stuart, in a burst of pure exhilaration, ran to see if she'd make it.

LATER, BACK AT HIS hotel, sitting at the makeshift lobby bar, which had three faux-wood stools and spaced-out bottles of cheap liquor behind the counter, he munched on a late lunch of soggy flatbread while waiting for the Dream Team to show. Their flight had landed two hours ago. Liam had texted, but Stuart hadn't heard from him since. It was a nine-minute drive to the hotel from the airport; the lines at customs couldn't have been that long. What was keeping them? Stuart needed their feedback on the pitch deck for tomorrow, especially after the changes he and Jack had come up with. He called Marie.

"I went for a run along the Strand."

"With whom am I speaking?"

"Ha ha. Anyway, it's beautiful here."

"How's the bite?"

"The bite's fine; it's me that's the problem. I must be clawing at it in my sleep."

"Oh, Stuart, you're going to eat yourself alive."

He clenched his fist a couple times. "It's fine. I shouldn't have mentioned it."

"The doctor said it would be tricky."

"I wish you were here to take care of me."

She let out a groan. There he went again. "Stuart, you've never needed me to take care of you."

He smiled. "Next time you should come with me."

"Next time?"

"I have a good feeling about this, Marie."

"You always do."

"Seeing that book on his desk, Marie. *Your* book—"

"Stuart, it's your book. I simply wrote it."

"Whatever you want to believe, Marie, when I saw it there, I almost lost it."

They fell silent.

"Stuart?"

"I'm here."

"Where is all this headed?"

He knew what she was implying. Admittedly and partly purposely, he'd gone full steam on this thing without bringing her along. She'd been less receptive to talk about work, and he'd been less forthcoming. It had, for the first time in their relationship, become easier this way. "Leverage," he said finally. "We deploy COMPASS for these guys, and it buys us six months' time to pivot into cybersecurity."

After a pause, "What cybersecurity?"

"The gaping cavern of opportunity that exists in that space."

"Did I miss something? I thought we were going bankrupt."

He didn't respond.

"Cybersecurity is not what you do, Stuart."

"It's what we do now, on the periphery of COMPASS." Funny, this was the first time he'd said it out loud, and it sounded just how he'd hoped it would—solid. He'd not talked to anyone about it, except for Jack the night before, not even the Dream Team. "We need different skills, like artificial intelligence and machine learning expertise, to leverage the assets we have; our customers' network data has been staring us in the face—"

"Jim's behind this, isn't he?"

"Oh, relax, Marie. This isn't a conspiracy. Anyway, the bottom line is that to build that expertise, we're going to need money, lots of money—"

"As I recall, the troughs are empty."

"Not when it comes to cybersecurity. This is a new ballgame."

Since when did we stop telling each other things? "I'm confused about what dream you're chasing, Stuart."

"The one where we're living in a house by the ocean. Maybe you've forgotten about it, but I haven't."

"I thought you said this wasn't about money."

He told her to forget it. Just forget it.

That house-on-the-ocean dream was so long ago. In and among all the other dreams. "This CEO thing has gone to your head."

"I know what I'm doing."

A text came in on Stuart's phone. Liam. "Biggy was escorted off to a detention center by Immigration over an hour ago, and I'm still waiting to hear something."

Stuart stared at the text.

"Stuart?"

"What do we do?" Liam wanted to know.

Stuart got off with Marie and sat thinking. *What. Was. Going. On?* This was the moment he would have called on a tenaciously relentless Yelena or a Smally, but he no longer had a Yelena or a Smally. He dialed Jack, who knew some people. A friend of a friend of a friend was an immigration lawyer, who wasn't available but recommended someone else who might be. They finally got in touch with someone who was willing to go to LAX, and she suggested that Stuart and Jack, who'd come right over to the hotel, stay put where they were. Stuart told Jack to go home, but he wouldn't. He sat in a chair and watched Stuart pace from one end of the lobby to the other. After an hour or so, Liam returned with Franco. Still no news on Biggy. Liam was as white as a ghost, and Stuart immediately thought of the babies and that he should not have asked Liam to come. Liam had asked for less travel, and what had Stuart said? "Just this one last time, Liam." Stuart wasn't sure who he hated more in this moment: himself or Marie, for always being right: *This CEO thing has gone to your head.* Liam needed to be in Singapore in case the social worker showed up at his home unannounced. The adoption was not a done deal. The babies could still be sent back. "I'm booking you a flight home," Stuart told Liam, who said that he'd already looked for flights home and had found none available. "You were looking in coach class. I'm booking you in first."

Laurie showed up out of the blue. She'd flown her prop plane down from Arizona, where she'd been beached after the Exchange project ended and working remotely on internal projects while dealing with issues she was having with her significant other. She found Stuart in the lobby, took a seat in the sectional across from him, kicked off her shoes, threw her socked feet up on the coffee table, and confided in Stuart a few things that he was not prepared to be told. Stuart listened and empathized and thought, *Are our problems not all the same?* She needed to work. *Real* work. The work was the thing. And why hadn't Stuart called her? She wanted to know. She *was* DevOps, after all—a big component of what NEWTV needed.

"I did call you. Why do you think you're here?"

"No one called me. I just came."

Stuart was confused. Well, anyway, he had meant to call her.

She did not buy that answer. "I used to be your first call, back in the times I don't want to remember. Do you remember?"

He remembered. Her implication was that since she'd become a she, he'd not treated her with the same level of reverence he'd had when she was a he. "Get yourself a long-term-stay room here, and welcome to the party, Laurie. You might be here for some time. How do you feel about football? As I recall, you were a Patriots fan."

Meanwhile, the Cowboy, who had gotten wind of Stuart's meeting with the CTIO and her team the following day, had begun a Twitter rant directed at Javelina and the "joker who started it."

"Did you see his latest?" Laurie asked, showing Stuart her phone.

"I won't give him the benefit of paying attention," Stuart said. Then he stared at her phone. The Cowboy was threatening to sue Stuart for "stealing" his IP all those years ago when Stuart had worked for him.

"He's toxic," Jack said.

"He's a flea on the ass of a dog," Stuart said. "Niraj took out more than fifteen patents for Javelina and COMPASS, both of which were developed years *after* I worked with the Cowboy. He's got no basis."

But still, the suit would be a drain on resources. Not to mention the money wasted on lawyer fees. Money they didn't have.

Liam urged Stuart to negotiate with the Cowboy, to take him for drinks, walk him off the ledge—now was not the time to pit the two companies against each other.

"Not having an IP strategy is a mistake you make only once" was Stuart's response. He shot down a Nespresso from a machine they'd found behind the unmanned bar. "While half of you were still on training wheels, my underfunded team and I were working on one of the first e-commerce payment platforms. It was way ahead of its time, long before anyone had ever heard of PayPal. We didn't have the money to patent the IP; we just had some really smart people who knew banking and technology and saw the potential of e-commerce, and we figured we'd raise serious money after launch, which would have allowed us to tap into funds from a major New York retail bank, and then along came PayPal, with one hundred million in VC funding and founders whose names I won't utter because I don't like the taste of shit in my mouth. They built a me-too platform—to this day, I believe there was a spy on our team who was feeding PayPal information—and launched it six months after ours, but with significantly more cachet, their backers and clients calling in all the favors, and took what little market there was at the time. This was in late 2000, remember; then they bought us for peanuts to add what IP they couldn't build to their portfolio. We had zero leverage, our retail bank having bailed from the partnership. And from the ashes rose Tesla, Palantir, SpaceX . . . You're fucking welcome! If the Cowboy wants a battle, he's going to get one!" Stuart pounded his fist on the table. The water bottles jumped.

At three in the morning, Stuart told everyone to go to bed, but no one went to bed. They were all seated in a corner of the lobby by the fake fire pit. Laurie wanted to know what tools they'd used to uncover the NEWTV hack. Stuart told her they, spearheaded by Franco, had built their own tools. That they were sitting on a mound of data of which they'd barely scratched the surface. Stuart, half delirious from jet lag and sleep deprivation and worry over Biggy, glanced at Jack, who gave him a nod, and then leaned in and said to the group, "Imagine what we could do with *real* intelligent automation." He turned to Franco. "No offense."

"None taken."

Stuart continued, "Imagine what we could do with intelligent automation based on artificial intelligence and machine learning, in terms of developing predictive analytics capabilities in identifying and shutting down diverse rogue network attacks before they do any real damage."

The lobby doors slid open. They all looked, but it wasn't Biggy. Liam turned back around, his frustration visibly growing. He glanced at his watch and asked, "But don't a thousand companies already do this?"

"They might have predictive analytics solutions, but the combination of the core COMPASS platform and the network data we've amassed through our MNS offering, together with the machine learning algorithms, will allow us to identify specific patterns and enable us to differentiate our services and emerge front and center in the growing cybersecurity space."

"And we have access to that network data? Legally, I mean?" Franco wanted to know.

"You can thank Niraj for that. He negotiated it into the contracts."

"He may be an asshole, but he's not stupid," Liam said, and everyone looked at him. No one had gone as far yet to disparage Niraj publicly. It wasn't how Stuart operated.

"As long as it doesn't leave our 'walled garden,'" Stuart said, "we can do with it as we please."

"We don't know shit about AI," Liam said.

"I know some guys," Jack said. "Some Ukrainians stuck out in Orange County."

"What's going on in Orange County?"

"They're out there building some kind of AI platform for a Saudi prince who lives in the hills there or something, only this prince seems to have left them on Fantasy Island, because they've been holed up at the Ritz-Carlton in Laguna Niguel, waiting around for him to show up and be more specific about what he wants. Three months like this."

"Sounds like a story I've heard before. How many engineers?" Stuart asked.

"Six. Not cheap."

"The money from NEWTV will give us leverage," Stuart said.

"Assuming we win NEWTV," Liam said.

"We'll win NEWTV. Just like Biggy will walk through those doors any moment now." Sometimes, Stuart believed that the power of absolute surety was what got you places. That by believing with everything you had that you would win, you won. And he did, in terms of Biggy anyway. At five, Arman from Iran walked through those doors, disheveled and trying to make light of the situation, though he was clearly agitated.

His name was the same as someone's on the no-fly list. Stuart handed Biggy something stiff. Biggy's hands shook as he held his drink but did not sip from it. "Are you a believer in the words of the Prophet Muhammad?" the immigration officer kept screaming at him, for eight straight hours, in which Biggy said little, and they finally let him go.

They took what remained of the bottle of Jim Beam outside and sat in rubber lounge chairs by the kiddie pool because everyone was too wired to sleep. Biggy's mind was in a spiral about his flight back to Singapore. If he left the United States again, could he ever get back in? His kid was here. Well, not here—Virginia. It was the first any of them had heard about a kid, and, true to form, no one probed. Biggy went on. The United States was his home, his refuge. The country that had given him asylum all those years ago, no questions asked—him and his brother. They'd been able to go to university. His brother was a doctor now. At one point, there in that detention room, the supervisor and then his supervisor had mused sadistically about sending Biggy back to Iran, where he belonged. He'd be persecuted if that happened. It was a threat. They were trying to scare him. When had everyone gotten so mean? This country he'd always felt so indebted to now thought him the scum of the earth.

It reminded Stuart of everything he hated about what had become of the United States, though what was he going to do, leave? Go sell his wares somewhere else? He'd already done that. And look where it had gotten him. Right back here.

THE NEXT DAY, WHILE Liam headed to the airport, Stuart, Biggy, and Franco, bleary-eyed and solidarity-fueled, headed into the CTIO's conference room, passing the Phenom on his way out. "Howdy, cowboys! You rebels want to grab drinks later?"

Stuart ignored him and kept walking.

The room was packed with network and security engineers, solutions architects, the compliance and risk management teams, governance, the CTIO, a good amount of gray around the table, more crumpled white dress shirts, certainly no acne. The few women who were there were stuffed into blazers and comfortable shoes, and Jack slouched far down in the back. Haggard, they looked as if they'd been in that conference room since the beginning of time. Laptops and phones, cast-off food wrappers, stale cookies, doughnuts, and coffee cups were strewn about the boat-shaped table, which looked as if it were sinking.

When Stuart walked in, the curtains were drawn to block out the glare from the always present sunshine and the roar of planes on their approach to LAX—the Dreamliner, Stuart imagined, making its final descent as he began his presentation.

Keep your enemies close, he quipped to himself, just before he started. It was what Niraj had always said, but Stuart was no Niraj. On the 65-inch HD screen, he re-created two scenarios of the NEWTV hack, one using COMPASS as an overlay on the Cowboy's platform, and one using COMPASS as its own platform. It was easy to see which one outperformed—it took all of about ten minutes for Stuart to eviscerate the Cowboy's platform.

"The December and February deadlines don't give you enough time to do what you need to do, which is blow up what you've got and start over with COMPASS as its own platform, so here's the plan I propose:

"Step one: Overlay COMPASS and create a work-around for the Cowboy's platform to meet the year-end AriaNet-NEWTV merged customer platform deadline. It's a Band-Aid but your only choice.

"Step two: Unplug the Cowboy's platform two months later for the Super Bowl stream in February. Another Band-Aid, but at least we'll curtail instability. Vita's MNS engineering team will use our new AI analytics tools to provide the around-the-clock monitoring you'll need as fifty million football fans log in all at once for three hours, to ensure no breaks or breaches or lapses.

"Step three: Once the Super Bowl streams successfully, next up is the revolution. AriaNet announces the SEC's approval of its merger with NEWTV, touting COMPASS as the solution enabling its secure, scalable platform, at which point we blow up the overlay *and* the underlying platform and install COMPASS++ the way it should have been installed in the first place."

There was some coughing and throat clearing.

"And how does this revolution work, exactly?" the CTIO asked.

"The opposite of how you might think," Stuart responded. "It's called iteration. This is how we've done it before, and it works. One workload—one tiny workload. Test it. Do it again. That's the beauty of the cloud: You don't have to wait eight weeks to provision a server, a firewall, or a database; it's all done with a click of a button. The cloud gives you a level of agility you've never had before. You can fail fast and you can fail a lot, if you keep learning. You don't have to spend millions of dollars to know if a workload or the underlying platform scales; you know right away because you fail right away. We'll show you how to take advantage of this. And once we do, once you prove one case a success to your business users, you're going to have a revolution on your hands."

Jack raised an eyebrow. Not exactly how he and Stuart had practiced the spiel the night before. Stuart had gone a little rogue about the "revolution," not to mention the AI tools on hand for step two, but one of his guys had just spent the night in a detention center, and then those twin babies . . . Stuart needed this win. He needed it badly, and he was fed up with all the bullshit, the Cowboy's crap, all of it. He was starting to wonder if Asia had turned him into a pansy.

The CTIO made a verbal commitment to Stuart that afternoon. The Cowboy was out, per Stuart's plan, at the end of the year.

"AI tools?" Jack asked.

"You mentioned Ukrainians?" Stuart responded.

CHAPTER 36
NOVEMBER 2012

THEY WERE MEETING ON A Saturday, on the down-low, because technically the Ukrainians were still working for the prince, and with the prince there would be no moonlighting. But they were bored, so bored. Bored and homesick. They all had US visas, thanks to the prince. But they wanted something real, something to sink their teeth into, and this was real. Jack, father of open-source—if he wasn't real, who was?

As Stuart recalled, Jack had always had shit cars, and this one did not disappoint: a dented and rusted-over Toyota Corolla with a surfboard strapped to the roof. It rattled all the way down the 405 freeway, while out the window shiny BMWs and Porsches whizzed past.

"What a waste," Stuart said, "this COMPASS layover we just sold them."

Jack did not dispute the point.

"Twenty years ago, we'd never have agreed to a compromise."

"We're different than we were twenty years ago."

"I guess. Maybe. Really?"

"Trust me, it's not a bad thing."

"Fine, okay. But please don't tell anyone. Not Marie, certainly. She still thinks I'm nuts, and I prefer it that way."

They drove up the long, winding entrance to the Ritz-Carlton hotel perched on the cliffs of the Pacific, where they were to meet Aleksander, the Ukrainian team leader, in the lobby lounge. Jack handed his keys to the unimpressed valet. Then he and Stuart ducked behind a couple of blond bombshells heading into the lobby, because Jack thought he recognized Aleksander in the black Range Rover now pulling up behind them, and Stuart did not want this guy to see the CEO of what was still considered a relatively hotshot, if burned-out, startup crawl out of a shitty Corolla. Toyota as a client had always sounded so sexy until this moment.

Three hours later, when Stuart and Jack left the Ritz, as waves crashed in the distance and a breeze swirled around them, Stuart was feeling very pleased to have found himself in sync with the Ukrainian on most aspects of the cybersecurity play, its value and future direction. Aleksander was a creative, smart, affable guy with whom Stuart immediately connected, even if he did look like a thug. And yes, the Rover was indeed Aleksander's—he'd made some money selling his previous venture to Rackspace.

They drove in silence, Stuart taking in all that Aleksander had said, like how little the industry still knew about deep learning, what it might mean to misclassify a hacker, or even a hack. Trolls were getting savvier. They were learning how to trick AI algorithms into believing they were authorized persons. So, possibly and ironically, building AI to identify rogue attacks on a system might make the system *more* vulnerable.

"Do not assume the machine thinks like we do, because it doesn't," Aleksander had stressed, the main point he'd wanted to get across. "Do not think we are superior to the machine, because we aren't. Do not think we complement the machine, because we don't, not anymore, anyway. Google's AlphaZero proved that."

Aleksander had gone on to say that while the AI Liam built to uncover the NEWTV hacker did its job, make no mistake, it was old-school, the first coming of AI, in which very explicit rules are set down for the machine to follow. But now, he said, we are in the second coming of AI; the machine follows not rules we've designed but rules of its own design. The capacity of processing power and the birth of cloud data storage cleared the way for that. Now, a machine might solve a problem *unlike* a human might, and we need to let it. People talk about empathy, judgment, and creativity, about how the machine will never have these human traits. And while it is true that a machine perhaps won't bear a cognitive trait the way a human might, that doesn't mean it might not bear this trait in a way that remains unrecognizable to us. We assume that our human design is the optimal design. Where does this inherent superiority complex come from? Who is to say that evolutionary forces won't create a more intelligent design for living that has nothing to do with humans?

This latter part of Aleksander's dissertation, about human design vs. the optimal design, brought out what Stuart considered a very lively and healthy debate on the subject of "ethical" AI. Where would Vita draw the line, for instance?

"There is no line," Aleksander had said. "Don't believe that the machine will augment jobs. It has been proven that a machine and a human working together aren't as efficient as a machine working on its own."

Jack had taken Pacific Coast Highway back to El Segundo, a longer but much more scenic drive that wound along cliffs through the towns of Laguna Beach and Corona del Mar, flattening out at the wide beaches of Newport and Huntington. It was stop-and-go with lights and beach traffic—people loaded down with beach gear and wearing flip-flops, surfers hoisting boards onto their heads as waves crashed beneath a blue and cloudless sky. Windows down. Marley in Stuart's head. Ocean air like a dream.

"Did you buy that stuff Aleksander said about evolution?" Stuart asked.

"You mean, do I think machines will rule the world?"

"Yes, that's what I'm asking. Should we be contributing

to our own demise? Or should we be doing everything in our power to stop it, like we should be doing about climate change?"

Jack was discerning the break in the waves and didn't immediately respond.

"It's wild to think about," Stuart went on. "How much we still have to learn. Another interesting puzzle to solve, one in a long line of puzzles that can and will ultimately be solved. So why should we not be the ones to solve it?"

Jack said, "Do you want to know what I really think?"

Stuart stared at Jack's profile, the wind blowing through what was left of his hair, waiting for him to continue. But he did not. He pulled over and into a parking lot lining a long stretch of wide beach. He got out, went around back, opened the trunk, dropped his jeans, and pulled on trunks. "Only a couple good waves left," he said through the hatchback opening. Then he tucked his surfboard under his arm and headed down some steps and onto the wide stretch of sand toward the ocean. Stuart sat motionless and watched him go, unsettled by the delay. He'd been eager to get back to the hotel, but for what? The Dream Team had their own lives; he had nowhere to be. He got out of the car, grabbing his computer bag because it was a rule of his never to leave it unmanned in a car, and trailed Jack down the cement steps, pausing at the sand as if it were some foreign object. Always the conundrum of what to do with the shoes, something Marie gave him endless grief about. Stuart liked the beach as much as the next guy; he just couldn't stand the feeling of sand between his toes. He sat down on one of the steps and took off his shoes, tucked his socks inside, rolled up his jeans, slung his bag diagonally across his shoulders, and, carrying his shoes in one hand, set out across the sand toward the water.

The beach was windswept, the sun starting its descent. Dogs with long, galloping limbs chased balls along the shore, waves curling in the near distance, a tumble of whitewash.

Surfers' Beach, a sign said, and now Stuart understood why Jack had agreed so readily to come to a work meeting on a Saturday when he could be with his family. Jack, who had sprinted with his board across the sand, was now running with it into the waves. Stuart watched him push his way out beyond the break. Pushing and pushing. It took some time, the sand growing cooler on Stuart's feet as he got closer to the ocean. Once there, he pulled up his shirtsleeve and dipped his forearm into the salt water because the *tokay* wound had reopened again, after another night of picking and clawing in his sleep. As with his cuticles, he could not seem to control himself. Once something was there to pick apart, it was hard to keep himself from going back to it. The salt burned. Jack had made it past the break. He was sitting up on his board, staring out at the horizon, where the sea met sky, waiting for the right wave. Waiting and waiting. And then he kept waiting, the swells coming and going, Jack staring out past all of them.

CHAPTER 37
JANUARY 2013

THE DANE, WEARING A CAPE over an elegant pantsuit, had come to the bodega to present Marie and Stuart with one of her paintings as a parting gift, though it was not certain who was parting or for where or if this was all completely metaphorical.

The Dane glanced around the place.

"Stuart's in El Segundo," Marie told her, presuming that was who the Dane was looking for, though the two had never met in person.

"Where is El Segundo?"

"Southern California."

"Is he coming back?"

"Back and forth. Both forward and backward. It depends on how you look at it."

The Dane nodded absently. She set the painting down by the door and walked into the living area as if on impulse. Cape still on, she began rolling up one of the Agra carpets. She suddenly found them too dark and morbid. Marie came and helped her, for lack of knowing what else to do.

After the rug was pushed safely to the side, the Dane stood up, hands on hips, and said, "I'm envisioning a bright and happy space." It was as if, with the rug gone, everything else had borne its true self. She walked to the mantel and with one hand swiped the tiny, dark Buddha statues into her cape. She then went and deposited them outside in the

Japanese garden. She returned and had Marie help her hoist onto the mantel the painting she had brought, in place of the Buddhas. They stood back and admired it for some minutes. A purplish mass of shifting violet whose shape would remain elusive to Marie. An elephant?

Soon after, they repositioned the couch to face the window, which the Dane proceeded to shut so that she could crank up the AC, because by now she was caked in a dusty sheen. The cape came off, at last. Then she fell onto the couch and announced that Giorgio had gone bankrupt.

Marie tried not to focus on the irony of that statement. Out the bodega door, she noticed the Dane's luggage piled up.

Or at least that was Giorgio's story, the Dane went on— he had money in the Caymans he refused to admit to.

Marie went to the kitchen and returned with ice water, at the Dane's request.

In the meantime, Giorgio was moving them all back to Italy to live with his mother. But Italy was where the Dane drew the line. She could not live with Giorgio's mother, and she had told him so, that she would rather leave him. "If you leave, you'll do so with nothing," he had responded. She knew he didn't love her, but she had not been prepared for him to call her bluff, for she had no intention of leaving the children. Her fingers trembled over the thick black pearls at her throat. "I brought along some heirlooms for safekeeping."

Marie, seated across from the Dane, had no words.

"I won't stay long," the Dane said. "Just until I figure out what I'm going to do." Then she went and examined her face in the antique wall mirror, as if there were no crack straight down its center. "Of course, the hedge fund is underwater."

Marie closed her eyes for a moment, for she had guessed that, as she might have guessed everything that would happen to her until the day she died. She had worked hard for that money. But what had money ever done for either her or Stuart but make life easier?

"Stuart's going to kill me," she said.

MARIE LEFT JIM A voice mail. He called back a few days later. Yes, he had something for her. He went on to explain a very orthogonal and esoteric business problem a friend of his was trying to solve. She'd been bracing herself for some complicated telecommunications-arbitrage play, but what Jim said was tanning salons. She took a quick moment to regear her brain. Tanning salons? His friend needed someone to help him develop a pitch for this groundbreaking, green energy–fueled tanning-salon business, and the first person who had come to Jim's mind was Marie. She spent an hour on Skype with this friend, who told her all about his plans for merging multiple small tanning salons into one, also known as a "rollup." She told his friend that she'd think about it. The worst part was that when she told Stuart about the idea of her flying to Texas to build a business plan for tanning salons with Jim's friend, he said that it sounded interesting.

Interesting? He wasn't listening, surely. Because if he *had* been, he would have heard.

TO TEXAS SHE WENT. Jim flew in for the first week to set the strategy, and they worked together as they always had, Jim attacking the idea in ways no one else might. Marie interpolating and translating his words so that the others could understand them, like translating from Japanese to Greek when all she spoke was English. And yet it clicked, she his missing gear. She wasn't sure what to expect about that other thing, his schoolboy crush. She was prepared for a resurgence, a sense of awkwardness on his part, or, worst case, his bringing up what he'd said to her all those years ago, but it wasn't like that. In fact, he seemed slightly out of sorts, more alienated from the humans than she remembered. Perhaps he was just older. He might not even remember what had happened, which made her wonder if she'd made it all up. Was anything that happened in the past real, or made to be in our minds? A dog had replaced Marie—a Labradoodle that accompanied Jim everywhere, sprawling over his lap or feet. Strangely enough, she found herself feeling deflated. Perhaps she'd needed a little flattery. Attention. The awkwardness of youth. But now the dog.

CHAPTER 38

MARIE MET STUART AT the baggage claim, even though she had no baggage, just a swimsuit in her carry-on for the ocean she'd planned on spending most of the weekend in. It had been cold in Austin. Cold and *dry*. Her skin was cracked, and her lips were chafed. She'd stayed inside. Gigs didn't have hours. She'd worked until the work was done. No breaks, lapses, or pauses. Until now. She wasn't sure why Stuart had demanded her presence in El Segundo. It was February, the platform merger had been a success, and now the Super Bowl. He'd be on call up until and through the game on Sunday, though he assured her that everything was ready, they were just going through routine tests at this point, and he wanted her there.

Flights were being called on loudspeakers all around them, general mayhem and chaos, and she came toward him slowly in some culmination of all the reunions they'd had like this one. Airports. An ache dull and worn. A week's worth of facial scruff grazed her cheek and then hovered there just long enough for the chemicals that lived at the base of their attraction to churn and combust into the scent that never failed to direct them back to each other. Then he handed her the coffee, and they got the hell out of there.

Behind them, the ghosts of two people falling into each other's arms.

The next morning, she swam to the pier and he ran along the shore beside her with a towel around his neck. They walked back along the Strand, she wrapped in the towel, pausing every so often to stare up at one of the mansions that spoke to them in some way. One for its clean lines and walled windows. Another for its beachy feel. Then that ridiculously gaudy one that looked like an Italian palazzo. Or the one in the shape of a container ship. There was even one house that had almost no windows. Why? People were weird, that's why. And anyway, what did it matter? Most of the houses were darkened, empty. Had they always been that way?

"It all feels so behind me now," she said, as they stood before one house with a beautiful mosaic window. "Behind me in a good way, I mean. A way in which I've grown bigger than all this. I think it was Asia, don't you?"

He tried to contemplate Asia, but for some reason, he felt spent and couldn't.

She looked at him. He seemed far away.

They continued walking.

"Will you rent a corporate apartment here if the Super Bowl proves a success?"

He didn't want to say anything. Couldn't. Not just yet. He was superstitious that way. Just three months ago, he'd thought Vita was done.

She knew what he was thinking: that he didn't want to jinx it. She changed the subject. "And the board?"

"They're off my back for now. In these past few months, with the revenues from the NEWTV overlay, we've stopped the bleeding. The financials have stabilized. The Cowboy's Twitter threats have cooled. And WIPRO is on the back burner."

"It's incredible, really. One day the world's going to end, and the next—"

"Riding high in April," he said.

She said, "Shot down in May."

"But I know I'm gonna change that tune, when I'm back on top in June."

Stuart's ode to Sinatra. "That's Life"—the song he liked to blast in particularly possessed moments.

"That's why I never give up, Marie."

The insinuation was that she did.

"By the way, have you heard from Jim? I've been trying to get ahold of him. I need his buy-in on the Ukrainians before we get too far down this road. He's going to have to help me sell it to the board."

"He's off on a trek along the Camino de Santiago."

Stuart stopped walking.

"You know, that pilgrimage in the North of Spain."

"He never told me he was going."

"He usually doesn't."

Stuart took off walking again, head down. A few minutes later, when he realized she wasn't there, he turned and came back for her.

"Don't tell me I didn't warn you about Jim," she said. "And anyway, you're already too far down this road."

She tightened the towel around her shoulders.

He rubbed her upper arms. "You're cold."

"I'm okay."

"You're shivering."

"Stuart," she said. "I'm going back to Singapore after my project's over."

It was something he knew but didn't want to acknowledge.

"There's nothing here for me any longer."

"I'm here."

At Rosecrans, they paused before the steep incline, two blocks they would have to scale to get to their car.

"Come on," he said. "I'll push you."

AT THE BAR. LESS than twenty-four hours before kickoff. Tacos and tequila and the team. There was not much for them to do now but stand watch over final test runs that were simply going through the motions. Laurie and Biggy had their laptops out on the bar counter, a beer on either side. Franco was strutting around in a Messi jersey out of protest—the team was mostly indifferent to American football, except Laurie, who wore her Patriots jersey—especially with Ronaldo doing his thing on one of the screens behind the bar, where people had gathered to shake their heads at one more spectacular goal.

Liam was also in town, having flown in for the cybersecurity sessions with the Ukrainians scheduled for the following week. "What do you think about this picture for our baby announcement?" His face beamed behind his glasses as he showed everyone the photo on his phone. Each jet-black-haired baby was lying blissfully in a blanket in a big cast-iron pot on the stove, the mother holding the lids up in each hand as if she were about to cover the pots and boil herself up a nice baby stew. Stuart couldn't remember the last time he'd seen Marie smile so deliciously. Then he told Liam that the photo might be problematic. Even though their adoption was all but secured, the filing *was* still pending, and Liam, with his driest wit, said that yeah, Stuart was probably right, and just as laughter broke out, one of the tests blew up and everyone's phones went off.

Franco tried solving the problem first, and when he couldn't, Biggy got involved. Liam. Unflinchingly, one by one, the others. No one seemed too concerned, though it was always so hard for Marie to tell. With Stuart, the world could be coming to an end and he'd say, "There's always a solution, Marie." Soon the entire group had dispersed to far corners of the bar amid grumbles and curse words. Stuart took a position over Liam's shoulder, everyone all at once immersed in that *other* language. Stuart was the last and final person to get out his laptop, while giving Marie a nice-knowing-you shrug. She needed no apology, nor pity, and, before bearing witness to what she knew to be Stuart's middle-of-a-coding-crisis petulance, she gathered her things and left.

A few hours later, at nine, the glitch was still not fixed. Liam roused the Indians in Jaipur, Stuart called Jack at home, and they all returned to the NEWTV offices. They spent the subsequent eight hours debugging and testing over and over while somebody made coffee runs and Stuart placated the NEWTV CTIO over the phone. Before they knew it, the sun was setting over the Indians in the East and rising for them out here in the West—Marie on an earlier-than-planned flight back to Austin—and then, eight hours later, it was the reverse: the Indians had spent all night and the Americans all day so that an entire country could begin logging in to the streaming platform to watch the Super Bowl without one glitch or lag. Every one of the team's bleary eyes was glued to their monitors as the servers loaded up real-time bandwidth with not one break or breach, though that wasn't to say that hundreds of hackers didn't try. But, thanks to Aleksander's help, the hackers met roadblocks at every turn. The COMPASS overlay had officially done its job, and now, once Stuart got word from the CTIO, assuming word would come from the CTIO, positive word—though Stuart never liked to assume these things—the team could at last get to work building for NEWTV what they'd come here to build for it: COMPASS++ with a kick-ass AI engine, driven by the Ukrainians, all this giving them the leverage and revenue cushion they needed to pivot to cybersecurity.

It wasn't until the third quarter of the game that each of them remembered their distaste for American football, but for Laurie, and they switched off their monitors and went back to the hotel, too wired to sleep. Someone had brought down a bottle of tequila. It occurred to them that they should celebrate. Stuart told everyone to take Monday and Tuesday off, and, three shots in, Laurie mentioned that she was flying her plane up to the Bay Area in the morning to see friends. Stuart, slightly intoxicated, guilt-fueled, imagining Marie already back at work, gone and lost and obsessing over her analysis—they'd not even had a chance to say goodbye—feeling this strange and vacuous sense of longing, asked Laurie if he could hitch a ride.

It was a decision he was now regretting. The Santa Ana winds had kicked up from the north, fires to the west. The world tasted smoldering and burned, and through it all the plane jolted and thumped. Stuart slammed shut his eyes and gripped the edges of his seat the entire way, reminding himself that he should not drink tequila with twenty-five-year-olds. That puddle jumper he'd forced on Marie in Bangkok came roaring back—how many lives did he think he had? She had threatened to leave him then, too, he remembered, after they'd landed. She was done with all this. She was done with it now. A lifetime of being done.

When they landed in San Jose, there was a message from the NEWTV CTIO asking Stuart when he could come in to talk about COMPASS++ and AI and MNS and all of it. The SEC had conditionally approved the merger with AriaNet. Stuart stumbled outside and puked onto the tarmac.

NEAR THE OLD FIRE station, his father lived in a home with other aging veterans. In a chair in front of the TV, with a basketball game playing, he took a moment to recognize Stuart, then lumbered to his feet to greet his son and did that routine where he tripped and fell over. The catch and hug—as if the only way one man could hug another without looking untoward was if it was an accident. Stuart helped his father back into his chair and said, very delicately and as he'd been coached earlier by one of the nurses, that perhaps it was time he got a walker. It was something they'd been trying to convince his father of for a couple of years now, since he'd taken a few spills. Not so unpredictably, his father said, "I'd rather die tumbling down five flights of stairs than use a walker, son."

"And I've been thinking about that, Dad. Because the thing is, you could tumble down those stairs and *not* die."

His father contemplated Stuart suspiciously for a few moments. "Always the clever boy."

"Just try the walker, Dad."

"I won't need a walker. I'm going to have knee surgery."

"Knee surgery? You said Pilates was strengthening your knee, that you weren't having the surgery."

"I've decided I want to give it a try. I've got to be able to walk, son, and don't worry, my fireman's pension covers most of the expenses—we take care of our own."

"But are you sure—"

"I'm sure."

"When?"

His eyes grew iridescent. "I forget. Soon, I think."

"Who can we ask?"

"Janice. You can ask Janice."

"Who's Janice?"

"My lady friend."

"I thought her name was Beatrice."

His father squinted. "Who's Beatrice?"

Stuart exhaled, long and slow.

"Janice is all right, though I mostly put up with her. She never laughs at my jokes. You can come if you want. For the surgery."

His father never asked Stuart to *come* for anything. He never wanted to be a bother.

"I'll make the trip, Dad, but I need to know when it is. Is there a doctor I can talk to?"

"Oh, don't bother. Forget I asked. I know you're busy with that company of yours."

His voice seemed thinner than normal when he said this. Stuart wondered if something else was going on.

"Are they treating you well?" his father asked.

"They who?"

"Those people—you know, those people you work for."

Stuart stared at his father as if from a great distance. There had been a day, early on, when he used to tell his father about his hopes and dreams, and even though his father could barely keep up with the state of the world that Stuart was describing, he always had a kind, encouraging word to say. "You're passionate about what you do, son; that's what matters." But somewhere along the way, when their relationship was reduced to phone conversations once a week and then once a month, it got too hard to convey to his father all the complexities of his life. For instance, that the bankruptcy option he'd just possibly skirted for his company was par for the course and not the end of the world. Not a failure. His dad had been a failure, according to his dad, a failed actor, which was why he had become a fireman. He was big on failure, had a scent for it. And for Stuart, it had just gotten too difficult to explain to his father that neither he nor anyone else, for that matter, had failed. Not if they had tried. Stuart finally just started telling his father that everything was all right even when it wasn't, and he could hear the loss in his father's voice because they both knew it wasn't the truth. How could life be all right? So Stuart called less frequently and his father called less frequently, even while they both thought only about calling each other more. It was an entirely unnecessary downward spiral, and oh, how Stuart missed those early days when there weren't all these layers of living between them.

"I asked if they're treating you well. Are they, son?"

Stuart, who'd been staring at something on the floor, looked up, having barely heard his father's question because he had so many questions of his own.

"Because if they're not, you just let me know and I'll show those kids a thing or two."

It was a little joke his father always told, and Stuart started to respond, but then his voice cracked. The emotion was unexpected but not out of nowhere. His father had saved children from burning buildings but couldn't for the life of him save his own son from those mean, elusive bullies. Stuart put his head in his hands.

"It's all right, son." A hand heavy on his shoulder. "I'm sure everything is going to be all right."

There wasn't anything wrong, Stuart wanted to say. *That's the thing, Dad, don't you see? Things are turning around, finally.*

On his way out, he went and found the nurse, who pointed to a Janice, who knew nothing about any knee surgery.

CHAPTER 39

WHILE JIM WAS OFF on his trek along the Camino, Marie, settled back in Austin, began unpacking the strategy she and Jim and Jim's friend had set out. She dug more deeply into the analysis involved in merging the salons with a green-energy core—how easy it was to fall back into the grind. The fight and the glory. The monotony and the thrill. How quickly her mind could churn value out of so little. Create numbers that worked. Stuart had been right. The project was interesting, especially the green component. But then, wasn't anything? If you sank your mind into what you were doing, couldn't you make anything interesting? Forget if it was useful. Did it need to be? Was riding around the country on a motorcycle useful? An old college boyfriend of Marie's had given her his very worn and coveted paperback copy of the book *The Art of Motorcycle Maintenance*, insisting that she read it. This boyfriend had journeyed through the Amazon and Machu Picchu while breezing through a double major of philosophy and mathematics. The margins were filled with his pencil markings, and sentences were underlined on every page, many of which were dog-eared. When she finished the book, she couldn't help wondering what this boyfriend was getting that she wasn't.

Now she knew. Riding around fixing a motorcycle was not unlike analyzing the efficiencies of green energy for tanning salons if you were fully present with what you were doing. The salon owners were all women. A rowdy bunch. They went out for drinks. The potential of this roll-up was all very new to them, the possibilities exciting. They didn't understand a thing that Jim or his friend had said. Marie explained it to them. They wanted to understand. The money they might make from this would send their daughters to college.

After six weeks, the business plan was written and Marie was set to return to Singapore with a check for $50,000. It was up to the salon ladies now to execute on the plan and achieve the targeted returns Marie had forecasted, the first part of which was to raise the funding with Jim's friend. But could these ladies proceed without Marie? Yes, they could, Marie assured them. They'd taken Marie out for drinks to say goodbye, and one of them, the really smart one, hadn't looked so sure. This woman could drink, this really smart one; a couple martinis in, and Marie didn't have to tell her what she was already reading in Marie's eyes—it was a slim chance that these ladies could raise the funds, much less achieve the anticipated returns. It was the reality of any startup.

ON HER WAY BACK to Singapore, Marie stopped in San Jose because Stuart had asked her to meet him there for his father's knee surgery, and she wanted to do this one last thing for him. But when her plane landed, a text from Stuart was waiting for her. He was on a flight to India. Something had come up; he'd call when his plane landed in Delhi. He'd be in San Jose as soon as he could. Marie was not pleased by this. Stuart's father had grown ornery and bitter with age and she did not want to be alone with him, though apparently there was someone named Janice now.

Marie rented a car at the San Jose airport and drove straight to the assisted-living facility, and it was just as she'd feared: the soar of anticipation in Stuart's father's eyes, followed by the sinking disappointment as he looked past Marie and saw no one behind her.

"I meant to call and ask when Stuart would be arriving," he said in that deep, trembling baritone. "What time should I pick him up at the airport?"

"Stuart's not coming for a few more days, Tom. Something came up at work."

He seemed out of sorts and disoriented, and his normally carefully combed-over hair was sticking straight up. "I don't need to pick him up?"

Marie fell limp to one side. *Oh, Tom,* she thought.

Tom had once commandeered one of those mammoth hook-and-ladder rigs through red lights and down wrong sides of chaotic San Francisco streets—don't try and tell him he couldn't drive. His obstinacy to keep driving had become as much of a problem as his determination to keep walking. In the parking lot, Marie had seen Tom's truck, the one Stuart bought him after executing a particularly lucrative stock grant, the kind of truck Tom had always dreamed about but couldn't afford. Luckily, he could never seem to find the keys anymore, thanks to Stuart, who'd taken them.

"No need to pick up Stuart from the airport, Tom," Marie responded. "He won't be here until *after* the surgery, which is when you'll need him the most. Speaking of which, I think we should go to the hospital now. Are you ready?"

He peered at her for a moment, before it struck him. "Ah, the surgery. That's why you're here. I knew there was some reason. I'm sure everything is going to be fine. You're not worried, are you?"

The question surprised her. "Why should I be worried?"

"Good," he said. "I'm not worried either."

He looked worried, though. He mentioned Stuart again, asking if he needed a ride from the airport, and then Janice materialized. Janice fixed Tom's hair and did all the responding, and Marie thought, *Janice! Beautiful, doting Janice! Where have you been all these years?*

THE SURGERY WENT WELL. Tom was moved to recovery and woke in good spirits. Marie had him speak to Stuart on the phone so he could tell him the good news, and the two joked about Tom's showing Stuart a thing or two the next time they were on the golf course together. Just like old times. But then later that evening, when the light outside the window faded, Tom's eyes began darting anxiously about the room. By night-fall, his gaze had settled on one particular spot where the ceiling met the wall. "Are there bugs up there?" he asked Marie.

"No," she said. "There are no bugs up there."

His eyes, wide with alarm, had landed on Marie now.

"What?" she asked. "What is it, Tom?"

He seemed afraid to say. And then, "It's just . . . It seems as if . . . Are you floating in the air upside down?"

She glanced to either side of her. "No, Tom."

He began fiddling with his IV, as if he were trying to rip it out. Marie jumped out of her chair and tried to restrain him. He fought with her. "I've got to go. Don't you understand?"

"There's nowhere to go, Tom."

They went back and forth like this.

"Fucking cunt," he seethed.

She stumbled backward, her reflection in his eyes. The devil. Marie called in the nurses, who assured her this was normal. All night like this. This was not normal.

The next morning, as sun poured into the room, Tom slept like a baby.

Marie, bleary-eyed and tormented, told the doctor what had happened. He assured her it was the anesthesia talking, that it was just a matter of time before it wore off and that Marie shouldn't worry.

Fucking cunt. Fucking cunt. Fucking cunt.

Tom woke around one and was himself again. He remembered nothing of the previous night. They shared a turkey sandwich that Marie had bought at the kiosk. He asked her when Stuart was coming. She said soon and handed him Wednesday's *New York Times* crossword. He dozed on and off holding his pen to the folded paper.

At one point, he roused himself and looked around and told her that Stuart didn't have to come all this way. "Where was he, again?"

"India, Tom. Stuart's in India."

His eyes narrowed, as if India was not computing.

"He works hard, Tom," she said, though she didn't know why she'd said that. She didn't need to say that, to defend Stuart when he likely did not deserve defending.

"I'm really proud of my son," Tom said. "I know he doesn't believe me when I say that, but it's true."

"He believes you when you say that, Tom."

"I'm so impressed with everything he's accomplished."

Accomplished? Marie half smiled. What had any of them accomplished?

"I was never good at accomplishing things."

"You're not alone, Tom."

"I never actually carried a child out of a burning building." He dropped his head back on the pillow. "But I did once use an ax to crash in the skylight of a syrup factory that was up in flames. It was supposed to release the air flow for the flames, but instead it brought down the entire building, almost taking me and my unit with it."

"That must have been scary."

"Janice was pregnant with Stuart at the time, and I remember thinking of one thing as I flew down the side of the ladder scaling the building—the irony of my son having to grow up without a father, when that was exactly why I became a father. To *be there*. In the way my father wasn't."

Janice was not Stuart's mother's name, for those wondering. Stuart's mother's name was Teresa. She lived in Spain and Marie had never met her.

"I suppose Stuart's probably told you that it became an obsession of mine to be a certain kind of father, and I may have gone overboard in my quest. I certainly never thought I'd have to raise Stuart alone, and I think I was angry a lot of the time about that. I regret a lot of things, but I did my best. Can you tell Stuart that for me?"

"You can tell him yourself, Tom."

He began fiddling with the pulse oximeter string attached to his finger, as if he were trying to knot it. When that didn't work, he used an imaginary string. But it wouldn't knot either. It was all so futile, his hands said finally, falling onto his lap in frustration. "I can't do anything. I've never been able to do anything my whole life."

Marie turned then and noticed, out the window, dusk settling in, and she quickly went and shut the blinds. But it was no use. A shadow had already crept over the room and Tom, and suddenly Marie was that woman to be wary of, and that woman Janice, just possibly out to poison him. He went from staring at the spot on the ceiling to staring at Marie floating upside down to fumbling with his IV to trying to get out of bed with his reconstructed knee still trapped in its device. The next four days went like this, Marie spending the nights by Tom's hospital bed to ensure he wouldn't injure himself attempting to get wherever it was he so desperately thought he needed to get to. A three-alarm fire? Stuart? All those unfinished tasks and failures?

"You've got to come, Stuart, and you've got to come now." Marie had slipped out of Tom's room. "Maybe if he sees his son, his flesh and blood, he'll snap out of it."

The line remained silent. He couldn't tell her about Niraj's return. Just couldn't. Not yet.

"Stuart, what are you waiting for?"

"I'm coming, Marie. I'm on the next plane."

A few more days passed. It's just a matter of time, the doctors kept saying. She asked for the neurologist, the pulmonary specialist, the orthopedist, the physical therapist, a psychiatrist. It's a matter of time, they all said. They had no idea.

It was almost as if Tom had purposely, subliminally, trapped Marie here, in this city by the bay, so that she could swirl around in a womb of memories. The mist and fog through which somewhere existed a house in Tiburon. A girl at the window, staring out at those seven hills across the bay, her father there somewhere, so close, and yet the girl rarely saw him. Her mother never took her there, or allowed her to go there. And yet it seemed so close. Close enough to swim to, certainly. So sure was the girl of this fact that she threatened often to do so. And then one day she did do so. Or tried to, anyway. She was ten, and a good swimmer. A strong swimmer. But she had no idea what she was doing. Her mother had to send a boat out to bring her back. She had hypothermia. Then pneumonia. It took her three months to recover. Her mother was so angry at the girl that she did it again.

There is nothing left of home. The woman I was. Of any of it. These were the darkest hours, in the dead of night, when Marie's thoughts spiraled alongside Tom's. How do you convince a crazy man that the red light squiggling across the room was not the great light but his heart monitor, the one attached to his finger attached to his hand that continually levitated into the air, as if on its own? With all the wonder of a child, he stared at that finger. Marie gently brought it back down.

Some time passed. A minute, an hour?

"Are you there?"

She sat up from where she'd been dozing in the chair beside him. "I'm here."

"Last night . . ." He paused. "Were you there?"

"I was here."

"You weren't at the house?"

She didn't say anything. It got to be that it was easier just to go wherever Tom was going in his mind, rather than break the news to him, which was that he'd not gone anywhere, that all this time he'd been here in this darkened hospital room, where no man should ever be.

"It was evening," he went on. "The street was so quiet. No cars. All the warm lights in the houses. I was wandering down the middle of the street, looking inside the windows. People came to their doors, welcoming me in. Strangers. Friends I knew once. The man who fixed the lift in my shoe. I think my father was there. Can you believe that? My father."

"I can believe it, Tom."

"Nobody cared where I had come from or where I was going. They just wanted me to come in and get warm. They wanted to take care of me."

Stuart had told Marie about Tom's childhood. It wasn't a pretty one. She reached out for Tom's hand. It was cold, but still strong. His face was ashen, a flicker of understanding in his eyes now searching hers.

"It wasn't real, was it?" he said.

She thought her hand might break. *I shouldn't have come*, she thought.

That night, she got a call from the Dane. "When will you be back?" The ficus plant had died. Giorgio had been calling. He wanted the Dane back. There was a pause before she asked Marie, "Should I go back?"

Marie had no answer. Who had the answer? "Don't go back," she told the Dane, who would not long from now go back anyway.

CHAPTER 40

AT THE COFFEE CAFÉ next to the Raghukul Tower, Niraj appeared to be a different man than the one Stuart had met in Bangalore. He didn't appear to be any version of the man Stuart had known for over twenty years. Never had Stuart seen Niraj wear a baseball cap, but that's what he was sporting now—a Yankees cap, no less—seated in a dark corner underneath a dusty canopy of big-leafed almond trees, hunched over a yellow legal pad. The pits of his untucked dress shirt were stained with sweat. The ashtray was full of butts and ash.

"I've been studying the cybersecurity pivot and have some serious concerns," Niraj said.

Something caught in Stuart's throat. He coughed a few times.

"There are a lot of unknowns about what we can achieve from the data. Those Ukrainians don't have a solid AI platform, besides the fact that they're not in the software network space. They don't understand our market. And this prince? What is it they're supposed to be building for him over there in Orange County? Do you even know?"

"Just because they're Ukrainian doesn't mean they're affiliated with the FSB."

"One might go so far as to say that what you're doing is irresponsible."

A few moments passed in which Stuart collected himself. Niraj had been back for only one week, and Stuart had to remind himself that it was going to take time. Plus, because

Niraj's doctor still wanted him to stay local, he'd not been able to fly out to El Segundo and see what the Dream Team and the Ukrainians had been hard at work on, COMPASS++ and the new AI engine, the progress they'd made in the five weeks since the Super Bowl. "Look, Niraj, the Ukrainians are coming out next week to work on the data schemas with Professor Meena and the new data-mining expert. You'll get a chance to work with them firsthand, and you can form your opinion then. We're going to start putting together the pitch deck, and you know I can't do this without you. I need you to buy in and be a part of this."

"I talked to the Dream Team. They're wondering if you know what you're doing."

Stuart pulled back. "Okay, well, that is simply not true."

"Do your clients know you're trolling through their data? That you have this kind of power over their networks?"

"You negotiated the contracts, Niraj."

Niraj didn't answer at first, and Stuart got the sinking feeling that Niraj didn't remember negotiating the contracts. "Did you ever think that what you're doing might be criminal?"

"You mean like hacking into a car?" Stuart wanted to say but didn't. Instead, he said, "We're the guys with the white hats, remember?"

"Black hats, white hats—you're both trolling."

"You're being paranoid."

"You're chasing after the fast buck."

"The pivot is a risk. I won't deny that. It's the only way I believe we'll get funded. People aren't buying the margins for MNS. Cybersecurity puts us in a different league."

"By the way, we can't sell to WIPRO if we're in the middle of a lawsuit with the Cowboy."

"I told you, the sale to WIPRO is off the table—"

"We can't do *any* kind of deal or transaction if we're in a lawsuit, including a funding event."

"The Cowboy's not going to sue. He's stupid, but not that stupid."

"You need to be prepared regardless. You need to have a contingency plan. Have you spoken with him?"

"I won't give him the satisfaction."

Niraj nodded and wrote something down.

Stuart frowned at the pad and the scribbles Niraj was making on the page. "Anyway, that's why you're back, isn't it? To take care of all these things."

Niraj looked at Stuart, then at the pad. He began flipping through the pages, which were brittle and warped as if he'd dropped the pad in the tub or sink. On them bled illegible scrawls, line items listing Stuart's inadequacies and all the things he'd failed to do.

Niraj began going through the items while Stuart stared at the pad, thinking how he'd not even had time to order coffee. He was also thinking how surreal this all was. Through the leaves of the plants he could see a couple of toddlers playing in the gutter, no shoes or pants on, their hair flying in the wake of passing scooters and *tuk-tuk*s. He wanted a cigarette. His father had babbled to him over the phone that morning, "There's this woman here, and she keeps asking me things, and I'm not sure who she is, but don't tell her that."

"That's Marie, Dad. You know Marie."

"She's nice, but I'm not sure why she's here."

"You see what's happening here?" Marie had taken the phone back and said.

Niraj flipped to the next page, at which point Stuart laid his hand down on top of the pad and said, "Stop, Niraj."

Niraj looked up and could not have missed in Stuart's gaze an emotion twenty years deep.

"Just stop."

Niraj looked down at his pad. Some moments later, he put it away.

The unfortunate part was that Stuart and Niraj couldn't even share a drink and break the ice that way. One of their fuck-all, Friday-night-in-Gangnam kind of drinks, because Niraj didn't drink anymore. They had to be big boys now.

"INDIA IS VITA'S FUTURE," Stuart told Professor Meena, "our new data-mining nucleus, and I'm not going to let anything compromise that."

They were on the balcony of a second-floor tea parlor on the end of the Walled City opposite from where Stuart had just met with Niraj. A gazillion percent humidity outside, and she wasn't even breaking a sweat, though she did look tired, worn, errant strands falling from her bun, and that sari looked like it could use a good cleaning.

"Next week, you'll see. Pitch decks are where Niraj shines his brightest. Just give me one more week, and you'll see that I'm right."

Professor Meena's face remained stern and just a little bit scary. "I have better things to do than cater to the whims of a CEO who doesn't know what the hell to do with himself. Last week," she went on before Stuart could say anything, "there was something wrong with a light switch in the data center. I was about to call a technician, but Niraj said that he could fix it. He spent four hours fixing the light switch." She raised a brow at Stuart. "An odd thing for a CEO to be spending time on, don't you think?"

Stuart did not disagree. But who knew? This was India, after all.

"Then, a few days later, I was having the technician come in to fix something else, and he happened to check the switch that Niraj had fixed and told me to shut everything down immediately. To send everyone home until he rewired it. The place was a fire hazard."

She paused to hold Stuart's eyes. As disconcerting as this was, Stuart had to bite his lip to keep from laughing.

She sat back and began tapping her index finger on the table between them. "Stuart, he almost blew the place up. I don't understand what's so funny."

Tap tap. Tap tap. Tap tap.

NIRAJ DID NOT DISAPPOINT. The Ukrainians came to Jaipur. They presented the work they'd done to date alongside the Dream Team, who piped in from El Segundo. Niraj listened to their spiel. Discerned. Had some interesting ideas. Great questions. Aleksander was impressed. They sketched out a pitch deck that Niraj would flesh out further with input from Professor Meena and the teams. Professor Meena's worries about Niraj seemed overwrought and premature, and, after all, Stuart reminded himself, she'd never worked with Niraj before. He did have a certain kind of flair.

They all agreed on a strategy for the next phase of the AI design. They wanted to have something strong to show Jim in a week when he returned from his trek along the Camino Santiago. With Jim's backing, they'd go back to the Vita board, and now that the NEWTV contract was boosting not only Vita's brand but its revenue, the board would have no choice but to give Stuart another shot at pitching the Japanese conglomerate's venture capital fund group.

At the end of their sessions, they all went out for drinks. Stuart was surprised to see Niraj imbibe, too, but he didn't see any harm in it. Who was he, two drinks in, to say? It was a relief to see Niraj and Aleksander hit it off, the two continuing to drink together long after Stuart had to leave. He had a long-overdue plane to catch, and thank God, because he'd heard one of the Indians mention something about a dinner party.

CHAPTER 41

LIGHT FLICKERED THROUGH THE windows when Stuart arrived at Marie's Airbnb in a torrential downpour, with water running down the streets, wind knocking him sideways as he got out of the car. She shepherded him in. Behind her, a bottle was open. She was frazzled and had a smudge on her face from trying, unsuccessfully, to make a fire. He squeezed her hands, brittle and cold. "You're chilled to the bone." Then he noticed her wet hair. The smell of salt, a hint of petrol. "You went swimming?"

"I needed to clear my head."

There was a gray film in her eyes, the skin around them chafed and red. "Out in the open?"

She nodded.

"How far?" And then, "You didn't cross, did you?"

"No. Not in this weather. How was he?"

"The same."

"What does the doctor say?"

"He'll come out of it. It's a matter of time."

She deadened her eyes. "It's been three weeks."

"You can go back to Singapore, Marie. They brought in a new night nurse. Dad seems to like her, though he keeps asking me if she's Asian." Stuart paced to the window.

"How long will you stay?"

He didn't answer. He was looking at his phone now. Fumitaka-san's name had popped up on the caller ID. He needed to get it. It was critical that he get it, but—

"Get it," she said. "Just get it, Stuart."

The fact was, he was afraid to get it. He'd been gone from Jaipur for all of thirty-six hours, and it was as if a switch had been flipped. When he'd left, everyone was in sync and on track, and he'd felt elated, as well as guilty and worried about what lay ahead. He didn't even open his laptop on the plane. He watched five movies and drank tiny bottles of vodka, trying to decompress from everything but, more important, prepare for everything he might face with his father in San Jose, only to step off the plane and have ten texts waiting for him.

The first was from Professor Meena. "Call me. We need to talk."

Then came a variety from members of the Dream Team, with questions about technical direction, and one from Aleksander.

This after he'd made a public announcement to the entire team—hell, the whole company, even—that he was going to be out of pocket for a few days and would *not* be responding to texts or email. This was his frustrating thought as he stood still in the middle of the terminal, staring at the texts for long jet-lagged minutes.

He called Professor Meena from the cab. Niraj had decided on a sudden change of course for the AI module and COMPASS++, and as a result, she was now to work with the data expert on a different project, one for Toyota, and so she was not sure how to—

Stuart cut her off. "I'll talk to Niraj. Stick with the original plan."

That wasn't even the worst of it, Professor Meena went on. Niraj was going around saying things like Stuart was running the business into the ground with this cybersecurity pivot, that he was spending cash on these Ukrainians as if it were going out of style. "It wasn't already enough that morale had spiraled since Niraj's return, but now this?"

Professor Meena lamented. Stuart reiterated that he'd take care of it, and they hung up.

He then had to assuage the Dream Team in the same vein, all on his way to the hospital, where he at last received a text from the man himself as his cab pulled up to the main entrance doors.

Niraj: "Where are you? We need to meet."
Stuart: "Meet where? San Jose? Which is where you know I am, because I told you this was where I would be."
Niraj: "We need to meet now, or there will be consequences."

Stuart stared at the text for a long harrowing moment. Then he shut down his phone and sat staring at the entrance doors repeatedly opening and closing, even though no one was coming or going.

Now, Fumitaka-san. Stuart stared at the caller ID.

Marie pulled up his shirtsleeve. The bandage had spots of yellow and brown. Then she noticed his fingers, chewed to the bone. "Oh, Stuart, what have you done?"

Setting down his phone, he said, "I'm gone for a few minutes, and the world comes to an end."

She pulled the sleeve back down. "Is it Niraj?"

He looked at her with desperate eyes. "Please don't say 'I told you so.'"

"He's not of his right mind."

"Marie, be careful what you say."

"I got an email from him a few days ago."

Stuart pulled back from her, as if she might be in on it, too. "From Niraj?"

"It's not like you and I have had a chance to talk."

"What did he want?"

"He wanted me to give him feedback on the first chapters of a new book."

Stuart frowned. "What book?"

"They were gibberish, Stuart. The chapters. It was almost as if they'd been written by a person unhinged."

He looked around for a place to sit, but he couldn't find one place he wanted to. The faded furniture, knickknacks, toys, and board games—it all felt so lived in, and not theirs. Stuart sat on the back of the sofa. "Why is it we've never bought a house, a place to come home to, Marie? Why is that?" The rain was drumming even harder now, and he looked up at the ceiling, as if it might cave in.

"You're tired, Stuart. You must be exhausted." She moved him to the couch and got the bottle of wine, but he didn't want a drink. "Why did Niraj come back in the first place?" she asked.

Stuart went and stood before the fireplace. "Why does anybody? I'm guessing he needs the work. Work is the only thing that keeps people like us sane."

"But he seems insane."

"Don't say that, Marie. Not out loud."

"He's going to derail this whole thing, isn't he?"

"Stop it, Marie."

"You're so close, Stuart. You've worked so hard. You can't let him do this."

He dropped to his knees abruptly, assessing the mess she'd made of the fireplace. All she could do was watch him, until at last he began the long and steady process of setting it properly. Rearranging the logs on the grate. The kindling. Crumpling the paper and then setting it alight, slowly, methodically. It took time, lots of time, and focus. He stabbed at it with the poker, but he was patient, so unfathomably patient, she thought, watching as the sparks began to kindle, as the flames began to grow, slowly, into a roar.

STUART CLUNG TO HER, passed out from a sleeping pill, but Marie couldn't sleep. She felt hollowed out from their lovemaking, her thoughts a harrowing spiral. She tried everything, but after an hour of tossing and turning, she grabbed her cell and checked the time. *Missed call.* It took a minute for the name to come into focus; she was sure she wasn't reading it right. Then her phone buzzed in her hand (her ringer was off). He was calling again! As quietly and quickly as possible, she got out of bed, threw on some clothes, and took her phone out to the living room. Her heart was pounding. She went to the farthest window and, against every one of her instincts, answered the call.

"I need to speak to him," Niraj said.

"Stuart's asleep," she said. "You shouldn't be calling, Niraj. It's three o'clock in the morning."

"He won't return my texts."

"He'll call you in the morning."

"I need to talk to him now."

She could hear street sounds, horns honking. "Where are you?"

"Walking," he said. His words were slurred.

"You've been drinking," she said.

She could hear him light a cigarette. The pull, the exhale of smoke. "This wouldn't be happening if Stuart had just listened to me."

"What's happening, Niraj?"

"Stuart changed," he said.

Through the living room window, she could see that the rains had ceased. "Are you all right, Niraj? Is everything all right?"

"He used to care about building something, not selling out to horseshit. It was Jim whispering in Stuart's ear all along, all this stuff about changing the world. It's a goddamn software-defined network, and now he thinks he's the messiah or something. Who is this Jim guy? You know, I never even asked what he had going on with the two of you."

"Hold on," she said. She grabbed a coat from the rack, put it on, and went outside. She did not want to wake up Stuart. If Stuart awoke and realized Niraj had called her, there'd be trouble, and she didn't want any of that. "I used to work with Jim, that's all."

"He's driving the company into the ground."

"Jim?"

"Stuart."

"You shouldn't have called, Niraj."

"I want to talk to him."

"What is there to say?" She stood on the porch and drew the jacket around her. "He trusted you, and now you seem to be on a mission to derail him and everything he's done. Why? All he did was stay steadfast in your place while you were recovering from a terrible loss. He kept the company going. He made decisions that weren't easy."

"He's hemorrhaging the company's cash. He's lost his mind."

She could argue with him, but what would be the point?

"I used to . . . We used to . . . And now . . ."

After a moment, she asked, "Now what?"

He couldn't answer.

"Work with him, Niraj."

"This company is mine as much as his."

"No one's saying it isn't. He brought you back, for God's sake. He needs your help."

He let out some kind of strangled noise.

"Are you okay? Do you need me to call someone?"

"I shouldn't have called."

"No, you shouldn't have."

She could hear him breathing.

"Stuart cares about you, Niraj. If that's what you need to know, then there it is. He cares about you very much."

He didn't say anything.

She had no idea where this conversation was going or why she was still on the phone with him. She wanted to sit down, but the steps were wet. She started walking. Maybe she could talk him down, remind him of how things started. "Remember that time Stuart was considering working for the CTO of JPMorgan Chase—or *I* was considering it for him, anyway—and that lit a fire under his ass and he went running to you? He was always running to you for career advice. I could suggest this or that, but it wouldn't be this or that until *you'd* suggested it. I secretly called you 'Guru.' Did you know that? No, I suppose you didn't. I guess the only thing I was ever sure about regarding Stuart was that he was frightened for his life at the idea of becoming 'one of them.' Did you know that in the early days, before I came to Seoul, I often wondered if you even existed? For so many years I'd only heard of you, this peer of Stuart's, not a friend, only a peer. I'm sure you knew this. He said you felt the same way, but I never understood it. After everything, how could you two not be friends?"

"Why did you show up in Seoul?" he asked. "Just like that. So suddenly. I've always wondered."

Why is it we do the things we do? "I was jealous," she said.

His end of the world went silent for a moment, as if he'd muted the sound.

A dog started barking from inside somewhere nearby. She walked more quickly. It wasn't true about the jealousy— she'd said that for Niraj, and now she regretted it. "I need to go. I need to get back before Stuart figures out I'm gone."

"Just a little longer. I have no one to talk to."

She felt the urge to cough from the cigarettes he was sucking down. It occurred to her that this was the first time she and Niraj had ever had an exchange that lasted longer than a few minutes.

"The truth is, I'm not going to be married. My fiancée's family backed out."

"You didn't love her, though, I'm guessing."

"Her promiscuity did not devastate me. We had an agreement, she and I, but I still wished for some decorum. Ask Stuart about her. I'm sure he'll tell you."

"He told me," she lied.

He went quiet, and for a minute she thought he'd fallen asleep standing in the middle of the street.

"Ah, what's the use?" he said. He hung up abruptly, and she let out a little gasp and stopped walking, unsure if she should call him back. Call anyone for that matter, or do something. A rustling scared her, and she turned around and started back. The same dog barked at her again. She kept her head down, her hands jammed into her pockets. She'd walked farther than she had thought. It took a while to get back. As she was walking up the porch steps, she looked up, and what she saw took her breath away. The moon, churning inside a charcoal cloud, hovered so low she thought she could reach out and touch it.

CHAPTER 42

IN THE MORNING, A BLESSED, blazing sun. Stuart hurried to the hospital and threw open the curtains of his father's room. The arm of the plastic lucky cat Stuart had bought at Duty Free started waving at his father, who lay in the most peaceful state of slumber Stuart thought he might ever have seen him in. One socked foot was sticking out from the bottom of the bed; the other moved up and down with the help of a robot programmed to keep the knee muscles working and the blood circulating. Stuart wanted to wake his father but could not bear the thought, so he sat and watched him. The nurse came in. He'd had a restless night, she told Stuart. He needed to sleep. Stuart went over and kissed his forehead. *Sleep, Dad.*

He went outside and called Fumitaka-san. He apologized for not having gotten back to him sooner and explained that he was in the hospital with his father, who was having some trouble. He paused to swallow a knot in his throat. He went on for some time about his father's condition, his obstinacy; how Stuart should never have allowed him to have the knee surgery at his age, not to mention the fact that Stuart hadn't shown up for it as he'd planned and as his father had asked him to; how his father never asked him for anything, but work had gotten in the way, and perhaps if he had been here for the surgery, perhaps if he had been . . . There was a long, drawn-out pause in there. Anyway, no one could give him any answers.

"You need to take him home," Fumitaka-san said, something no one else had said.

It hadn't occurred to Stuart to simply take his father home. What home would he take him home to? "I'm sorry to have laid all this upon you, Fumitaka-san. I don't know what came over me. Please forgive me. Please, let me tell you about our sessions in Jaipur with the Ukrainians last week, how extremely productive they were—"

"This is not the time to talk about business," Fumitaka-san said. "Be with your father."

"My father will be sleeping for some time, and for me, working will be the best distraction."

"Niraj came to see me yesterday," Fumitaka-san said.

Stuart was silent for a moment, before he asked, "He came to Tokyo?"

"He showed up at my office with a yellow legal pad, wanting to meet. We spent thirty minutes together because I could bear no more than that. He had a list of issues, and he started to go down the list, but I quickly cut him off. I didn't understand why he was coming to me with these issues about you—"

"Fumitaka-san, please accept my apologies for Niraj. I did not know he was coming to see you."

"The fact that Niraj went behind your back . . . This is not how we conduct our affairs in Japan. This is a private matter between you and Niraj. There is no honor in this. I sent him home and then called you directly."

"Again, I am very—"

"I feel great shame not only for Niraj but for you, Stuart."

Stuart closed his eyes. *Niraj is going to derail this whole thing.* "The truth is, Fumitaka-san, Niraj and I have been having issues for some time, even before his father's death."

"You need to find a way to come to terms with Niraj. To make amends. I do not want any further part in it."

Stuart felt the blood rise up through his neck and face. "Of course. Absolutely. You have my word. This will never happen again."

"Meanwhile, I suggest you get a lawyer and start documenting your conversations with Niraj. This is a delicate matter, and an unfortunate one. But you have my support, Stuart-san, if it comes to that."

This surprised Stuart, though he wasn't sure why, as Fumitaka-san had always been kind to him. They hung up. Stuart stood there, gathering himself. Then he drove back to the Airbnb and picked up Marie and drove her to SFO for her flight back to Singapore. She cried silently the whole way there, his hand interlaced with hers, both of them squeezing.

She'd not told Stuart about Niraj's call. It would anger him. And she didn't want to be with Stuart when he was angry. He was already in a state of distress about his call with Fumitaka-san, Marie's departure, and now, out the window, the sun beginning its harrowing descent.

He looked at her. "I shouldn't have left you alone with my dad. It was a mistake not to be here."

She didn't say anything.

"Are you going to be okay?"

"No," she said. Marie-speak for "yes."

Stuart pulled up to the curb of the international terminal. She got out, and he came around and held her.

By the time Stuart got back to the hospital, dusk had fallen. He entered his father's room with a feeling of having succumbed to whatever might lie ahead with Niraj, or Stuart's father. He was braced for anything, but what he found was his father and Janice holding hands and laughing at something they were looking at in the crossword. The bugs were gone from the walls, and the blue was back in his father's eyes, as he looked at Stuart and said that he wanted him to know how proud of him he was. That maybe he'd not said it enough to him when he was younger, but that he wanted Stuart to know now that he'd always been proud of him.

CHAPTER 43

STUART NEVER CONFRONTED NIRAJ about his meeting with Fumitaka-san. He didn't see the point. Nor did
Niraj, apparently. As his unpredictable temperament continued to spiral downward, he and Stuart avoided each other.
Meanwhile, Stuart and Professor Meena began diligently
documenting respective interactions with Niraj that they
deemed less than appropriate. While the COMPASS++
development teams—now spread out across Singapore, El
Segundo, and Orange County—were spared Niraj's antics,
thanks to lack of proximity, Jaipur was floundering in chaos.
Niraj, who had taken an apartment in Jaipur, took to showing up at the office sporadically, inserting himself into SRE
meetings where he knew little of what was going on and
demanding not-insignificant changes in whatever direction
had already been agreed upon. Then, in follow-on meetings,
he'd berate those same SREs for jobs they'd done as he'd
specifically asked them to do.

Stuart finally got up the courage to ask Niraj to resign.
"Why should I resign?" was his response. He threatened
to sue. Then he went to JS with his yellow legal pad, but
Fumitaka-san had already aligned JS with Stuart. Stuart did
not know what favor Fumitaka-san had had to call in, but it
must have been a big one.

After many documented moments like these, as well as
repeated incidents that were starting to damage the reputation of Vita's board members, it was agreed that Niraj would

have to go. No one wanted a lawsuit, however, so Stuart trod as delicately as he could. In the darkest part of his mind, he worried that Niraj might implode, explode, or, worse, attempt to blow up the office building again. Stuart didn't believe Niraj would, but he no longer believed he was dealing with the same Niraj he had known for twenty years. That Niraj seemed lost to him now.

Above all, Stuart wanted to keep things amicable. Fair. Stuart felt partly to blame, and he knew Niraj had nowhere to go, no plush cushion to fall on when this all came crashing down. Plus, Vita was his creation, too. Stuart couldn't deny this, and he imagined Niraj fighting until the bitter end to stay. For four long and grueling weeks, their negotiations went on. Niraj had engaged a lawyer friend, through whom all his communication with Stuart now passed. Stuart offered Niraj everything he wanted—his full stake in the company and priority, after their investors, in any returns the company made in the event of a sale or other transaction.

In the end, strangely, there would be no drama. Niraj "resigned," signed the papers, and disappeared. No one knew to where. Delhi, presumably, but Stuart wouldn't know—Niraj blocked him from all social media connections and did not return his calls. It was an absence that would haunt Stuart for some time.

Two weeks after Niraj left, Stuart got word that the AriaNet-NEWTV merger was stalled. While the SEC and FCC had conditionally approved it, the States had now blocked it. They claimed that the merger would decrease competition for broadband and cellular services, not increase it, and that customers would fall victim to unwarranted price increases. The claims from both AriaNet and NEWTV to protect competition were insufficient, and therefore the litigation would be protracted, with no merger in sight until it was resolved, which it might never be.

The AriaNet-NEWTV COMPASS++ project was put on hold indefinitely, and Jack was moved to another department. As a consequence, a quarter of Vita's projected revenue was also on hold.

There wasn't much for Stuart to do but send the Dream Team back to Asia and start letting some of the COMPASS++ platform team go, including the data-mining consultant. Halt work on the AI module. Scale back, again. Close down the Tokyo and El Segundo offices. MNS in India was back on track, now that Niraj was gone, and had become a well-oiled operation, not to mention revenue generator, under the direction of Professor Meena and her band of lady SREs. WIPRO increased its offer—the work Vita had done on the Super Bowl had upped Vita's brand value. It was offering four times revenue, versus the two it had offered before. Though it put no value on the AI module—WIPRO wouldn't even know how to spell "machine learning"—the network data, MNS, and COMPASS++ platform all contributed to the higher valuation. There would be an earn-out component to the deal, meaning that Stuart would have to stay for the full two years and achieve biannual revenue targets in order for Vita investors to get their full due. And after all the ugly, untoward bullshit that had gone down with Niraj the past two months, the board was insisting that Stuart take the offer. Something they'd insisted before, to no avail. But this time they weren't alone in being done with Vita, willing to make some of their money back with minimal upside and move on. Stuart had had it, too. Niraj had left a bad taste in his mouth.

Though the WIPRO deal had yet to go through, Marie was already mentally packing up their bodega, at once rejuvenated by the idea of moving to India, where Stuart would be based for the two-year earn-out period. She felt as if fate had taken over, as if Professor Meena and her sharp, penetrating gaze had forged open some unknown path for Marie, one buried in the recesses of Marie's mind and enmeshed with the vision she still often had of the boy standing before the Taj Hotel, waiting for her.

As the rumors spread about India, the Dream Team began sharing their respective qualms: they were startup guys, not corporate guys; they had no place at a WIPRO. There were rumblings about jumping ship—Biggy going back to finance, Laurie flying off in her prop plane to Vegas, and Franco opening up a hot-air-ballooning business in Seoul—but Stuart assured them that their share of the WIPRO earnout would no longer be laughable, as it had once been. It was nothing you'd go touting to the Cowboy, who'd made ten times what they were set to make for selling his shit company, but no one liked to so much as mention that. Nor would any of the Dream Team be required to relocate to India, like Stuart. That was a bullet he had taken for them. They could continue working from Singapore or wherever.

But then none of that might even be relevant. Aleksander called. Turned out the prince was not a mirage after all. He'd shown up in Orange County, finally, and Aleksander had gotten him all excited about the cybersecurity idea, COM-PASS++, and the AI module. He wanted to hear Aleksander and Stuart's pitch ASAP, before he returned to Saudi Arabia and turned into a pumpkin again. He was sending his private jet over to Singapore to pick up Stuart and whomever he wanted to bring along and take them back to Orange County.

"When's the last time you were on a private jet, Marie?"

She wasn't talking to him.

"I'm just going to hear him out."

Stone-cold mute.

"Fine. It's probably better for you to stay here. I'll be back in three days, anyway."

His phone rang. He didn't look at it.

It rang again. This time he looked at it. Liam, always managing to call at the most inopportune moments. And yet Stuart couldn't help but smile inwardly, imagining Liam's reaction when Stuart told him about the prince, about how the Dream Team might not be headed out to pasture just yet, after all.

"Stuart," she said.

He looked up, and with the full bore of his gaze, he said, "Come with me."

"Stuart, I'm not coming with you."

"Then marry me," he said.

She said, after a pause, "Oh, Stuart, please."

"I'm serious," he said.

"How is marriage going to change anything?"

He didn't have an answer.

"Stuart. What I'm telling you is that this is the stop on the train at which I get off."

The smile vanished from his lips. She did not look away. Nor did he. He could—should—believe her, but what was the point of that? It would be like believing in death. Sure, he knew he was going to die, but he didn't actually *believe* he would die, that it would actually *happen*. If he believed that, he would go nuts, bonkers, crazy. No, whether she married him or not, Marie would be with him on that train, always.

"What, you're going to go to India by yourself?" he asked, though it wasn't a question. Of course, she would go off to India by herself. He knew this. He knew she knew he knew this. She was apt to do anything she wanted to if she put her mind to it. He'd always known her to be capable of going further than he. It was what he loved about her. That one day she would leave him, if she had to. That one day it would be his turn just to show up, as she had just shown up in Seoul back when this story began.

STUART MET LIAM AT the expat bar. They each ordered a beer, and before Stuart could mention the prince, Liam told Stuart that he'd received a job offer from Amazon Web Services. He paused before he added, "In Seattle." They were sponsoring him for an H-1B work visa. A solid offer with good benefits. Stuart should not have been shocked or disappointed, but he was both. Liam's dream had always been to start a life for his family in the States, and Stuart had hoped to be the one to give him that life, but he couldn't compete with what Amazon was offering. Even the WIPRO offer wouldn't make up the gap in the value of Amazon's stock options. The prince, however . . . If he came through and funded Vita 2.0, Fumitaka-san and the board would have no choice but to go along. He wanted to tell Liam, heard in his mind himself telling Liam, *Now is not the time to jump ship. This wasn't over, after all. This could very likely be your ticket to the States, Liam, all of our tickets.* All this swirled in Stuart's mind while Liam waxed on about old times and how long he and Stuart had worked together and how he appreciated everything Stuart had done for him. Everything he had taught him. He admired Stuart. Always had. And Marie. The both of them. The way they lived their lives. But Liam was not one of those people. Never had been. So, in the end, Stuart said nothing about the prince. In the end, all he could do was wish Liam well.

AUTHOR'S NOTE

I WENT OFF MY BEATEN PATH and dove deep into tech for this novel. Real tech. Tech so real you don't even know it exists. And I wanted it to be true, too, which involved a significant amount of research. Endless discussions with Francesco about cloud computing, and I want to thank him and all those who schooled him. It's not easy to teach a relentless layman about cloud computing, especially one bent on getting it right. I would like to thank my copy editor, Annie Tucker, for her deftness in clarifying some of my very long-winded, unwieldy sentences while staying true to what she calls my "distinct" style. To my mother for always insisting on reading everything I write, for her curiosity and relentless pursuit of knowledge—even if it's about software-defined networking! Thanks to the She Writes Press and SparkPress author community for all their comradery, support, and honesty—we are so lucky to have each other's back! To Brooke Warner, my publisher, and Lauren Wise, my project manager, for their smart, intelligent guidance, and for, alongside my publicist Crystal Patriarche, their indefatigable, singular mission to support and inspire the work of independent women authors. And finally, and most importantly, thanks to you, reader, for giving my quirky little book a try.

ABOUT THE AUTHOR

BEFORE BECOMING A FULL-time writer, Jackie Townsend received her MBA from UC Berkeley and worked as a financial consultant in the Bay Area alongside her Italian husband, who worked in Silicon Valley and other parts of the world before starting and running his own tech company. That career, both exciting and exhausting, fuels Jackie's novels and essays, as well as the blogs she posts at jackietownsend. com, as do her travels and exposure to foreign cultures. Meanwhile, her husband continues the pursuit. Jackie's previous two books, *The Absence of Evelyn* (SparkPress) and *Imperfect Pairings*, both won or placed in a variety of Indie Awards. She is a native of Southern California who lived for many years in the Bay Area before she and her husband landed themselves in New York City, where they live today.

SELECTED TITLES FROM SPARKPRESS

SparkPress is an independent boutique publisher delivering high-quality, entertaining, and engaging content that enhances readers' lives, with a special focus on female-driven work. www.gosparkpress.com

Attachments: A Novel, Jeff Arch, $16.95, 9781684630813. What happens when the mistakes we make in the past don't stay in the past? When no amount of running from the things we've done can keep them from catching up to us? When everything depends on what we do next?

Those the Future Left Behind: A Novel, Patrick Meisch, $16.95, 9781684630790. In a near future in which overpopulation, resource depletion, and environmental degradation have precipitated a radical population control program, people can volunteer to be culled at a young age in exchange for immediate wealth.

The Absence of Evelyn: A Novel, Jackie Townsend. $16.95, 978-1-943006-21-2. Nineteen-year-old Olivia's life takes a turn when she receives an overseas call from a man she doesn't know is her father; her mother Rhonda, meanwhile, haunted by her sister's ghost, must face long-buried truths. Four lives in all, spanning three continents, are now bound together and tell a powerful story about love in all its incarnations, filial and amorous, healing and destructive.

Hostile Takeover: A Love Story, Phyllis J. Piano. $16.95, 978-1-940716-82-4. Corporate attorney Molly's all-consuming job is to take over other companies, but when her first love, a man who she feels betrayed her, appears out of nowhere to try to acquire her business, long-hidden passions and secrets are exposed.